M000188124

STEALING THE FUTURE
Book I of the East Berlin Series

'A compelling re-imagining of East Germany's peaceful revolution in 1989—exploring what might have been. As Europe grapples with the consequences of austerity, this novel poses questions both about the lost chances of 1989, and about how we organise our society—questions that are becoming more relevant with each passing day.'

Fiona Rintoul, author of *The Leipzig Affair*

'An authentic atmosphere of tension and uncertainty ... The brilliance of *Stealing the Future* lies in the honest portrayal of a young country and its idealistic inhabitants struggling to keep alive their dream of freedom, justice and equality in the face of international and domestic opposition.'

Jo Lateu, *New Internationalist*

'Creates the perfect atmosphere that existed around the fall of the wall: the sense of hope dashed by the awful reality of reunification.' Peter Thompson, *The Guardian*

'An intriguing and gripping page-turner of a thriller—believable and exciting. More than that, though, it's an exploration of power—political, economic and electric power; and what it might be like, day to day, to put our ideals and hopes for self-determination into practice.' Clare Cochrane, *Peace News*

Max Hertzberg, sometime Stasi files researcher and more recently a social change trainer and facilitator. This is his first novel, having previously co-written and edited *How to Set Up a Workers' Co-operative* (Radical Routes, 2012) and *A Consensus Handbook* (Seeds for Change, 2013).

Visit the author's website for background information on the GDR, features on this book and its characters, as well as guides to walking tours around the East Berlin in which this book is set.

www.maxhertzberg.co.uk

STEALING THE FUTURE
Book I of the East Berlin Series

Max Hertzberg

 WOLF PRESS

C 2 3 4 5 6 7 8 9 10

Published in 2015 by WOLF PRESS.
www.wolfpress.co.uk

Copyright ©Max Hertzberg 2015.

Max Hertzberg has asserted his right under the Copyright, Designs
and Patents Act 1988 to be identified as the author of this work.

Cover design by Stig: www.shtiggy.wordpress.com.

Cover photograph copyright © Tim Lucas, licensed under the
Creative Commons Attribution 2.0 International Licence.

Maps derived from OpenStreetMap. Copyright © OpenStreetMap
and contributors. www.openstreetmap.org/copyright.

Text licensed under the Creative Commons Attribution-Non-
Commercial-No-Derivatives 4.0 International License. View a copy
of this license at: www.creativecommons.org/licenses/by-nc-nd/4.0/

Wolf Press, 22 Hartley Crescent, LS6 2LL

A CIP record for this title is available from the British Library
ISBN: 978-0-9933247-0-3 (paperback)

Set in 10½ on 12pt Linux Libertine O and 11/16/24pt Linux Biolinium O
Printed and bound by Createspace LLC..

The German Democratic Republic
showing the situation of West Berlin and West Silesia

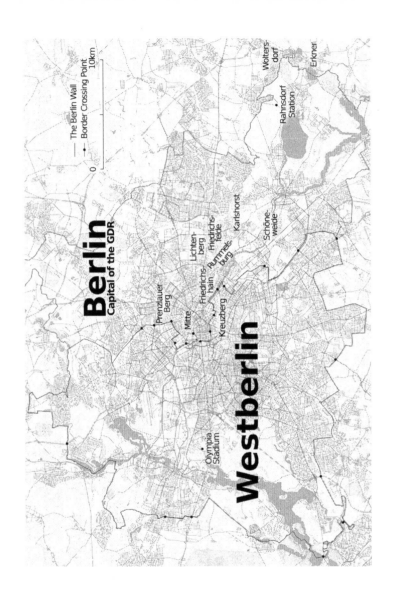

Berlin
showing West Berlin and
Berlin, Capital of the GDR

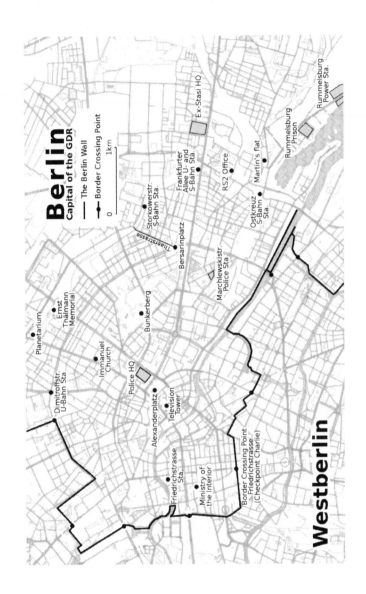

Central Berlin

DAY 1
Wednesday
22nd September 1993

Sunshine and darkness march across my path, the car diving through bands of light and shade. My eyes struggle to adjust to the glare flickering through the trees lining the road, but after a few more kilometres, peering through the dusty windscreen I make out a pair of petrol pumps, a prefab hut. The Trabant rumbles across the concrete slabs and the attendant comes out, wiping his hands on his overalls.

"What have you got?" hoping for anything.

"Don't know what you call it, thicker than what we use for heating, I suppose," he rubs his face with an oily rag, looking away, up the road, out of the sandy town. "It works, though. I cut it with grain schnapps—you'll get home."

I turn away, gesturing with a cigarette by way of an excuse, and wander over to the other side of the road. Lighting up, I watch him lift the bonnet, then fill the tank from a canister, still talking about the fuel. The radio in the car chatters to itself: ... *protests continue throughout the Soviet Union after President Gorbachev was impeached yesterday. It's not clear whether or not Gorbachev is under house arrest, but reports indicate that he is negotiating with both the army and the KGB.*

I could go back to the car, turn a knob, silence the newsreader. But turning my own thoughts off will be much harder. I'm tired, *dead tired*.

Not the best turn of phrase.

The image of the body on the rails hangs before me in the blue-grey haze of the cigarette. The head crushed, the feet crushed. Not crushed, no ... I need a better description. I tap ash off my cigarette.

Smeared.

There was nothing left to indicate the shape of the head or feet: bone, flesh and brains smeared along the rails and around the heavy steel wheels. The smell of blood might have been there, merging with sand and hot metal.

Above the torn body a steel lattice work, thirty storeys high, half a kilometre long. So big it had pulled my attention towards it—I hadn't known where to look: the body, or the mining machine. Rusty girders merged with the dusty air over the exposed coal seam. My mind, silted with sand and blood, refusing to take in the impossibility of what my eyes were seeing. Looking from one to the other. Corpse. Machine. Corpse again. Both just too far from everyday life experience: I had no reference points, no context to help me understand them.

I force my mind back to the present, the practicalities of the case. Breathing in smoke, breathing out questions.

Who was the person this body used to be? Local cops were sorting that out—papers pulled from the victim's pockets identified him as the politician Hans Maier. Fingerprints should confirm his identity. Maier had made a big thing about his persecution in the 'eighties by the secret police, the Stasi: there'd be files, prints would be on some record, somewhere.

But why was a politician dead on the tracks? And why had the local West Silesian police called their Saxon colleagues in? Odd, considering the pressure that we were facing from West Germany over the Silesian question.

Thinking things through, I feel a tension tightening my shoulders and neck. I feel lost. Out of my depth. And above all, bloody scared.

15:24

I was back in Berlin by early afternoon, and went straight to the office in Lichtenberg, parking on a patch of wasteland a couple of streets away.

As I entered the building I could feel how my concentration sharpened: the smells of the staircase—polished lino, *Optal* disinfectant and the warm earthiness of brown coal smoke. Up the stairs, past the discreet sign marked *RS2*, and through the door.

"Hi Bärbel, can you get everyone together—my office?"

The secretary nodded. "Not everyone's around at the moment, but give me a minute or two."

Into the toilets, sluicing my face in the rusty water over the cracked sink, then a glance in the mirror. I still looked tired, but at least I was a bit calmer. I'm at home here, I told the stranger in the mirror. He said it right back, so he must have been me.

What I've found out, what I fear, perhaps I can pass it on to the rest of the team—let them deal with it. The stranger in the mirror looked furtive, then guilty. That's not the way we do it any more he seemed to be saying to me. And he was right. Still, once I'd told my colleagues it would become a shared responsibility.

"A problem shared ..." I said to the mirror, and headed back to my office.

We usually met here, it was the biggest room on the floor, but it was dark, the net curtains dusty, hiding more of the light than they needed to. Using the moments before my colleagues arrived, I fished out a piece of paper, only written

3

on one side, and a stub of pencil from the chaos that lived on and around my desk. I made brief notes about what I'd seen.

I'd just finished the short list when Klaus came in, smoking one of his cigars. He said nothing, but went over to the corner, lowering himself on to the most out of the way chair, then putting his feet up on another. Erika followed, grimacing at the smoke already hanging in the air, waving her hands in front of her face, but looking towards me.

"How's it going? You don't look so good–"

"I'll tell you in a moment, let the others get here first."

"There's only the three of us here right now: Dieter's away, and Laura is at the Ministry. But here comes Bärbel."

The secretary sat down in the corner, a sheet of paper on her knee, pencil poised to take shorthand minutes.

"Klaus? Can you put that cigar out—I can't think with that stink."

Klaus shrugged, nipped the cigar and laid it gently in an ashtray. "What's up?" he asked.

"I didn't want to wait till tomorrow's meeting. I want to know what you think of this one. What's everyone doing at the moment?"

"You'd know if you hadn't missed our meeting this morning. But I guess this has something to do with it?" Erika, somewhere between disapproving and sympathetic.

"OK, can we get started?"

Erika and Klaus were looking at me now, curious, concerned. Klaus slumped in his chair, Erika sat forward, her hands in her lap, eyes searching my face. I needed to learn to hide my impatience better.

"I've been on the road since just after midnight. I've been to West Silesia and back," I said it as though I'd been all the way to Siberia, not West Silesia, just a few hours south of Berlin.

Erika's eyes widened slightly, her hands moved a fraction on her lap.

4

"Are we even allowed into West Silesia at the moment?" asked Klaus, studying his fingertips, acting nonchalant. But I could see the tenseness around his mouth.

"Probably not. I got a call from the Ministry of the Interior, so I didn't ask, just went.

"I don't know how the Ministry got hold of it, I guess from the Saxon police, trying to pass the buck. It was near Weisswasser. A body: the politician Maier. The big fish in the WSB," the *Westschlesische Bund*—the West Silesian Union, the party behind the move to split West Silesia from the rest of the GDR, our East German state; wanting to become a West German enclave, like West Berlin, deep in our territory.

"What were the Saxons doing there?" asked Klaus, looking both sceptical and confused at the same time.

"Not sure. I'd like to know that too. I guess the local West Silesian cops just panicked, and called their ex-colleagues. They haven't got the forensic set up, and all the records are still in Dresden, so they'd need to rely on the Saxons anyway.

"The body was found on the rails that one of those open cast mining machines run along." I didn't say it, but his body hadn't been found until the whole thing had run over him. Dozens of wheels had dragged him along. The head and feet were crushed. "Identity papers were found on the body, and they're checking his prints to confirm. We should find out more in the morning."

Klaus looked tense, exhaling audibly. I felt exactly the same way. If the body is Maier's, then we'd have a problem. The Silesians might accuse the GDR government of doing it, the West Germans will use that as leverage—and the kind of leverage the West Germans were after was the kind that would make us give up West Silesia.

"I still don't get why they're so interested in Silesia."

The West Germans were pumping money and technical support into the Region. They were clearly still annoyed that three years ago we had held a referendum and voted not to be taken over by them. The whole world had expected us to gratefully allow ourselves to be swallowed up, but instead, we decided to remain independent. To remain the German Democratic Republic. To continue the social experiment we'd started the autumn before.

"We may be about to find out what their interest is. The whole thing scares me—the Ministry asked me to go and check it out, which must mean that they suspect foreign interference. And we'd better hope it's the West Germans, because it isn't going to be the Poles, and that just leaves the Russians."

Erika was picking up on my fear: "Do we even have the experience to deal with this one?" She was watching me, a frown creasing her face. "But there's something else bothering you too, isn't there?"

"I don't know, a gut feeling. But that body. It was awful," I didn't continue, but my thoughts ran on.

That place, barren, empty. Just dust and industrial equipment. Part of the moon, an immense rocket launcher collapsed across a sandy pit that stretched to the horizon. Underneath all of that huge machinery, underneath the rusty steel and the wheels, a dead man: broken, fragile, pitiful. Maybe I was just tired, but it really got to me.

"You're right, it could have waited till tomorrow morning," I tailed off, feeling pathetic.

"No," Klaus sat up. "You're right to tell us about it. This could be a big one. Or just a coincidence. Why don't you tell us how far you've got, then get back home and catch up on some sleep?"

"Not much to tell, I have some film of the crime scene." I took the small camera out of my pocket, and tossed it on top of the mess on my desk. "He was probably killed elsewhere and the body laid out on the tracks." Other than that, just questions: why Maier? Why now? Why were the Saxon cops

6

there? "The senior officer present, *Unterleutnant der Kriminalpolizei* Schadowski made it all sound reasonable. First of all he didn't want to talk to me, but when I showed him my RS pass he was all 'Herr comrade *Oberleutnant*'. I guess these silly titles they gave us can be useful." The other two grinned, glad of a chance to break the tension: even in these times of change official pieces of paper and officer status bought influence.

"There's so many more questions, but I can't work it all out. Too tired. Sorry, it's not much to show for a day's trip."

"That's fine, thanks Martin. If you want you can go home now. I'll take the film up to the police technical support offices for a quick turn-around. Klaus and I will have a think about what else we need to work out. Let's look at the photos and sort everything else out at the meeting tomorrow."

I looked at the other two, wishing I could follow their suggestion. I didn't feel up to these all night missions any more, they belonged to another time, a younger time. Perhaps a more idealistic time.

"No, I've been asked to report directly to the Minister. I should have gone straight there, but I wanted to talk to you first."

I got up and went to the door. Bärbel had already left the room, I could see her through the doorway, sitting at her desk. She'd put her notes in front of her and was reaching for the phone. Before I could leave, Klaus had stopped me.

"Before you go, one last question: who sent you down there?"

"You mean at the Ministry? It was the night duty officer."

Klaus nodded, his eyes unfocussed, far away, deep in thought. Erika and I watched him for a moment before I turned again and left.

I left the Trabant where it was and walked down to the station to get the S-Bahn train. I'd had enough of being cooped up in the small car. I also enjoyed getting the S-Bahn: once you got close to the centre of town the train went along a viaduct, giving a chance to look down on Berlin from on high, peer through first floor windows as you trundled past. My favourite bit was going between the museums—classical buildings between Marx-Engels-Platz and Friedrichstrasse, the pockmarked rendering of the Bode Museum contrasted well with the glimpses of the exhibits that could be seen beyond the windows.

Once past the museum I got up and waited by the doors until we entered the station. Pulling on the handle, I heaved the heavy sliding door open and stepped off the still moving train. Down onto the platform, a slight skip to keep my balance. Moving with the crowd out into the open, I followed the street then crossed Unter den Linden. The Soviet Embassy stood huge before me, red flags hanging limply in the still air. Down the side of the Aeroflot offices, and round the back to where the Mauerstrasse started. The first building on the left was also imposing, but in a more antique style than the monumental Soviet mission behind me. From either side of the door a trio of flags hung: red and black flags flanking the new GDR flag, a black, red and gold German tricolour sporting the *Swords to Ploughshares* emblem of the opposition. All over the country variations of this flag were to be seen: the round crest often replaced by something else: black stars, red stars, sometimes even a black A in a circle, or a hole where the old communist hammer and compass had simply been cut out.

Next to the main door somebody had chalked on the wall. *Where there is authority there is no freedom*, I smiled, nodding at the sentiment, and went in. Showing my pass to the policeman standing guard on the door I went straight up the wide staircase to the first floor. The smells were the same as in my offices in Lichtenberg—*Sigella*, *Optal* and brown coal—but the lino here wasn't worn into brown patches, and the stairs and banisters were polished stone. I told the secretary that I was here to see the Minister about the body in West Silesia, and without looking up from her typewriter she gestured at the row of chairs against the wall.

Instead of sitting down I took an empty glass from the table in the corner and wandered off to the toilets to get some water. I didn't hurry back, but stood in the corridor, enjoying the majesty of the staircase and the light coming in through the windows. Behind me I heard the door to the Minister's office open. I turned to see him shaking hands with a man carrying a briefcase and wearing a light green suit, well cut from slightly shiny material. The suit obviously came from the West, and so did the wearer.

I made no attempt to be discreet, remaining where I stood, watching as the visitor headed off downstairs. He showed a certain confidence, suggesting he was no stranger here.

"Martin, you'd better come in." The Minister seemed uneasy as he ushered me into his office.

"Have you come to see me?" seated behind his large desk the Minister was more at home, less confused.

"I've just returned from West Silesia. The night duty officer sent me down to have a look at Maier's body, said I should report directly to you on my return."

I couldn't be certain that the Minister already knew about Maier's death but I reasoned that he would have been briefed by now.

"Mmm ... yes, it was you they sent down," he seemed to be talking more to himself than me.

"I'm sorry?"

"Do you have a report for me? Perhaps you could just hand it in to the secretary." He leafed through the pile of papers in front of him, then looked up, slightly irritated that

I was still there.

"I came straight here, I haven't had time to write a report. I thought you might want to know immediately."

"Yes, that's very kind of you. Well, you'd better let me have it, I suppose, since you're here now."

He hardly seemed excited about what I had to say, just nodded absent mindedly as I told him what I'd seen. I left out my reactions to the size of the mining conveyors and excavators, the helplessness of the broken body. I kept it all businesslike. At the end of the account he nodded once more, and asked me to let him have the written report by the end of the next day.

"And Martin? No need to worry about this, it's all in hand. What I mean is, there's no need to prioritise it over your other work. We can handle the liaison with the Saxon police and the Round Table sub-committee."

Without looking at me, the Minister returned to his papers, and I returned the glass to the secretary.

17:38

The Minister's attitude perplexed me—but right now I was feeling drained, and happy not to have to think about Maier. After all, the Minister himself had told me not to worry.

We went way back, the Minister and I. It's not like we were close or anything, but still, must be more than ten years. Benno was his name, not that any of us called him that any more. We used to call him Benno or Pastor Hartmann, but nowadays we generally just called him 'the Minister'. Not sure why that's the case. He used to be the vicar at one of the churches which gave shelter to opposition groups, a safe place to meet. But he had been more than that—he took part in some of the demonstrations and events that activists organised. Some said he only took part in those actions when he was guaranteed exposure to Western journalists, and that he'd soon disappear once the cops showed up. There were often snide rumours and jokes circulating about him in opposition circles, usually when he was mentioned in one of the West Berlin papers. I didn't pay much attention at the time, but did notice that when the revolution really got going in November 1989 he very quickly managed to get a place on the Central Round Table that began by advising the government, and soon became a part of the government. Most of us involved in the opposition movements at that time were working flat out, organising demonstrations, creating news sheets and leaflets, helping new people to get involved, showing them how to design and print their leaflets and set up their groups. We didn't have time to sit down and negotiate with the Communist Party about how to run the state. But a few people—some who had been very involved in protest and resistance over the years, others merely on the fringes—started working with the Party. Most of them now occupied leading positions in what central government was left. A lot of power had been devolved down to the local level, but a few state functions remained stubbornly centralised: foreign affairs, customs and border controls, taxation and policing, in which somehow I had become a small cog.

It was the end of the working day, the sun was starting to hang low in the sky, just visible over the top of the buildings opposite. I decided to walk down the Mauerstrasse to get to the underground line that would take me up to Prenzlauer Berg. I hadn't been up there for a while, and I fancied a quick beer in a small bar, something different from the workers' pubs in my native Lichtenberg.

As I went down the steps onto the platform, I could feel the warm air being pushed out of the tunnel by an oncoming train, the same smell of hot metal that had been there this morning in the mine pit. I hopped on, finding a seat on the long bench along the side of the carriage, feeling slightly

11

nauseous, lost in my thoughts of that sandy, dusty hell.

It took a few stops for me to become aware of my surroundings again. Lots of people got on at Alexanderplatz, and I amused myself by playing Spot The Westerner. The number of Western tourists had increased dramatically in the last couple of years, and it looked like I wasn't the only person heading up to Prenzlauer Berg in search of a cool bar.

The train laboured up a steep ramp out of the underground and onto an elevated section of track, stopping almost immediately at Dimitroffstrasse station. I got off and walked down the steps to the Schönhauser Allee. I crossed the road, and took a few turns at random, pausing at the neighbourhood Round Table's noticeboard. They'd provided a short summary of decisions at the top of the board, with references to the relevant parts of the latest minutes posted below. Sometimes it felt like our whole lives were being taken over by meetings, and even if you weren't at a meeting, the chances were somebody would expect you to know about what had been talked about in it. I liked the way this noticeboard provided a quick overview of the decisions—at the end of a long day at work I didn't usually have the time or patience to read about the proceedings of every relevant meeting.

I turned away from the noticeboard, not bothering to read all the notes, and still wanting a beer. It was a bit too early for the clubs to open, but I should be able to find a drink somewhere not too far away. After a few hundred metres I stopped in front of a tenement block draped in flags and graffiti. Even by the standards of East Berlin this building was in a bad state. Balconies had fallen off or been untidily removed, and on the pavement lay a pile of bricks and dusty rendering. It looked to be one of the squats that had been opened in abandoned and derelict flats at the start of the revolution. Curious, I went into the entrance, and saw a crowd of punks drinking in the yard. Two of them were setting up a ladder below a broken light, stopping every so often to gulp down a mouthful of beer. When the ladder was in place, one climbed up while the other fed him electric cable. On the other side of the yard I could see the door to the cellars in the side wing. It had *BAR* crudely painted on it in smeared red paint. A few steps led down into a damp corridor. A bodged rack held leaflets, all jumbled up, and off to the side a door lay across two trestles, with a crate of beer on it. Above the improvised table a slogan was daubed in the same red paint: *People who talk about revolution without understanding what is subversive about love, and what is positive in the refusal of constraints, such people have a corpse in their mouth.* Quite a mouthful, corpse or no: sounded like the Situationists to me. Something to ponder on while I had a drink. Next to the crate of beer was a jam jar with a slit in the lid. I put a Mark in and took a bottle, looking around for a bottle opener. There was none, but a young woman appeared next to me, her head shaved at the sides, the remaining hair forming a wide mohican, drooping over to the side and painted with washed-out red food colouring. She smiled at me, grabbed the beer out of my hand, and took the top off with her teeth.

"Nice trick."

"You gonna get me one then?"

Another Mark in the jam jar, and the punk took a bottle out of the crate, opening that one too with her teeth, then tapping my beer with her own.

"Prosit!" She smiled, looking slightly coy under her ragged hair, poor teeth giving her mouth a lopsided look.

"Prosit!"

I tipped my bottle, allowing the beer to trickle down my throat, and let out a sigh.

"Hard day?"

"Like you wouldn't believe. What's happening here?"

She mustered me as if she were trying to work out

whether I was a cop. I must have passed.

"We're holding a talk on energy use in the GDR; you know, the energy crisis, pollution, brown coal. For the demo on Saturday. We're holding more talks on the theme too, every night next week in different squats and bars." She was enthusiastic, stumbling over her words, keen to impress me.

"Demo?"

The punk moved over to the leaflet rack and pulled out a tatty flier. Badly mimeographed, a line drawing of a power station spewing out clouds of smoke which made up the word DEMO. Underneath that: *For a sensible energy policy—in East and West. Alexanderplatz, Saturday 25th September, 14.00.* On the back was a mass of text, originally typewritten, but hardly legible after its journey through the smudgy copier. I read it over while I swilled down my beer.

"Thanks," I said, screwing the scrap of paper into my pocket.

"You coming on Saturday then?"

"You know, I might just be there."

Not sure why I said that, maybe it was because of the impression the open cast mine had made on me. Whatever my reasons, it seemed to please the punk. She smiled at me again, and I stuck my hand out.

"I'm Martin."

"Karo," she said, shaking my hand.

I'd nearly reached the door when she called out.

"Hey, Martin!"

I turned back.

"Cheers for the beer!"

I gave her my best smile.

DAY 2
Thursday
23rd September 1993

... at 8 o'clock on Thursday the twenty-third of September, here's the news on Radio DDR I.

***Moscow**: The Second Crisis of the Union in the USSR has deepened after President Gorbachev called elections for both Soviet Parliaments. Delegates of the dissolved Soviet of the Republics have refused to leave the parliament building despite water and electricity supplies being cut off.*

***Berlin**: The Ministry for Foreign Affairs has formally lodged a complaint with the West German Mission in Berlin concerning the delivery of military hardware to the breakaway Region of West Silesia. So far there has been no response from the West German Mission nor from the Inner-German Ministry in Bonn. A press conference will be held at the Palace of the Republic later today.*

And now for the water levels and draughts on the inland waterways ...

08:07

I had just got the coffee ready when the others came into my office for the morning meeting. There were only four of us, plus Bärbel, who sat in the corner without a word, pen in hand. We shook hands with each other as we sat down and I turned the radio off.

I looked over to Laura. "Did the others fill you in on what happened yesterday?"

"It sounds quite horrible—are you OK?"

I smiled, nodding towards the package marked with a police stamp that Erika was holding.

"Yes, I caught up on some sleep last night. But I'm not looking forward to seeing those photos."

We passed the pictures round. They were gruesome, but didn't tell us much. They just showed the body of Hans Maier, head and feet crushed, torso and legs ripped and oil-stained.

"I asked Dresden to forward Maier's police and Stasi files," said Erika. "They arrived with the overnight courier."

"Have you had a chance to look through them yet?"

"Not really, just a quick look—but it was enough. See for yourselves."

She put another package on the table, an A4 envelope, and pulled out a few pieces of paper.

"These are the photostats of the files the police have managed to pull so far." Erika looked at the top piece of paper, which had a letterhead reading *LdVP Sachsen*. "We've got copies of his F 16, F 22, a Disciplinary File and his I 210—his written declaration of commitment. That's all they could come up with at short notice—they said they'd carry on looking."

I sifted through the pieces of paper. Apart from the declaration, none of them actually had any markings on them to indicate which was which. I glanced through the handwritten declaration, the usual pompous phrasing: *On the basis of my Marxist-Leninist convictions, I, Johannes Friedrich Maier swear to collaborate with the Ministry for State Security in order to secure and strengthen the GDR ...*

"Of course, we should look in the central archive in the Ruschestrasse, but for the time being, this is what we have: the F 16 file has the person's real name. The reference number is in the top right hand corner," continued Laura.

I looked at the file. Johannes Friedrich Maier, along with various addresses where he was registered during the last twenty years. The reference number began with a Roman numeral.

"What department was HA XVIII?"

"That was the department monitoring heavy industry," said Laura. "It makes sense—Maier always claimed to be a victim of Stasi tactics, but at the time he was a big fish in the *BMK Kohle und Energie*—the combine that did all the building work at power stations. He was in the main offices in Hoyerswerda for several years."

The next file card didn't mention Maier by name—it just had his reference number stamped in the corner. His codename: MILCHMÄDCHEN, date of birth, first contact in 1964 by HA I/12. The most interesting entry on this card was the field marked "IM-Category/Offence". The entry was simply "IM"—*Inoffizieller Mitarbeiter*, informal collaborator. This, along with the written declaration told us that he'd worked as an informant for the Stasi, and it looked like he'd been recruited in 1964.

"What was Maier doing in 1964?" I wondered aloud.

"Looks like he was doing his National Service in the army," answered Laura. "I put together a summary of his activities yesterday."

"You have been busy!"

A grunt from the other side of the table was Klaus's first contribution of the morning. I looked up.

"Yeah, these two got excited about doing something interesting for a change," he gestured towards Erika and Laura.

"Well, it's good to get a head start, you never know what we'll be saddled with next," slightly defensive, from Erika.

I could understand her irritation—Klaus rarely said very much, so when he did, it felt like he was making an

17

important announcement. Light hearted criticism from him could sometimes feel like a serious accusation.

Klaus fell back into silence, and Erika and Laura busied themselves with flicking through the papers.

The final photostat must be the Disciplinary File. It had Maier's details, including his full name rather than his code-name. The file was dated summer 1988, and scanning through the text I could see that Maier had been reprimanded for having an unsuitable relationship with another asset, and had been told to end the affair. There was no further information than that.

"I've never seen one of these before—why has Maier got one?" I asked.

"It's interesting, I thought they were only used for Stasi full timers, not for informants. But Maier was just an IM, not a paid officer—looks a bit strange. If we had the VSH card then we could double check, but they didn't send it. Maybe it got lost." The answer came from Laura, who had become something of a Stasi files expert.

"None of this seems to help though, does it? Half the files are missing, and the ones we do have don't really tell us anything." Klaus was studying the cobwebs up in the corners near the ceiling, probably in an attempt to avoid Erika's indignant glare.

"I guess it doesn't really matter anyway. The Minister asked me to write up a report on my trip to Silesia and to leave it at that," I looked around at the others, all staring at me.

"What, he told you to drop it?" asked Laura.

"Yeah, I'm not to worry about it."

"Hang on, wait a moment," Klaus suddenly leaned forward, like he had a point to make. "Did he actually tell you to stop working the Maier case?"

"No ... not in so many words. But he definitely meant it."

"So, what did he say?"

"That I shouldn't worry about it, erm ... and not to prioritise the report, despite the fact that he wants it by the end of today."

"OK," Klaus looked around at us jubilantly. "So, we can carry on working on it. After all he didn't tell Martin to drop it–"

Erika looked troubled, holding up her hand, palm outwards, as if to stop the flow of the conversation.

"But it's clear that he meant we should leave it. Presumably he's got someone else working on it? We shouldn't just go against him like that. And anyway, what's the point?"

Klaus shrugged, sitting back in his chair again and crossing his legs. We all sat looking at each other, slurping coffee from our mugs. All except Bärbel who was still making notes in shorthand.

"Now that I think about it ..." I started, wondering whether I was saying the right thing. "He seemed sort of, shifty. Like he was unhappy that I was involved, and couldn't wait to get rid of me."

"Doesn't have to mean anything. Probably just a bit stressed or busy. I think it's safe to assume that the case is being dealt with, no doubt by another department. Klaus—do you really think we should carry on looking into Maier's death?" Laura asked in a matter of fact way.

She saw herself as the grounded and rational one in the office, and she wasn't wrong about that. She had a mixture between a bossy character and a need to keep busy, and see others around her being kept busy too—I think this led her to chivvy us along, make sure we were doing our work, that our meetings didn't go off topic and down sidelines. It could be annoying, but on the whole I think we appreciated having her around—she kept us on our toes.

"No, not really. It just all sounds a bit weird. But no, I think you're right," Klaus looked down, concentrating on fiddling with one of his evil cigars.

"OK, so shall we leave it there then?" Still the voice of reason, Laura was looking around at us, checking that each of us was agreeing. "Right, so that's that. What else have we got on the agenda today?"

After the meeting I decided to write up the report on my trip to Weisswasser, get it out of the way so that I could concentrate on the stuff that I ought to be doing. It didn't take too long, after all there wasn't too much to say. I went to West Silesia, I saw a body and a mining machine, the police seemed to be taking care of everything so I came home. I didn't bother mentioning that we'd had a look at Maier's Stasi files—it didn't seem relevant, particularly since we weren't actually going to do anything with that information.

I finished the last page and pulled it out of the typewriter, putting the top sheet with the others in a file to take to the Ministry. The two carbon copies went in another pair of files, one to keep here, the other for the central RS archives. I sat back in my chair and peered through the dusty net curtains. It was a nice day out there, the sun was shining, the sky blue. Shame to be cooped up in the office, I thought, much better to be outside.

10:23

I handed my report to the secretary, I could have sent it in the internal post, but I had enjoyed the short walk from the S-Bahn station to the Ministry. I was about to leave when she did that thing with her hand again, the disdainful wave at the chairs. I looked at her, and waited while she decided whether she was going to tell me what she wanted.

"If you would take a chair, the *Staatssekretär's* assistant wishes to speak to you."

The secretary handed my report back to me, and I took both the file and a chair, like a good little boy. So Gisela Demnitz, the assistant to the senior civil servant at the Ministry, wanted to see me. She was the person I usually dealt with, the one with the responsibility for all the peripheral agencies in the Ministry of the Interior.

She didn't make me wait long—a buzzer on the secretary's phone sounded, and she informed me that Frau Demnitz was ready to receive me. I walked along the corridor and went into Frau Demnitz's office after a polite knock. She was sitting behind her desk, a standard woodchip number, with grey steel legs.

"Herr Grobe," she said, as she stood up to shake my hand. She and I were still on formal terms, perhaps because she'd always worked for the Ministry and valued the traditional protocols of government.

I sat down in the chair opposite her, the desk between us. Frau Demnitz fiddled with some papers, peering through the horn-rimmed glasses perched on the end of her nose. Finally she looked up and addressed me.

"Herr Grobe, I understand that you have been receiving information from the police officer responsible for the Maier investigation in Dresden. I can only assume that you requested this information while you were in personal and contiguous contact with the comrade *Unterleutnant* yesterday, but I am certain that I need not remind you that the Minister has explicitly stated that there is no need for any further involvement on your part. The Minister has in fact asked me to inform you," and here she looked at her notes, presumably in an effort to get what she was about to say exactly right, "that the investigation is in hand." Demnitz paused before starting her next sentence. "Additionally, the Minister wishes to instruct you to take over the liaison between this Ministry and the Four Powers. In its wisdom the Central Round Table," and here Demnitz broke off to give what I'm sure was a disparaging sniff, "has advised that such a task should be carried out by this Ministry. Your instructions are to provide the formal framework for contact between the German Democratic Republic and the military missions of the Soviet Union, the Republic of France, the United States of America and the United Kingdom. You will begin this afternoon. A meeting has been agreed in principle with Major Sokolovski of the Soviet Army Western Group of Troops in Karlshorst. I would be obliged if you could contact his office to confirm the time and communicate the details of your appointment with this office."

Frau Demnitz handed a file to me, and I gave her my report in return. She held out her hand, and I took it as I got up, but before I'd made it to the door I was called back.

"Herr Grobe," and this time it was definitely a sniff, "while I am sure we appreciate the fact that you have prepared this report in a remarkably short frame of time, I would like to ask you to provide us with a more comprehensive account. If you would be so kind?"

11:58

Coming through the door to the offices I could see that Bärbel was not there, and that the post had been delivered. It was in a pile on the secretary's desk. I shuffled through the letters and parcels. There was only one for me: a fat letter from Dresden, *LdVP Sachsen* stamped in the top left corner. It was from the Saxon police. Perhaps this was the information from Dresden that Demnitz had been getting so excited about? It did make me wonder how she'd known about the letter even before it arrived, but the obvious answer was probably the right one: Schadowski had been on the phone with someone from the Ministry.

I went into my office, tearing open the envelope and poking my hand into it. The cover letter included an inventory identifying the contents of Maier's pockets when his body was found. None of it looked familiar, even though I had probably looked at it all when I was down there. But at the time I must have asked for the list to be sent to me at the office, because otherwise it would have bypassed me and gone straight to the Ministry.

A second sheet informed me that fingerprints had been taken from some scraps of paper (copies enclosed) found in Maier's pockets. These fingerprints had been identified as belonging to Chris Fremdiswalde, DOB: 17.09.1973, place of birth: Löbau. Currently registered as living in Thaerstrasse in Berlin-Friedrichshain. He had been arrested in 1987 for theft at his school in Hoyerswerda, and a photo of Chris at the time of his arrest had been included. There was no explanation of why the police had bothered to compare his fingerprints with those on the papers in Maier's pockets—there must be some close connection with Maier, otherwise they couldn't have come up with the fingerprint match so quickly.

The other items in the envelope didn't look particularly interesting. There was no diary, only a few scraps of paper that looked like shopping lists. Except one, which had a date, the 25th September, along with the time 14.00, and a name: Alex. Looking at the note, I pulled out the crumpled leaflet that Karo the punk had given me the night before: *For a sensible energy policy—in East and West. Alexanderplatz, Saturday 25th September, 14.00.* I stared at both pieces of paper for a while. Why would Maier be interested in a demo here in Berlin? True, he'd been involved in the mining business, but that was before the revolution, three years ago, before he'd become involved in politics and the business of Silesian devolution.

I shovelled the bits of paper back into the envelope and tossed it on to the pile that I called my in-tray. Time for some proper work. But before that I had an appointment to confirm with the Russians.

Fortunately my meeting with the Russian liaison officer was in Berlin-Karlshorst. It could have been worse—I might have had to go all the way to the Soviet Army headquarters in Wünsdorf, about thirty kilometres south of the city. I'd got here with the office Trabant, parking it near the S-Bahn station, and wandering through Karlshorst to arrive at the grey steel gate sporting a red star. One of the guards posted in front checked my pass and ushered me in, the gate clashing shut behind me. I was in a small paved yard, Soviet soldiers in dress uniform and fatigues hastened between the main building and various side wings. No-one paid any attention to me, and not quite sure where to go I just headed in through the main entrance.

Behind the tall wooden doors the hall was both large and high, with expansive bay windows at the back, and a wide staircase to my right. Soldiers bustled around here too, looking both purposeful and efficient, clacking over the polished parquet. Not even sure who to ask for, I stood just inside the doorway, and flicked through the file Frau Demnitz had given me. It contained nothing but the addresses and telephone numbers of the headquarters for each of the Four Powers, each on a separate sheet. When I looked up I noticed that a soldier, wearing fatigues and a cap, was standing right next to me. He spoke in Russian, and although I tried to work out what he was saying, I really hadn't a clue. He held his hand out, pointing at some chairs just to the side of the stairs, before he too moved purposefully off. I watched him march away, and as he went past an open doorway another soldier caught my attention. It was the eye patch that did it—a very noticeable fashion accessory. And now I looked more closely at this second soldier, I noticed the blue flashes on the collar and the blue stripe on his shoulder boards: KGB. Now that I was looking at him I could see that he too was mustering me with his only eye. A curt flick of his head, acknowledging my existence, then he moved further back into the room, beyond my line of sight.

I hadn't quite got to the chairs when someone else spoke to me, this time in German.

"Lieutenant Grobe! Very pleased to meet you. I am Major Mikhail Vassilovich Sokolovski. No relation."

I didn't understand who he might not be related to, and didn't like to ask for fear of causing offence. But the major in front of me had a smooth and clear way of speaking German, which was also a good way to describe his appearance. Dress uniform, red flashes, very neat. Several rows of medals did his chest proud, indeed the medals would have looked cramped on a narrower chest. He held his hand out for me to take, a huge paw of a hand that could easily crush mine, but thankfully didn't. The major pointed the way upstairs, arms gesticulating the whole while, underscoring the small talk he was using to show off his flawless German. I was far too busy looking around me to pay much attention to what he was saying, something about a cultural event at the embassy.

I'd never been in a Russian military base before, and it was not at all how I'd imagined it. Outside rigidly controlled 'cultural events' the population of the GDR had been kept well away from the Russian brothers. To us, the Russians were different, alien, scary—and even after nearly three years of revolution I found it hard to believe that I was standing here in the Soviet Military Berlin HQ. But it all felt rather informal, I could see through open doors how soldiers and uniformed secretaries were shouting down phones, taking down dictation, typing away at noisy old typewriters, and all the while the endless stream of people moving around, carrying papers, boxes, radio sets, furniture—anything you could imagine. Nobody bothered to salute the major as we went past.

We reached an office at the back of the building,

overlooking a large parade ground surrounded by flag poles. The major gestured that I should take a seat while he closed the door. Turning to a filing cabinet he took two glasses and a bottle of vodka from the top drawer. He set the glasses up on his desk and filled them to the brim before handing me one.

"Before we start, a toast. I propose we drink to the architect and inspiration of the colossal historic victories of the Soviet people; the banner, pride, and hope of all progressive humanity. To the great leader and the teacher of my country and yours: *da zdravstvuyet* Joseph Vissarionovich Stalin!"

My glass tipped in shock as I listened to his words, recognising the style from a time not too long past. The major laughed loudly at my reaction.

"No, my friend, times are different now! A small joke is allowed between friends, no? But perhaps you had better make the toast?"

Still not quite sure what to make of this man who looked so formal, yet started our first meeting with a joke about Stalin, I stood up, glass (adequately replenished by the major) in right hand, looked him in the eye, and tried my best:

"In these uncertain times let us drink to continued and fraternal co-operation between our people!"

Again, the loud laugh, and Sokolovski tipped back his glass, swallowing the vodka in one go. I nervously followed his example.

"Good, very good, *tovarishch,*" he said. "My colleagues might at this point recharge the glasses, and make another toast. They find it amusing that you Germans, so very exact and proper in all you do, are unable to get beyond even the tenth toast without falling over. And I? I consider myself open to the civilising influences of your culture, so instead I give you the bottle, and we shall meet again. We shall talk about whatever it is we need to talk about, and have many more toasts."

He shook my hand, opened the door and ushered me back out into the busy chaos beyond.

This was pretty perplexing, but I considered that I had made contact and that, at least so far, I had neither questions nor reports for my Russian liaison. All in all, the major was probably right: we were finished for now. At least it meant I could go back to the office and get on with writing up that report.

I wandered out of the building and to the gate, the sentries merely nodding as they let me back out into the street. Arriving back at the car I looked down at the bottle of vodka in my hand. That's enough vodka for one day—I opened up the bonnet, took the cap off the petrol tank and poured the Russian alcohol in.

DAY 3
Friday
24th September 1993

Moscow: For the first time since the crisis began, large numbers of KGB forces have been seen on the streets of Moscow. The KGB issued a statement saying that they have mobilised troops to assist militia and internal forces in their efforts to keep public order in the Soviet capital. It remains unclear whether or not they support President Gorbachev who remains under house arrest in the Crimea.

08:11

A nice short morning meeting today—that suited me, I was getting anxious about the backlog of work that was building up on my desk. We all had ongoing projects we were already working on, and there was no need to divvy up any further work. The others thought it unfair that I had been ticked off by Frau Demnitz, which made me feel a bit better, and they were surprised about the liaison task I had been given.

"She asked you to do liaison by yourself, or did she mean we should take on that task jointly?" Erika asked.

"Just me. But as far as I'm concerned we can share it. Sounds boring, really. Anyway, I've already been to see my Russian counterpart, it was quite strange. He toasted Stalin, then laughed at me and threw me out!" My description garnered a chuckle from my colleagues but I could see that they thought I was exaggerating. The meeting moved on to more general matters before we ended.

There had been nothing to decide today, but even when there was we very rarely voted. Most decisions in the *Republikschutz* departments were taken in the small teams that were working on any particular topic, but if we thought a case might have an impact on any other team we would check in with them first. Here in RS2 we generally talked any issues through until we found a way forward that worked for everyone involved. It used to be quite a frustrating process, but with time, as we got to know each other, to understand how our colleagues ticked, it all became both easier and quicker. Knowing each others' quirks and interests—along with Laura's help in making sure that we didn't talk for hours about something that didn't matter—meant that we'd become quite efficient in our decision making.

I was just making a start on a report about my visit to Karlshorst when the phone rang. It was the Minister's secretary informing me that a meeting had been set up with Major Clarie at the British Army offices in the Olympic Stadium for this afternoon, at 4 o'clock. It looked like the Minister wanted me kept busy for the next few days.

After the phone call I found it hard to concentrate on writing the report. And if I was to be in West Berlin this afternoon then I didn't really have enough time to get involved in any of the other pieces of work waiting for me. I found myself looking again at the stuff the Saxon police had sent me, I was particularly intrigued by the slip of paper with tomorrow's date on it. Alex, 14.00—it just had to be the Energy Demo. Or, at least that seemed the most likely. It could just be that Maier had been planning to meet someone called Alex on Saturday afternoon. But I wasn't convinced.

Thinking about it—the demo, with its focus on brown coal;

the site where the body was found; Maier's own past in the brown coal mining industry—I couldn't get rid of the feeling that there were too many coincidences. I shook my head, trying to rid it of questions. I wasn't the one investigating the murder. Not only did I not have any part to play in the investigation, but I had already been warned off by Frau Demnitz. And I'd agreed with my own colleagues not to pursue the case.

10:47

I caught the tram heading down to Rummelsburg, finding a seat as we creaked round the corner and under the railway tracks. Brown coal was a seam running through this case, and even if I wasn't actually involved, well, I asked myself, why shouldn't I express an interest in a matter that clearly had the potential to become a security issue for our Republic?

I could see the twin chimneys of the Rummelsburg coal power station beckoning from way down the road; but they were much further away than they had seemed—it was several stops before the tram finally arrived at the main gates.

I showed my pass to the works guard and asked to speak to the director. A short wait, then I was met by a guy in a suit who took me to a high Art Deco building made of slim, reddish-brown bricks. Everything about it was narrow, it was huge, but its ten storeys made it look tall and lean, the same as the windows, stretching virtually from marble covered floors to the soaring ceilings. We clacked our way across the marble to the stairs. On the first floor the walls were covered in glassy green tiles, the floors with well polished red lino. I was ushered into an office, where another suit sat behind a dark antique desk. The suit rose and took my hand, beckoning me to sit down.

"How can I help you?"

Good question. I'd come on a whim, unprepared: I wasn't too sure myself what I was doing here. Curiosity perhaps? A desire to see with my own eyes another part of the workings of the brown coal industry? A hope that mere proximity would help my brain make some connections? But curiosity, a desire to follow up on a hunch—those weren't really the things I could admit to.

"The *Republikschutz* is interested in the impacts that the West Silesian crisis might have on the electricity supply in the Republic," I ad libbed.

"It's already having an effect." The director sat back, crossing his hands over his expansive belly, it was clearly a favourite topic of his. "Most of the power produced in the Silesian Boxberg power station is used in the south of the Republic: Saxony, Thuringia. Up here we get coal from the mines south of Spremberg, mostly from West Silesia. They've been dropping hints about setting a 'market price' for the coal that they send up to us. As I've already informed the Ministry for Coal and Energy, in the case of West Silesia seceding from the GDR we would lose over half of our national coal reserves, and half of our generating capacity to boot. We are already importing some coal from Poland, but that would have to increase—the Welzow field doesn't have enough capacity to feed the Schwarze Pumpe power station, and the West-Elbe fields are still supplying Espenhain and what's left of the chemical industry," the director continued, his mellifluous voice outlining technical details and statistics that were far beyond my ability to understand, never mind remember. The gist of it was that most of our coal reserves and a huge amount of electricity generating capacity were in West Silesia, and therefore at risk.

After a few minutes of this shop talk I interrupted: "But if West Silesia became independent then they'd have too much generating capacity for their own use—surely they'd be happy to sell it on to us?"

"You'd think so, but there is talk of an extra-high voltage transmission line running from West Silesia to West Germany, presumably in order to export the electricity to the Western markets."

West Germany wasn't suffering from any shortfall in energy supply, so why would they be interested in importing power from West Silesia? Except, of course, to make life difficult for us.

12:33

Deciding not to go back to the office I went home. Arriving at the flat I could see a note on the door, just like the old days before I had a phone. A neighbour had taken a call for me, and left a message on the notepad hanging from the door frame. "Katrin called, please phone back".

I turned the key in the door and opened up. Going in, I crossed a beam of sunlight, making the floating dust dance in my wake. Putting the still warm bread rolls I'd just bought on the table, I went to the stove to boil some water for coffee. Standing in the kitchen, looking out of the window and enjoying the warm, yeasty smell of the rolls I watched a local S-Bahn train squeal around the curved tracks below. Its dull red and grey paintwork swallowed the low sunlight, the passengers behind the smeared windows barely visible, a shadow puppet show. The train passed, and the weeds between the tracks waved their goodbyes. Turning around I stared at the telephone that had just started ringing.

"Grobe."

"Papa! It's me."

"Hi Katrin, what's up?"

"Oh nothing much, just got a cancelled lecture, thought it would be good to see you. Besides, I've got something to talk to you about. Have you got the day off?"

"I've got a few hours free. Why?"

"Listen, do you want to come out here? I'll buy you coffee."

I really wanted to go to bed for a short nap before I had to meet the British major, but I knew I would probably lie there staring at the ceiling, thinking. And even if I did manage to nod off then I wouldn't sleep tonight and would be grumpy all day tomorrow. No, better to get out and about, enjoy a bit of time off. I turned off the stove and headed back out the door. I hadn't seen Katrin for a couple of weeks, and I was heading over to West Berlin anyway: the Olympia complex, where I was to meet the British liaison officer, was in the British sector.

I walked as far as Ostkreuz before catching the train, hoping the stroll would wake me up a bit. I didn't go to the western part of the city very often, there wasn't much for me there. The heady days after the Wall was opened had long gone, we knew we could have bananas whenever we wanted them, and we knew we couldn't afford them. We knew that the people who populated the other half of our city were mostly better fed, better dressed and better housed, but they weren't as happy as we were. Looking around at my fellow East Berliners you could be forgiven for disagreeing—we were a dour bunch. But we had something the people in the West had never had. They had experienced dictators, as we had, and they now had a stable democracy—which we had never had. But they scrawled a cross on a piece of paper every few years, and let the politicians do what they wanted. Their bodies had never surged with the adrenaline and endorphins that come from the power of revolution. We may be the poor cousins on this side of the Wall, but when it came to living life, we were rich.

Changing trains at Friedrichstrasse station was nothing like it used to be. Nowadays it was as simple as changing platforms. Not so long ago—so recently we could still measure the time in months—the short distance to the trains to the West couldn't be bridged by a few steps down a corridor and up some stairs to the platform. In those days it took years to get the piece of paper that allowed you to pass the border controls. Years of tears, and usually a one way ticket. In those days most of those who left on the westbound train would never return.

As the S-Bahn whined along the viaduct I looked down at the Wall that still drew the boundaries of this double city. The barbed wire and fences were gone, and the first line of the Wall—whitewashed concrete slabs marking the eastern edge of the border defences—was being dismantled. Behind that there were rows of potatoes, beans and other vegetables growing around the watchtowers and fence posts. The outer wall, facing West, was being maintained while the nation debated what to do with it. It was permeable now, people could pass through a number of new border crossings, but trucks and vans from the West weren't welcome. After the Wall opened up in November '89, West Berliners started coming over to the East, buying up subsidised products and taking them back to sell on the street markets. This quickly led to shortages in the capital, some claimed it was a deliberate attempt by West Germany to destabilise the GDR further—as if that were possible in those days when the communist state was already teetering, pushed by a population hungry for change.

So for the time being the Wall stayed, an economic barrier that gave us space to breathe and grow into the country we wanted to be, whatever we might turn out to be.

A few stops later I got off the train, and following the instructions Katrin had given me on the phone, I made my way to the café.

Tables and chairs were set out on the pavement in front,

all populated by young people in their young clothes, wearing their young faces. Katrin was inside. We hugged. This was a new thing, at home people mostly just shook hands when they met up, but Katrin had started hugging me after she moved to the West. I sat down at her table, and she pushed a cassette tape across the wooden surface. I put my hand over it and drew it towards me.

"What's with all these cassettes? I mean, it's not that I don't appreciate them, in fact I'm rather enjoying them. But, well, why?"

Katrin was sipping a hot chocolate, I nursed a black coffee, no sugar. I could see how my daughter had noticed that I'd deliberately sat with my back to the tray of pastries on the counter, and I think she knew that I was having to try hard to ignore their sweet, sticky call. I couldn't afford one, nevertheless I hoped that Katrin wouldn't offer to buy me one either.

"Promise you won't go off on one?" Katrin, nervous, looked at me. I wondered what was coming as I constructed a lopsided smile (the one Katrin called my Zen-face), and nodded.

"It's just, after mum ... well you had your hands full. With me, queuing for food, cooking, working in the factory. And after all that you'd go out, some meeting in some crypt, some church hall, or your friends would come round, and you'd turn the radio on loud and hold your whispered conversations around the kitchen table. But you weren't listening to the music. You never had time for music, even though I knew you loved music. West music, East music, the lot."

This made me think. *The old days.* Strangely, life was simple and straightforward, then. A tug of nostalgia coming from somewhere deep in my chest set my thoughts off on a tangent: *did I miss those days?* I think I've still got my Zen smile stapled to the front of my face, but just by looking at Katrin I could see that it had slipped a little.

35

"I had the blues: Engerling, Cäsar, Bodag ... it's just, after that Udo Ludendorff guy did that song about the train to Pankow, and why can't he do a gig in our Workers' and Peasants' State ... it was so unreal. Patronising. *Westmusik*."

"Lindenberg."

The smile must have gone by now, the Zen-face turned into a question-mark.

"Udo Lindenberg. That was the guy's name. And he just didn't get it. How could he, a Wessi? But that's just it. You listened to the West Berlin radio station RIAS, and heard the shit stuff. Anyway, Lindenberg responded to Freya Klier's appeal for help in '88."

I had to admit, that was true. When the singer-songwriter Stephan Krawczyk was arrested along with several others for trying to join a demonstration on Rosa Luxemburg day, his wife Freya Klier, who'd already been released, went on Western TV to appeal for support for him and the other interned activists. Lindenberg was one of those Westerners who put pressure on the Communist government to let them go.

"But the *Puhdys*?" Katrin would never let go of what she considered my poor musical choices. "Have you still got that album, *Das Buch*? God, it's dire!" She pulled a face, then changed tack. "No, the point is. You were doing all that stuff for me, for us, for all of us here in the Republic, I mean, over there," a gesture, through the window, vaguely eastwards, and I wonder whether this is the point to break in, defend the Puhdys, but I'm glad I didn't, because:

"And here I am, I'm at uni, meeting all these people, finding out about all these things, hearing all this music. And I feel you missed out, and, yeah, I know, music isn't such a big thing, but it kind of is too." Another pause, then: "So, it's my way of saying thanks."

I wasn't sure where to look. I'm not good at public emotion; too many years of not wanting to give the state a way into my life, not wanting to give the Stasi a clue to my weaknesses. But I could feel a tear begin in my right eye.

"Thank you too," I manage, blinking rapidly and looking away from my daughter.

Katrin smiled. Genuine, not frustrated. A little nervous still, experience telling her to keep something back.

"But, is it your Republic, still?" I ask, without thinking. Now I'm sort of looking at my daughter. "I mean, there you are in West Berlin, with all your new friends, your new clothes, your new money. Your West student's grant from the West government ..." A pause, what I've just said sinking in. "No, I'm sorry, I didn't mean it that way. It came out wrong. Sorry. I meant, when are you coming home?"

But that, too, was the wrong thing to say.

"Papa, I'm just at the other end of the city! You can come out here any time you want!" But, seeing my face, she stopped. It wasn't about the physical distance. It was about the symbolism. The Wall is still there, no matter how many holes we'd punched in it. She was in the West, I was in the East. Same city, different countries.

"Papa," she said slowly, "maybe I should have come back that winter. Things were changing, but all I could think about was that the system was breaking you. I didn't want to go the same way. I wanted to study, but they wouldn't let me. You know all this."

Her face pointed at the table, but her eyes turned upwards, checking how I'd react. I think my face had gone hard, immobile—the calm look I'd been trying to keep up had definitely gone. Katrin was drawing circles with her fingertips on the dark wood, as if the Zen that had slipped off my face had landed on the table in front of us, a pool of viscosity that she could dab her fingers in. It was obvious to us both that we were each thinking of the day she left. The furtive goodbyes, nothing said aloud in case the Stasi were listening. The knowledge that once she crossed the border into Czechoslovakia, on the way to Hungary, and from there to the West, once that first frontier had been crossed there would be no return. We would probably never see each other again. I remembered the desperation, the claustrophobia that had driven her away. I remembered my feelings that day: crushed, hurt, betrayed. *Don't shed any tears for them* they told us, ordered us, on the TV and radio. Don't shed any tears for those who couldn't stay in this stagnant land. But I still cry when I remember that awful day four years ago. And I know Katrin does, too.

"Do we have to do this every time, Papa? We always do it."

I could hear the frustration, the pain, the anger in her words. And I could feel answering emotions rising up inside myself too. It was the state she was angry at, that old GDR, run by pensioners. Stalinists. But she was angry at me, too. The daughter of a known dissident had not been allowed to stay on at school after 16, not to do her exams at 18, nor go on to university. She'd never said it aloud, but that was my fault. It was my choice to do the things I'd done, and she had been made to pay for it.

Were families always like this, rubbing each other up the wrong way, accusing each other without words, the past a ghost that is always present? Having the same arguments again and again, hurting each other in the same places time after time? We always said, and left unsaid, the same things. Katrin was the only family I had left, I didn't want this.

"It's just, some of us are trying, Katrin. Some of us *stayed*," there was an emphasis on the word stayed, as if I had pushed my emotions into those letters before forcing them out of my mouth. "We pushed the *Bonzen* out, we kept the West out, and we're making a real, independent, democratic state. Probably the first in the world! You know this! You know we need people. Young people. We need people like you, Katrin! You can study at the Humboldt University in the East. We lost tens of thousands of young people that autumn. You should have stayed. We need you."

I should have kept my mouth shut, I knew it as soon as I'd said the words, I knew it before I'd even said those words. At times like this, I feel like I'm my own angel, hovering overhead, watching, seeing everything, my own face, her face, hearing my own words. The angel could see how I took a bite out of my own daughter with each syllable. I see it, but I always seem powerless to stop the mess I'm making.

"*Stayed?* Like you? And what are you doing now?" She was angry, her words sharp with barbs. "What's your contribution to the glorious revolution? Get off your fucking high horse. You, you spy! That's what you are, creeping around, look you even have a sad trenchcoat! A spy, no better than the fucking Stasi!"

This had to hurt. The angel watched my face become hard, my eyes glazing as I absorbed the shock.

"You don't mean that."

"Well, it's true, isn't it? They got rid of the Stasi, and they realised they still needed it, so they asked the sheep to put on the wolf's clothing, didn't they? The Minister of the Interior himself, good old Benno, he was the one who asked you! Didn't he?"

"No! You know that's not how it was. How it is. You know!"

"So if it's not true, what exactly is it you do? I mean, I have no real idea what my own Papa does!"

"You do know, I'm with the RS."

"Yeah, but I mean, it's just another of those weird combinations of letters that could hide anything! Tell me, tell me what it is you do? What have you been working on this week, yesterday, today?"

I could have told her about the Russian major, made her laugh about the Stalin toast and my summary dismissal from his presence, but my mind seemed stuck on the Maier case. I recalled that feeling of fear that I'd experienced on the way back from West Silesia. It was a fear that I hadn't had to feel for a few years—I used to know it so well, this extra sense, almost anticipating it, welcoming it. An old friend. You knew where you were with that fear. It was from the days when we didn't know whether the Stasi were listening, whether the Stasi were watching, whether the Stasi were coming to get us. It reminded me of why I was doing stuff, back then. Daring to disagree, to find out about stuff the state didn't want us to know. But nowadays it just made me feel sick.

"It's ... it's confidential. I can't tell you. Sorry," it sounded lame, even to me, even without my angel's ears listening to my own words. But I couldn't share this with Katrin. She was safe now. Here, in West Berlin.

"You know what, it's all rubbish. All shit. You and your new society, based on *trust and openness and honesty*," this last bit in a different voice, sarcastic. "And there you are, in your secret job, doing secret things for the secretaries in the secret ministry!"

I just sat there, head sagging, face inches from the table.

"Shit. Look, I've gotta go. I've got a lecture in half an hour."

I didn't look up as Katrin stood up, put her coat on, gestured to the waiter and paid. She looked at me, I could tell, even though I was still glaring at the table, shoulders hunched inside the trench coat. Without another word she turned, and left the café, swiftly negotiating the chairs and tables, away from where I was still slumped, fingertips just brushing the cassette on the table.

I nudged the cassette round so that I could read what was on the label. It said simply: *Thanks*, with a smiling acid face drawn next to the word. Sliding the tape off the table and into my pocket, I moved towards the door. Nowhere near as elegant as my daughter in completing this manoeuvre, bumping into tables and the backs of chairs, drawing questioning looks from the chattering students. I was no longer at home in a young persons' café. When did that happen? Or was it my clothes, my hairstyle, my smell; identifying me as from the East? I made it to the door in one piece, and hoping to make an exit without causing any further scenes, I pulled the door open. Too hard: it slammed against the coat stand behind it, and I slid out, not looking back to see what the students thought of my awkward exit. There, to one side of the door, stood Katrin.

"Katrin! Oh–"

"It's OK, I'm going already."

"No! I mean, please. Wait. You're right. I should share more. Open up a bit. One more chance?"

Katrin hesitated, a vague smile peering through her tears. She looked towards the bus stop, back at me. Maybe she did have a lecture to go to.

"OK, do you want to go back in?"

"No, it's true what I just said, it's confidential. I shouldn't be telling you, so I definitely shouldn't be talking about it in a café in the middle of West Berlin!"

Katrin smiled. A grin that reminded me of her mother when we first met, before the care and the worry crept into our relationship.

"Let's walk a bit, here, this way. And you can tell me why you're so cagey these days."

She took my arm, and steered me down a side street, as if I were an old man needing to be helped home after getting lost. It must have presented a strange sight: an attractive young woman, in trendy, Western clothes walking arm in arm with a bulky, grey headed man clad in cheap, nylon-mix clothing. But I guess everyone in West Berlin has relatives in the East, so maybe it was normal. From the side street we turned into another street. The tall buildings—delicate in yellows and creams, stucco patterns and reliefs gracing the façades—looked down on us.

"I'm sorry about before. I shouldn't have made fun about

41

your coat—I mean, it's not like you were the only one in a beige trenchcoat hanging around there." A few more steps, another street corner, cross the road while I wonder where she saw another Ossi, then: "You know, I will come back. I am coming back."

I looked at her, waiting for her to continue, not wanting to break in on what I hoped she was going to tell me. She'd never before spoken to me about her plans for the future. Not since she'd left.

"But I'm really enjoying being here, at the *Freie Universität,* being in West Berlin. It feels like, after all the years of, of ..." she was struggling to find the words: "*suffocation,* I can finally ... unfold. I know that amazing things are happening, over there, back home," again the vague eastwards gesture. "And I want to be part of that. I will be. But this is *me*-time. Does that make sense?"

It made a lot of sense and I wondered, if I were younger, would I be doing what she was, or would I be in the midst of this new society we were building in the East? I was thinking of the endless meetings with the other residents in my tenement block. If I were in my twenties, would I want to sit there and plan everything from the communal kitchen garden to insulation measures? Maybe the answer was yes. There were some younger people in my block and while I could see that they sometimes switched off (usually when Frau Priepert from upstairs was talking about noise levels or cleaning rotas for the communal areas), they were actually really engaged. Without them we wouldn't have the bike workshop in the cellar, without them we wouldn't have links with the farm on the edge of the city—the farm that brought us food. Last week when I got home they were hanging off ropes, repairing the rendering on the side of the building—it looked dangerous, the work slapdash and piecemeal, but watching them I felt a sense of pride. And the building desperately needed this attention after years of neglect.

While my mind was wandering, Katrin had continued talking. She was telling me about her course, the other students. I tried to keep up, but I had somehow become fixated on the bike workshop. I made a mental note to take my old bike there, and get it sorted out before the weather turned too cold.

"But you shouldn't think you can get away with it that easily," grinned Katrin. "Tell me all your secrets!"

I often had a strong feeling with people who knew me well, particularly ones who cared about me, that my face simply betrayed those thoughts I wasn't even consciously thinking. Like now, I guess I had been hoping Katrin would be sidetracked by her stories of student life, and that I wouldn't have to tell her about West Silesia and the dead politician. Had she read that on my face? Was that the reason for the sudden change of subject, back to me.

"Well, I had to go down to West Silesia. It's all kicking off down there."

"Yeah, tell me about it! A student in my seminar group is from Görlitz, she says they have guards on the Silesian borders now. They're wearing West Silesian uniforms, but are actually BGS." *Bundesgrenzschutz*—West German paramilitary border police.

I was surprised Katrin had heard about this, I'd only heard the rumour last week. So far we weren't clear whether the West Germans had actually put their own troops on the Silesian borders, or whether they were just providing training and military hardware. Either way it was a confrontational move, an incursion on our sovereignty—West Silesia was still, officially, part of the GDR.

"So, I go down there, because there's a dead politician, probably murdered-"

"Who?" Katrin interrupted, attracted, as so many are, by the gruesomeness of violence.

"I shouldn't say," but the look on her face, how could I not

43

say? "Maier. That slick one. But don't tell anyone!"

Katrin had gone quiet. Her keen curiosity had been shed the moment I said the name.

"Fuck!" she said quietly, almost whispering.

"Yeah. Things are going to get interesting now."

"Do you know who did it yet?"

"No, not yet. But the Saxon cops are involved, so it won't just be the Silesians dealing with it by themselves."

West Silesia was small, very small, and just didn't have the resources to deal with a difficult case. Or alternatively, I reckoned the investigation, if left to the Silesians, would come up with whatever result best suited the politics of the day.

Katrin seemed distracted, she looked at me. "Thanks, Papa. Thanks for talking. But I have to go—that lecture. You can find your way back to the station?"

"Hang on, you said there was something you wanted to talk to me about?"

"Oh! Look, I should go, we'll talk another time!"

15:22

I wandered around a bit more after Katrin left, stopping at a Currywurst stand to get a coffee. I stood by the booth, enjoying the weak sunlight, but not enjoying the weak coffee that I was sipping from a cardboard cup. I was next to a crossroads regulated by traffic lights, and every couple of minutes a shrieking, roaring stream of motorised metal hurtled across the junction, first from one side, then the other. It was loud and smelly, and made me appreciate the fact that there were so few cars on the road in East Berlin. A couple of years ago we probably had as much traffic as here, although the cars were neither as large nor as shiny, but the collapse of the Eastern European trading bloc, Comecon, in January 1990 meant that we were now paying market prices for the Russian oil we imported. The price of petrol and diesel had shot up, and on top of that it was rationed, the lion's share going to industry and agriculture. There were attempts to find other fuel sources, using feed maize and sugar beet, but we needed the land to produce food for ourselves and to earn hard currency through export. Fuel for personal transport just wasn't a priority. Raising the sour coffee to my lips I smiled—it was ironic, just a few years ago our tiny plastic cars with their two stroke engines symbolised freedom. Now we had real freedom, political freedom, and we didn't have cars. Or, at least not the fuel to put in them. I wondered if there was an inverse relationship between freedom and the number of cars. If there were, then I had to feel sorry for the people here in West Berlin.

Upon reaching the dregs of both my coffee and my ruminations on transport and freedom I set off again, looking for an underground station.

Exiting at Olympia I asked around until I found the British base on the Olympic stadium site. A guard wearing fatigues, rifle slung over his soldier, examined my RS pass and told me to present myself at the gatehouse beyond. A second check, this time of both my RS pass and my identity papers, then I was asked to wait. After a few moments a sergeant came to fetch me, asking me, in English, to follow him. We crossed a grassy courtyard and entered a red-brick single storey building. It looked fairly new, no more than 10 years old, and all the paint work was fresh, but somehow the overall impression I had was of shabbiness. Inside the building the ceilings were low, and the brickwork unplastered, just covered in glossy grey-green paint. A wooden door with a frosted glass window stood partly open, and the sergeant knocked, then saluted to whoever was in the room.

"Mr. Grobe here to see you, sir," he reported, not pronouncing the final E in my name.

45

"Very good, show him in will you? Thank you."

The sergeant looked over to me, gestured towards the open door, muttering something which could have been *sir*, then disappeared back outside. I went into the room to find a major sitting behind a large desk, head bent over some paperwork, pen in hand, poised perhaps to sign or correct. He looked up as I shuffled in, a vague smile playing at the corner of his lips.

"Martin! Welcome, Tom Clarie, Tom or Clarie to friends, but never both. Defence Intelligence Staff, yes, quite, really ought to be SIS that receives you, but somehow we get the honour. This is your first visit, I understand? Well, yes, welcome!"

He'd spoken in German, and was now getting up, his fatigues rustling as he pushed his chair back and extended his right hand, damp and limp. I took it, saying my name, then feeling foolish because he was clearly already in possession of this basic fact.

"Please, please sit down. A cup of tea and a biscuit, perhaps?" his finger hovered over an intercom system on his desk, and he slowly, almost reluctantly moved it away when I shook my head. My stomach was unhappy about the cardboard coffee I'd had less than an hour ago, and it certainly didn't like the thought of some over-brewed tea made with a tea bag, and definitely not with milk in it. But I was intrigued by being offered just one biscuit, and wondered what kind of biscuit it might be.

"I'm very pleased to meet you. I gather you are my counterpart from the other side? Quite odd, we used to deal with the chaps from your Ministry for Foreign Affairs, but actually you're from the Interior Ministry, aren't you? Well, the world changes, as we've so clearly seen these last few years, what, old boy?"

I really didn't know what to say, this chap seemed to be straight from the Babelsberg film studios. His German was

46

perfect, but with a deliberate English accent: an oversized plum in his throat. Although his fair hair and blue eyes made him look more Prussian than British, his language was that of an officer and a gentleman. Fortunately Major Tom (as I had already christened him in my head) ploughed on, neither waiting for nor expecting a response.

"Now do forgive me, but I'm actually frightfully under prepared—not something that you would expect from a British intelligence officer, eh? But we got a call from your office first thing this morning—they seemed awfully keen to get us chaps to meet up a.s.a.bloody-p. if you see what I mean. So, all things said and done, I've been caught on the hop. Just reading through my notes from the last liaison meeting, actually, but perhaps you have something for me?"

Major Tom peered at me over gold rimmed spectacles, as if he hoped I might just have the answers that had eluded him throughout his career as an intelligence officer.

"Er ... no. I gather that this is more of a social call, so we can get acquainted," I improvised, not understanding why the Minister felt it so urgent that I meet the Russians and the British.

"Ah! Splendid, splendid. Very civilised, actually. So there's nothing in particular you feel we have to talk about right now? Splendid."

He glanced around the office as if to find something to talk to me about. My eyes followed his, and settled on the bookshelves. Several shelves held weighty tomes on economic theory, everything from Mill to Marx, by way of Keynes, Locke, Smith, Friedman and Proudhon.

"You're interested in economic theory?"

"Why, yes, actually. Are you a fellow economist? Not strictly in my job description, but a firm economic understanding is essential in this post, I find. Take your country, very interesting indeed. Sadly I don't get intelligence reports on economic affairs, and what one can read in the papers over here is pure propaganda, not worth wrapping your fish and chips in it, as far as I'm concerned. But tell me, is your government really not going to privatise industry? Surely you need the capital investment?"

"Actually it looks like things are going the other way: most workplaces are being mutualised, sometimes formally by some kind of agreement, but often just because of the impact the Works Councils are having."

"Oh, really?" the major interjected politely, but without enthusiasm.

"Even though a lot of the larger factories and organisations still have a hierarchical structure, the Councils are involved at every level of decision making, and represent the workers." I persevered. "That means everyone can be involved in every decision, whether that's to do with production or work conditions. I think it's inevitably going to lead to some kind of syndicate system—as people get more confident, and more aware of the kinds of decisions that need to be taken, and why. We're all getting more involved in running our own workplaces."

"But that's not going to sort out questions such as what needs to be produced, and in what quantities," Clarie was more interested now, warming to the debate. "The communist planned economy failed, so you need some other way to make those decisions."

"Yes. The Marxists were arrogant, thought they knew best. But the capitalist systems of the West aren't any more efficient—look at how resources were wasted in the boom years of railway building in your country, or the redundancy and waste prevalent in the West German healthcare system. And capitalism isn't efficient in allocating resources either— isn't it immoral, having both poor people and rich people in the same economy? In the GDR that would be unconstitutional. No, the economy has to be structured from below, by the people, just like everything else in our country. We need to get the balance right—between what we *can* produce and what we *need* to produce, and like everything else in our society that's going to take a lot of negotiation. Think of it as central facilitation rather than central planning."

"But that's impossible—surely one of the reasons that the planned economy system failed was because it's simply impossible to calculate all the factors!"

"Maybe, but it doesn't have to be perfect, just better than the alternatives. And let's face it, Adam Smith and his followers haven't done such a great job of it either," I gestured towards the *Wealth of Nations* on the bookshelf. "There's no perfect information to allow supply and demand levels to be correctly recognised, the whole system skews supply towards those with the greatest access to means of payment, rather than those with the greatest need. And we're not starting from scratch, pretty much everybody in my country has an understanding of what is broken in our economy, where there are shortages or gluts in production. We need to build on that, find new ways of sharing information on production and to make decisions together on the larger economic issues."

"Shades of Hertzka, if you ask me," Clarie paused long enough to look pleased with himself. "But it's rather naïve to expect everyone to become an economic expert."

"Not really. Every household already makes economic decisions. I think we need to experiment with how best to share economic information, honest information, and trust that people will behave in more rational and fair ways—whether they're deciding what to buy, or what they should be producing in their workplace."

"Seems a bit optimistic to me, if you don't mind me saying, old chap."

"Perhaps, but I think it's got a better chance of working in a society that is already making those links—being involved and making decisions together at home and work."

Clarie just grunted, I'd lost his interest. His eyes wandered the bookshelves again. I could tell he was unconvinced by what I was saying, but I didn't mind. After all, just a few years ago anyone dreaming about a grassroots revolution in our country would have been called a naïve fantasist. It was all a big experiment, and it probably wouldn't work too well, but as I'd said, to justify itself it only had to be marginally better than the alternatives.

Finally the major's eyes returned to the desk in front of him, and he shuffled together the papers he had been looking at when I came in. Picking them up, and slapping the sides of the bundle of papers against the desk to square them off, he casually waved them at me.

"Minutes. Presumably you've read them, have you? Your predecessor, our meetings, I mean?"

"No, I was only tasked with liaison yesterday, the paperwork hasn't caught up with me yet." In fact, until now I hadn't even thought that I ought to look through the minutes of previous meetings.

"Well, I'm sure you know the ropes already, no need to tell you about it all? Basically you and I will stay in touch, any problems with the MLM or BRIXMIS, you know? And we'll see each other on the 7th as well, along with the others."

The 7th of October, Republic Day, when we celebrate the founding of the GDR, it used to be a day of official marches past the Communist Party leadership, nowadays it had become a 24-hour street party. But now it sounded like I'd be wearing a tie and jacket and getting bored at some formal international function in the Palace of the Republic.

"Of course old Mikhail Vassilovich will be there too, you know from SERB?"

It took me a moment to work out that he meant Sokolovski, but SERB? (not to mention MLM and BRIXMIS!) I was feeling rather out of my depth, and annoyed with the Minister and Demnitz for dropping me into this without even a proper briefing.

"Naturally, we won't talk about anything that matters, like the small problem you folks are having down in West Silesia," Major Tom's face took on a cunning cast, "Unless, of course, you actually feel we may have something to contribute?"

"That's a very kind offer, and we may take you up on it." I considered for a moment, then: "Is there anything you feel might be of use?"

"Well, of course, these things are usually quid pro quo, old chap! But, since we're new friends: I do sometimes wonder what would happen if our old friends the Russians, and your old friends the West Germans got together, perhaps with a little help from those chaps at the Stasi ..."

Major Tom winked at me, then pressed a button on his intercom system.

"Sergeant, could you bring one of the specials in? Thank you." Turning his attention back to me, the major continued: "In recognition of our new relationship, and the hope that it will be a long and fruitful one, ah–"

A brief knock, and the door opened. The major got to his feet and took a bottle from the hands of someone standing just outside.

"Here we are, yes. Fruitful. Quite."

Another bottle of alcohol, this time whisky. The label said *Talisker, 20 years*. Whatever that meant.

I was already feeling ignorant and ungracious, arriving empty handed and not knowing anything about what I was meant to be doing here. I had the feeling that if I stayed much longer my ignorance could only become more obvious, so I made my excuses, shook the major's hand again (which he didn't seem to be expecting, becoming flustered and red faced), and exited, bottle in hand.

Three trains and a short walk later I was back in my corner of Berlin, between Friedrichshain and Lichtenberg. Walking slowly down the middle of the cobbled street in the last light of the day. My mind was still in the West, on Katrin and Major Tom. What did he mean by what he said about the Stasi, the West Germans and the Russians getting together? Did he have any useful information, or were they just empty words? It didn't make any sense to me—the Stasi had been disbanded three and a half years ago, and why would the West Germans want to work with the Russians? I couldn't think of any way of finding out, short of asking Major Sokolovski.

Round the corner, and there was my building, one of the last of the old tenement blocks, standing proud against the sea of new-build flats that had washed down from Lichtenberg. Heaving open the solid wooden door, I went past the letterboxes without thinking; trying to switch off and glad to be home, working out what music to put on the record player, whether and what I could be bothered cooking for dinner, whether I'd make do, again, with bread and sausage with beer. David Bowie on the stereo with some sausage and beer sounded about right. *Ashes to Ashes* would fit the bill, I thought of the lyrics, and had to giggle at the idea of the terribly English major on drugs.

As I reached the bottom of the stairs, I caught sight of the row of metal boxes, just out of the corner of my eye. It was enough to make me hesitate. And the hesitation was enough to make me turn back and look in my letterbox. There wouldn't be anything in there for me, and if there was, it would be a bill. I poked my fingers through the slit, exploring, checking for a letter. The tip of my index finger brushed paper, something scraping my fingernail, another rough surface pushing against the pad of the finger. Not the smooth wall of the metal box; two letters! Between index and ring finger I fished out first one letter: West Berlin postmark, West German stamp. Handwriting unfamiliar. Fingers of the right hand pushed back in through the slit, this one a little more difficult—a small package of some kind—requiring more care and effort to manoeuvre it through the narrow slit. I recognised it before I even had it out of the letterbox—another of Katrin's tapes. I smiled as I held it in my hands, looking forward to another musical journey courtesy of my favourite and only daughter.

The other letter was intriguing though—who, other than Katrin, would write to me from the western half of this ghost town? Absent mindedly climbing the stairs, I looked at the address of the sender, up in the top left hand corner of the envelope. A postbox number in the West Berlin postal district 61—was that Kreuzberg, over towards Schöneberg? Letting myself into the flat, I dumped my bag and the letters in the hall, went into the kitchen and put a pan of water on to boil, then went back and picked up my mail. I opened Katrin's package first. A cassette, marked *Seduction*, and just a slip of paper with the words: "Don't be cross with me! K." scribbled on it.

Turning my attention to the other letter, I ripped open the brown envelope. Inside was another envelope, addressed to: *Chiffre* "Alone in the East", c/o Zitty Stadtmagazin. There was no stamp on this second envelope, and "Alone in the East" was written in English. I turned the envelope over in my hands before opening it: cream coloured, made of expensive cartridge paper, the kind we so rarely saw here in the East. A faint smell of Western scent came off the thick ribbed paper, heavy musk, mingled with lavender and the lighter notes of rose. No name, but an address, also in Kreuzberg in West Berlin, was written on the back of the envelope. I opened it up and unfolded a single sheet in the same thick, creamy cartridge paper as the envelope. The scent was even stronger now, very feminine, but not light.

Dear "Alone in the East,"

I was touched by your lines in the lonely hearts column. Perhaps you'd like to meet? I'm 39, no children, looking for adventure and a fresh start in these exciting times. I enjoy cooking, going for walks in the forests around Berlin. I'm looking for someone to read me beautiful books, enjoy the bronzes and reds of autumn, and watch the sun go down over the river. Sounds like we're made for each other.

Hope to meet soon,
Yours affectionately,
Annette Ruhle

Katrin! She'd only gone and put a lonely hearts ad in a magazine! And a West Berlin magazine at that! I stormed to the telephone and dialled her number. Down the line I could hear her phone purring, but nobody picked up. She'd still be at her lectures. Slamming the receiver down in its cradle I turned round, looking out of the window. The sun was setting, and although I couldn't see the sun itself, the little corner of sky that I could see was turning pink and purple, as if it had been beaten up. My lips curled upwards as I realised what a stupid simile my mind had delivered, and I looked at Annette's letter again. Katrin had meant well, I conceded to myself, as my ire died down, and, well, perhaps I could even meet up with this Annette? I had no time to spare, and I couldn't imagine that someone who could afford such expensive writing paper would be interested in an Ossi with no access to convertible currency. I held the paper up to the light and admired the watermark, noticing the writing—clear, regular, well formed letters, slanting slightly forwards, written with a decent fountain pen. The scent made its way again to whichever parts of the brain were responsible for smelling, and registered as pleasant, interesting. Yes, even sexy. Perhaps? Perhaps I would write back? I knew I wouldn't, but the thought entertained me. Looking at the letter again, I turned it over—there was the address again, the same as on the envelope, and under that, a telephone number. What did I have to lose?

I read the short letter again, went through to the hall, put the letter on the table next to the phone, lifted the receiver, and dialled.

19:01

After the phone call I went back into my living room, sitting down in my favourite chair. I thought about Annette and the strange week I'd just had. I was glad it was Friday now. It would be at least Monday before the Minister could give me any new tasks.

But in the meantime I could do with a drink. I thought of the whisky that Major Tom had given me, and getting up with a sigh, I fetched a glass from the kitchen, putting Bettina Wegner on the record player as I went past. Sinking back into the chair, pouring myself a measure, I toasted the living room at large: "*Drushba!*" To friendship.

Day 4
Saturday
25th September 1993

Berlin: A demonstration has been called for this afternoon in the capital of the GDR. The protest has been called by several environmental groups, including the Umweltbibliothek *and* Grüne Liga *with the support of the Central Round Table. Speakers from both the GDR and West Berlin are expected to talk about the impact the Silesian crisis is having on electricity supplies.*

09:26

Saturday. A day of rest, of enjoyment—even in this hard working little Republic of ours. But I went into the office this morning to write up the report on my trip to West Silesia; it was a dull morning, overcast, the window spotted with rain—I wasn't missing anything outside. Opening the outer door to the office I could see a light burning. Erika was sitting at her desk.

"Morning, Erika—you here again?" I propped myself up in her doorway, looking at the pile of papers she had in front of her.

"Speak for yourself! Are you planning on doing a bit of *subbotnik* too?"

"I've got some catching up to do—I've hardly managed to do any proper work this week, and I have to write up this report for the Minister again."

"What happened to you yesterday afternoon? I was wanting to ask you about this stuff I'm working on."

"Yeah, the Minister's secretary phoned. She told me to go and see the British."

"That's odd," Erika was surprised. "How did it go?"

"Oh, same as with the Russian—he didn't have much to say. I wasn't really sure why I was there. But the British liaison officer and I did have a chat about economics, well, to be honest, I had a bit of a rant and he was polite enough to listen to me. He compared what we're doing with something called 'Hertzka'."

"Yes, that makes sense—but it was a someone, not a something. He wrote about an economic utopia. It's an old book. He outlined ten principles, including free association, profit sharing and democratic control. A bit like the small workers' co-ops that are being set up here. He had a fetish for transparent economic information—accounts, trade movement, stuff like that. Terribly patriarchal and imperialist though."

I looked at Erika in surprise, maybe she was the one who should be talking to Major Tom, it certainly sounded like she knew more about economic history than I did.

"The thing is, after this chat about economics he said something strange, I can't work it out. Something about the Russians, the Stasi and the West Germans being behind the problems in Silesia. He didn't drop much more than a hint, then he changed the topic before I could ask him about it."

"Do you think he knows anything, or is he just playing games?" Erika was looking out the window. The clouds were breaking up now, and the rain was easing off. "I've been thinking more, about Maier. Maybe you and Klaus were right. Maybe there is something fishy about the whole thing. Do you still feel the same way?"

"Yeah, you could say that. I mean, first of all I get sent

down to West Silesia, then the Minister seems to want to distract me and keep me off the case. Now we've got some British officer dropping hints about the situation down there, talking about an international conspiracy. If I thought the Minister had someone working on it, that'd be fine, I'd get back to my usual work. But why is he trying to put me off? I mean setting Frau Demnitz on me, and this liaison stuff, it doesn't make sense to ask me to do it: I can't speak Russian, and my English is nearly as bad. Klaus speaks both languages, and both you and Laura are way more diplomatic and clear than I'll ever be—any of you would do the job far better than I can."

"Did the British guy have anything else to say?"

"Not much, just that hint about the Russians and the West Germans. I guess he might have been joking."

"Not really a joking matter. But a scary thought nevertheless—something to think about. Which reminds me, I was thinking of going to the big demonstration this afternoon—there might be a link to where they found Maier's body. Bit of a long shot, but it might help to clear things up in my mind. You fancy joining me?"

"Yes, you're right about the possibility of a link. I got a message from the Saxon police yesterday." I told her about the scrap of paper with Fremdiswalde's prints on them. "No idea who this Chris Fremdiswalde is, but I think it might be to do with this demo."

"When did you get this message? Didn't you think to tell us?"

"We agreed we weren't going to do anything about all of this, so I just put it to one side and forgot about it."

Erika pulled a face. "Right that's settled, I'm definitely going to the Alex this afternoon. You coming with me?" Erika had her legs crossed, one foot tapping the air. Excitement, if I knew her at all.

"Mmm, love to, but I'm going with someone else ..."

I must have blushed or stuttered, because Erika was straight in there.

"Really? Who're you meeting?"

"Oh, nobody, really. Sort of got a date."

"A date? Great! That should take your mind off things. Who is it? Where are you meeting her?" Erika's eyes were shining, and it made me wonder why she was so interested in my private life all of a sudden.

"It's a woman from West Berlin. She said she was coming over for the demo, so we agreed to meet up there."

"You're taking her to the demo? What kind of date is that?" she teased me. "Well, might see you there then!"

I needed to make a start on the revised report for Frau Demnitz, so I headed over to my office, thinking about Erika. We were very different kinds of people, but out of all my immediate colleagues, I think I liked her the best. Like all of us here at the *Republikschutz* she was from the ranks of the old opposition, chosen mostly for our scepticism of the security services, and first hand experience of being on the receiving end of the Stasi's tactics. I hadn't had much to do with Erika in the old days, being thrown together only in the last year when the *Republikschutz* was expanded. Before 1989 we'd seen each other at various gatherings, and maybe a couple of times on some of the bigger actions, but she'd been active in one of the women's groups so we'd never had the chance to work together on anything. That was a shame, because I enjoyed her company now. She was easily flustered, took her time thinking things through, but she was dependable and thorough, both qualities I appreciated.

Sitting down at my desk I stuffed some paper into a typewriter, winding it through until the top of the page was in the right position, then started typing. I left out Major Tom's hints and the Saxon police reports, just describing, in laboriously overblown detail, my trip to West Silesia and my impressions and initial conclusions. I typed it up, making the usual two carbon copies for our own records, then took it in to Erika.

"Here, have a look at this. I've kept it basic still, just padded it out with useless detail. What do you think?"

"Yeah," said Erika, frowning in concentration as she read through the report for a second time. "Makes sense to me to keep it simple. The Minister knows that you've been getting reports directly from the police in Saxony, but probably won't appreciate hearing that you've been drawing conclusions from them. You've got to get it to him by the end of Monday? In that case I think we should check in with the others at Monday's meeting. There'll still be time to change it if needs be."

It seemed a little overcautious to me, but I shrugged agreement and put the report and the carbons in an envelope and left it on my desk for Monday.

Back home I put water on to boil and stepped into the shower. Like most people living in pre-war buildings I didn't have a bathroom, just a shared toilet on the landing. The only place to have a wash was at the kitchen sink, so I'd rigged up a shower cubicle in the kitchen. It worked well enough, but it did take up a lot of space.

I was quite excited about meeting Annette and wanted to look my best for her. I couldn't remember when I'd last had a proper date, but it was certainly years ago. After a quick wash I got out of the shower and poured the boiling water into the sink for a shave. Looking at myself in the mirror, I smiled. No longer a spring chicken, but plenty of life in me yet. It felt good to be going to meet a woman, even if our first date was a demo. Perhaps we'd go for a coffee afterwards ... My mind wandered, taking in all the possibilities that this afternoon might bring. What would she look like? She sounded really nice on the phone. Self assured, perhaps a little bossy, taking control of the conversation early on. Typical Wessi. But it felt nice to have someone directing the conversation—a little businesslike perhaps, but if it had been left to me I would have stuttered and stammered and said ridiculous things. Yeah, it felt like it might be a good one.

13:17

I got to Alexanderplatz far too early, nervous about being late. We'd agreed to meet at a quarter to two, under the World Clock. With a half-laugh Annette had said that it was a romantic thing to do, and I didn't disagree. But here I was, half an hour early, wandering around the square, killing time.

The cops weren't exactly out in force, just a couple of small groups at either end of the square to keep an eye on things. A makeshift stage had been set up near the *Centrum* department store, and Western media teams were positioning their microphones on the speaker's stand. It was nearly a quarter-to when I realised that I'd forgotten to buy a *Berliner Zeitung* newspaper—I was to hold a *Berliner Zeitung*, Annette was to have a copy of the West Berlin *taz* paper. That way, even if there were lots of people under the clock, we could still recognise each other. I struggled down into the underground station, swimming against the mass of people crowding up the steps to the square for the demo, along the long pedestrian tunnels, pushed to the side, pressed against the underwater-green tiles lining the walls. I managed to get through to the kiosk, then back up and out into the square. This time going with the flow, but slowly, too slowly.

I dashed across to the clock, paper clasped under my arm, peering through the scrum that was gathering. There! A tall woman, reddish blonde hair tied back in a pony tail, holding a *taz* folded up in front of her, the red print of the title

61

contrasting with her light coat. I paused for a moment, watching her scan the crowds, and feeling a smile climb onto my lips, then I dived through a gap.

"Hi—you've got a *taz*!"

She laughed, "Yes, I'm Annette. And you have a *Berliner Zeitung*, so you must be Martin."

She had an infectious smile, broad, welcoming, splitting her face almost in two and showing her strong teeth. It was impossible not to smile with her. She had laughter lines in the corners of her green eyes, between them a nose that was slightly bent to the left as if she'd been a boxer in a previous life. She hooked her arm through mine, her long fingers tickling the inside of my elbow.

"Shall we get closer, so we can hear what the speakers have to say?"

Without waiting for an answer, she set off towards the stage, pulling me along in her wake. I lost the *Berliner Zeitung* along the way, but I noticed that she kept a firm grip on her *taz*. There was a good crowd of people already, many holding banners and placards—the *Watt-eater* goblin from the 1950s energy conservation campaigns was a favoured motif, along with other messages encouraging a reduction in energy use.

"Why did you suggest the demo?" I asked, not particularly interested, being too busy looking at her smiling face and shining eyes, but feeling that it might come across as rude if I stared too much and talked too little.

"Well, it's something I'm interested in—in West Berlin we get our electricity from you, but air pollution and water pollution are an international problem. Just because there's still a Wall it doesn't mean that the pollution stops at the border, or that we have no responsibility for it. Besides, I do part time research for the AL, and energy is my area."

Annette worked for the AL, the *Alternative Liste*, the West Berlin branch of the Green Party, and currently a coalition partner in the West Berlin Senate. In the past they'd been very supportive of the GDR opposition, but had been less keen to help out since we turned down the offer of merging with West Germany in early 1990, although parts of the party still had close contact with the Round Tables.

The first speaker had stood up, standing by the lectern. I recognised her—she was part of the *Arche* network, now working with *Grüne Liga*, and had long been involved in researching alternatives to using lignite brown coal for electricity generation. She started with a summary of how, since the early 1980s, the GDR had electrified train lines and converted most power plants to make more use of the domestically mined brown coal in preference to oil imported from the Soviet Union and the non-socialist economies. The speaker then went on to talk about the current use of brown coal.

"321 million tonnes of brown coal were used in 1985. By 1990 this had been reduced to 260 million, and we're on course to go below 200 million tonnes by 1997. The open cast mines that are swallowing whole villages, and even now are gnawing at the edges of Leipzig—they aren't our only problem. In 1989 our power stations produced nearly 2 mega-tonnes of sulphur dioxide, but by fitting sulphur filters we will cut this by a third over the next two years. We are overhauling our brown coal power stations to double their efficiency. Conversion of power stations to combined heat and power stations is already providing yet more savings.

"This all sounds very positive, particularly when we add the following facts: rationing of fuel for personal transport decreased transport related smog by nearly 60% this summer; less demand for energy from the military has reduced overall demand by a further 15%; and increased recycling and re-use decreases the embodied energy of products in circulation.

"But the fact is we are still using open-cast brown coal, with its high sulphur and salt content. Our electrical appliances and machinery—at home and in industry—use on average 20% more energy than those conforming to international standards. At current rates it will take up to 20 years to replace these.

"But we don't have 20 years!

"The following speakers will address the problems of acid rain killing our forests, smog in our cities, sulphates and iron in our water and the impact open cast mining is having on our landscape. Last, but certainly not least, we'll talk about the fact that if West Silesia secedes from the GDR we will lose nearly half of our brown coal reserves."

As promised there followed a series of speeches that were both illuminating and depressing. The final speaker, an academic from the Humboldt University, spoke of the impact the loss of the Silesian coal fields would have on the GDR economy. Imports of brown coal from the Czech Republic and Poland would be required until production at our other coal fields could be increased. He remarked that efficiency savings and the building of renewable energy sources such as wind turbines on the Baltic coast will take time to realise, and if West Silesian secession happens before these measures are in place, the GDR would inevitably be bankrupted.

He didn't need to spell out what that would mean: the end of our social experiment, and unification with West Germany.

Just like in 1989 events were moving so fast that we didn't feel we could keep up. In those days we didn't have time to dream or strategise, only to react. We were caught up in a whirlwind of enthusiasm and energy. But this time round it felt like we may not even have any time to react.

The first speaker took the microphone again in a bid to give the event an upbeat ending.

"Just a few years ago we came on to the streets to protest against an undemocratic and centralised government—a government that was incapable of listening to us, the people.

Once again we are here in the name of the people. But now we are in a time of change. Now *we* hold the power. Now it's up to us." The speaker waited until the cheers died down, the cries of *Wir sind das Volk!* slowly ebbing away as she held up her hands, asking to be allowed to continue.

"The time when we trusted the Party—or anyone else—to take the decisions for us has gone!"

Again a roar of applause and cheers. I looked at Annette, she was cheering with the rest of us, even though she was just a visitor to our revolution. But maybe she felt that she could help us with our work?

"With or without West Silesia, we can't rely on dirty fuel. Brown coal has to stay in the ground! We can't afford to switch the nuclear power stations back on. Uranium has to stay in the ground! We can't afford to use this much energy. We must use less—we have to stand our ground!" She spoke in waves, ebbing and flowing, peaking each time she said the word *ground*, the crowd's cheers and cries the sound of surf crashing on the beach.

"Go back to your neighbourhoods, back to your workplaces. Talk to your neighbours and colleagues. Discuss what you've heard today. We need plans to reduce our consumption. We need plans for more efficient energy use. We need plans to improve and replace high energy input machinery. This isn't the first time we've had to deal with difficult questions. As a nation we are talking, sharing and discussing difficult topics: the Wall, our constitution—"

She clearly had more to say, but a young woman had gained the stage and was talking to the speaker. It was Karo, the punk that I'd shared a beer with on Wednesday. After a brief discussion the speaker passed over the microphone. Karo took it, and stood, looking out at us, nervous, the arm holding the mike shaking. Her eyes scanned the crowd as if searching for someone she knew, then she started.

"My name is Karo, erm, I'm from the *Thaeri*, a squat in

65

Friedrichshain. I've just come back from the Czech Republic. I've been working with a group of people fighting the new nuclear power station at Temelin. They're called the Energy Brigades, and they're brilliant! They've been going round their neighbourhoods and villages, helping people install insulation in their houses and flats. And they've helped out with improving people's heating systems in their homes. It sounds boring, but they've halved domestic energy use! Their aim is to save so much energy that there won't be any need to build the new nuclear power station there. And," she gestured to the side of the stage where a couple more punks were watching, they reluctantly came up and joined her next to the microphone stand. "These two comrades have come up from Bohemia to show us how to do it. On Monday morning we're going to the Friedrichshain Round Table to negotiate a budget for energy brigades here in Berlin."

It's not like Karo was proposing anything new, but her enthusiasm was infectious, and she earned herself a round of applause.

"Do you know her?" Annette asked.

"Yes, I had a drink with her a few days ago. Why?"

"Oh, you were just looking proud," Annette was showing her smile again, teasing me.

"You know what? I am proud. Not just of Karo, but of all these young people. Where would we be without their energy and enthusiasm?"

"You're not so old yourself, and Katrin said you're still pretty enthusiastic."

"Katrin? You know Katrin?"

Annette looked sheepish, her smile turned off for a moment, her arms hanging by her side and her eyes lowered.

"I promised her I wouldn't tell you. She helped out at the AL over the summer, and she told me about you. I liked what I heard. I saw her the other day and she said you'd put an ad in the lonely hearts column in *Zitty*, so I thought why not?

She encouraged me, said we'd be perfect together."

Katrin! She was going to get an earful when I managed to get hold of her!

"Well, I'm glad my daughter has taste," I squeaked, and I'm sure that I blushed.

Annette treated me to her special smile, put her arm through mine again.

"Shall we go and get a coffee? This looks like it might go on for a while."

I looked up at the stage, and I could see that a line of people wanting to take the mike had formed. I nodded. A coffee with Annette sounded good to me.

We walked under the train tracks and over to the television tower, a tall stick of asparagus standing in the middle of East Berlin. The lift—a small metal cube operated by a uniformed attendant—clunked and clicked up the tower, making Annette visibly nervous.

"Does it always shake and make such noises?" she asked in a low whisper, worried about offending the attendant.

"Probably. Haven't been up here for years."

We reached the revolving Telecafé level, and waited for the *Dispatcher* to place us, eventually being directed to a table next to the window, looking down on Berlin below. It was still cloudy, making the city appear dull, overshadowed. But the line of the Wall was clearly visible—follow the Unter den Linden as far as the Brandenburg Gate, the Wall stretched out either side, then doubled back east, embracing the old centre before heading off into the hazy gloom. Annette stared out, past the Red *Rathaus*, over to Kreuzberg on the other side of the Wall, south of where we sat, but to our minds, West.

"It's strange. I mean, I live, what, two kilometres? Not far from here. Closer than you do." Her eyes flicked to the south-east, towards Lichtenberg, and I had a brief sense of unease that this woman who I'd known for less than two hours knew where I lived.

"But," she continued, "we still live in two completely separate worlds. Different societies, at least. Just a few years ago I was glad to be living in the West. Then I wanted to be back here, with you all. Now I wonder whether it might not just be best if you joined us, if we became one Germany again. That way you wouldn't sit shivering at home, starving."

Her eyes sought mine out, genuinely curious, and seemingly unaware how hurtful her words were.

"I saw you just now, down there, cheering with the rest of us. Don't you feel this, this ... power we have, as a people? Is that not worth shivering and starving for?" I could feel my arms moving around, gesticulating, taking in Berlin that lay at our feet.

"But is it really, or are you just being idealistic? It's not going to work, is it? Really?" Again her words stabbed at me, and I wondered whether it was my pride or my hope that she was wounding.

"I think it will, if we're given the chance. But what did you mean? When you said *back here*?"

"I was born here. My parents came over here in the '50s. Full of hope. They wanted to help build the better Germany. Idealism, it was, a sense of duty. Just like Bert Brecht and Maxie Wander and all the others who came here to take part in the great experiment."

"But they left? They didn't stay, and nor did you?"

"No. We went over to West Berlin when I was still little. Just before they built the Wall. My parents said it was all a sham, they couldn't be part of it any more. A power game run by Moscow and the Communists. And now I wonder whether this is just a rerun of those first, naïve years. I wonder whether my parents would have come back again?" She was still looking out at Kreuzberg. The revolving bulb in the tower, the restaurant we were sitting in, had turned further, and she had to look back over her shoulder.

"Where are they now?" I asked.

"Dead. Both of them. I think they died of broken hearts, broken dreams. My dad had a heart attack, and my mum went soon after."

"I'm sorry. But you know what? I think they'd see the differences this time." Why is it always so hard to find the right words when people talk of death? I avoided her eyes, preferring to watch the toy trains running into and out of the station far below. The green and black carriages of the long distance services, and the off-white and red of the local S-Bahn, stopping to pick up passengers.

"Would they?" She was looking at me now, intensely. Staring into my eyes, as if she could find the answer there. "Has that much changed? You still have the same propaganda, the same exhortations to work hard, to go without for the good of the country."

"I think it is different. I think your parents were right back then. At that time it was all a sham, it was all about control and blindly following a broken ideology, no matter the cost. But we're doing it differently this time round. There's no ideology, other than listening to each other, working together. There's no leadership of the Party, no dictatorship of one class over another. The days when the Party was always right, they've gone for good."

"So how's it different? Because from where I'm standing it doesn't seem all that different." She was still looking deep into my eyes, searching for answers, perhaps hoping I could persuade her.

"Well, look at the way we work now, and live together."

"Ah, yes! The famous collective decision making process! You should see the stories about that in our newspapers!" She laughed, but I didn't find it funny. For me it was all deadly serious.

69

"Well, it's not easy. But if we can build our society on the basis of active participation, where everyone has a part to play in deciding about the things they're involved in, that's got to be better, hasn't it?"

She saw now how earnest I was, suppressed the smile on her lips and changed the subject.

"What is it you do again? Katrin mentioned something about diplomacy," she looked confused.

"Well, that's part of it. But I'm in a team that keeps an eye open for anything, or anyone, who is trying to undermine what we're doing here."

"And what do you do when you find something out?" Annette was looking sceptical now, call it paranoia if you will, but I was sure she was thinking *Stasi*.

"We're not police, and we don't have the power to prosecute—that's one thing we learnt—we don't want to be like the Stasi," I said defensively. "We tell the people who are affected, so that they're aware of the problem. So, for example, we suspect that investors are coming over from West Berlin, trying to persuade people to vote to allow their flats to be privatised. Presumably these Westerners see some way to buy in and make a profit."

"So, what do you do when you find this happening?"

"We work out what's going on then if there's a problem we'll go to a residents' meeting, and tell them what the Westerners are up to. If we suspect anything illegal then we'll pass it on to the police."

"And this is really happening? Why isn't there a law about it?"

"We're having to change our whole legal system: it's a massive job, it's going to take time. Some of our law dates back to the nineteenth century—even the Party didn't get round to changing all of our laws, even though they had 40 years to do it in! We have to look at each law, see whether it's democratic. And anyway, we're just not used to all these capitalist tricks; our laws are so full of loopholes that anyone who's out to make a fast buck can practically do what they want."

Annette looked thoughtful. "I see. I hadn't thought about it that way. We're so used to people trying to sell us stuff and rip us off we don't even notice it any more. What else have you had to deal with?"

I didn't want to talk about what I had been thinking about so much over the last few days, so I told her a story about how confused we were about pyramid schemes when they first cropped up. We'd needed to get an expert in from the West to help us get our heads round them.

Annette laughed, showing her teeth again, the laugh subsiding into a big smile. It was impossible not to laugh with her, even though I suspected she was laughing at our naïvety.

"And what's happening in West Silesia? It's never out of the news, but I'm not sure I understand it at all."

"I don't really know what's gone wrong there. We're hearing lots of rumours, the West Silesian Round Table is saying that the administration there has sidelined them."

"Yeah, I read about it in the paper, but I didn't understand that either, I mean, I'm not even sure I know what a Round Table is."

"It's just another way for people's views to be represented, parallel to the Regional and national parliaments. Each level of Round Table and Works Council sends delegates to the next level up. They're there to keep an eye on what the elected representatives are doing, provide a sounding board, and a way of passing information and ideas to and from the grassroots."

"But that's really complicated! And what are you going to do if your Round Table tells you something you don't like about your *Volkskammer* representative?"

"It's simple. If anything goes wrong, say our representatives aren't keeping to agreements, or aren't checking in with us on important or controversial stuff—we can require them to come to a meeting, or even recall them and elect somebody else."

Annette had to think about this for a while, then: "OK, I can see that's better than the system we have in the West, but it is really complex, isn't it? And do people actually care what's happening?"

"Yeah. They do. Since 1989 people have been really engaged. And it's not like the parliaments are doing their thing and nobody knows or cares what's going on. The issues get debated in the Works Councils and in the neighbourhood Round Tables. And that gets passed on to the Round Table delegates who are working with the elected representatives.

"But you know what, I think the biggest change is that we're distributing the decisions and the resources as far down the chain as possible. So the national *Volkskammer* parliament and the administration in Berlin aren't even responsible for that much any more—mostly foreign affairs, tidying up the legal system, debating constitutional changes, stuff like that. Things that matter on a day to day basis, like transport and food, are decided on a Regional, District or even Neighbourhood level."

Annette smiled at me, and her eyes danced, sparkling with amusement: "I'm sorry, this is meant to be a date, and here I am, asking you all these boring questions."

"You know, it's kind of nice to talk to someone who isn't involved. At work, at home all we talk about are details, but you and I are talking about the bigger picture—the structural stuff. I don't get to think about that too much," I smiled back.

"But there's something else that I'm curious about: Katrin says you like the Puhdys?"

I grimaced. I definitely had to have words with Katrin ...

DAY 5
Sunday
26th September 1993

Görlitz: It has been confirmed that the body found in Nochten open cast mine last Wednesday is that of Johannes Maier, the Party Secretary of the West Silesian Union. There has been speculation about the whereabouts of Maier since he failed to speak at a WSB rally on Thursday evening. A spokesperson for the West German Interior Ministry described his death as 'suspicious'. Meanwhile in West Silesia, the Regional parliament has agreed to a WSB sponsored directive dissolving formal links between the Round Tables and the Region's political structures. The West Silesian Round Table has announced a protest rally later today in the capital Görlitz.

09:25

I woke in a positive mood—the date with Annette had gone well, and it was nice to feel that the future might hold something more than just work and meetings. I decided to allow myself a lie in, staying in bed, reading a book and drinking *Mocca-fix*, soundtrack courtesy of Panta Rhei and Engerling.

Just before midday the phone rang, so I levered myself out of bed and went to answer it, wearing only socks and an old pullover.

"Grobe," there was no answer. I tried again, "Hello?"

A couple of clicks then the line was dead. Nothing surprising there, the telephone system had been overstretched for years and had never worked particularly well. Still, it was good that I was up, it was time to head over to the weekly neighbourhood potluck. Every Sunday afternoon residents of the block would bring a dish and meet up in the *Kulturbund* rooms next door. It gave us a chance to have a chat about any issues without making a meeting out of it. The idea was that if we could sort things out face to face then petty grievances and requests wouldn't need to be discussed formally at the block plenary. It was also a chance to get to know each other, spend a bit of time building trust and friendship.

I usually enjoyed these get-togethers, despite not being a particularly gregarious person—the food was generally good, and if we hung around for long enough, sooner or later the Skat playing cards and *Kornschnaps* would make an appearance. Unfortunately, I was quite often working, even on a Sunday afternoon, or too knackered to be bothered to show up. It was nice to be able to turn up, not just in a good mood, but with enough energy to look forward to the event.

I arrived with a bowl of potato salad. There would probably be at least two or three other bowls of potato salad there, but I had leftover potatoes already, and it seemed the simplest and quickest dish to prepare. Besides, you couldn't go far wrong with potato salad.

Margrit from upstairs was talking with the old ladies from the ground floor. I greeted Margrit with a hug, and the ladies with a handshake. They cooed over me for a bit, telling me how they hadn't seen me for ages. I asked after their cats, not actually interested, but knowing that the cats provided these ladies with their main distraction between the Potlucks. After a few minutes the ladies started swapping knitting pattern tips, forgetting that I was standing there. I felt my social duty had been adequately fulfilled and went back to Margrit who was deep in conversation with Dirk from the top floor. Dirk seemed unusually friendly, in a good mood, slightly hyper.

"Hey Martin, your Bärbel's coming along today," Margrit turned, including me in the discussion.

"Who? Do you mean my secretary from work?"

"I'm not *your* secretary, Martin, and you know that. I'm the departmental secretary." This from Bärbel, who had just come in through the side door.

I didn't really know Bärbel, despite having seen her nearly every day for months. She didn't actively take part in meetings at work, she'd usually just sit quietly in the corner and take notes, pretty much invisible to us all once we'd got involved in discussing work rotas and cases. I hadn't really reflected on this strange relationship before, and it made me feel a bit uncomfortable now I was encountering Bärbel in an informal setting for the first time.

"Hi Bärbel, of course. That's what I meant. Departmental. Errm, good to see you."

She gave me a tight smile, and turned to Dirk, giving him a hug, and offering Margrit her hand when Dirk introduced the two. Dirk then ushered her away towards the side table, offering her an *Apfelschorle*; mixing apple juice and sparkling mineral water for her. I could hear him explaining that the apples were from trees along the nearby railway embankment. It sounded like he was trying to impress her, and she looked like she was prepared to be impressed, or at least pretend to be.

I turned back to Margrit, who had been quietly observing how I was watching Bärbel and Dirk, an amused twinkle in her eyes. I had always rather liked Margrit's eyes. One was hazel-green, the other blue, although I was never one hundred percent certain that they were always the same colour. I often found myself wondering what eye colour was entered on her identity card. Her hair was frequently dyed, a dark red or black which really showed her eyes up even more.

"Nice shoes," I said, looking down at the brown tooled leather.

"Yes, my aunt sent them from the West. You don't really know her, do you?" she asked, looking towards Bärbel who was smiling over her glass of *Apfelschorle* at Dirk.

"No, I guess not. Is it that obvious?"

"Mmm," Margrit murmured, nodding absent mindedly. "But she'd like to get to know you."

I looked over towards Bärbel, who was giving Dirk a lot of attention, nodding and smiling coquettishly at whatever he was saying. I'd never noticed Bärbel showing any interest in me, and there was certainly no evidence of anything now.

"Nah, don't think so, I mean look at how she's flirting with Dirk."

Margrit didn't say anything, just looked at me with those remarkable eyes of hers. She was good at this, making me feel uncomfortable, and I was relieved when five or six more residents crashed through the front doors, carrying trays and plates and bottles. I saw Eli, Robert, Steffen and a few others, but they were all milling around and laughing too much to make identification from this end of the room easy. They had obviously been drinking, probably been in the park or the small bit of grass in the yard at the rear of the building, where the washing lines were. They were in good spirits, and hungry. Without much ado the plates were first stacked on the table, then were doled out and everyone dived into the food. Pea soup, soljanka, roulade, red cabbage, a leaf salad, potato salad (only one today, apart from mine), a couple of loaves of dark rye bread and even some bread rolls from the day before, rock hard inside, the crust shrivelled, anaemic and rubbery.

We tucked in, conversation dying down for a few minutes

while we all tried out the various dishes. There weren't too many of us today, so we fitted around one table. The young families of the building weren't represented at all.

"They're all at the *Pionierpalast*," said Frau Lehne, one of the cat ladies. "There's some event going on, little Steffen was so excited about it."

Frau Lehne was interrupted by the door opening, and a tall, thin man, with longish curly hair and dirty blue denim work-clothes came in. He looked around the table, and, his eyes directed somewhere above our heads, put his hands behind his back, as if he were about to recite a poem.

"Good day, comrades. And a good appetite. How does it work here? I mean, with the food?"

He had a Thuringian accent, and looked hungry, slightly desperate. Dirk stood up, and gestured towards the table with the serving dishes.

"Are you hungry, brother? Join us, we have food."

The man looked hopeful, but avoided looking either at us or the food, even at Dirk, who was now well within the stranger's field of vision.

Dirk crossed over to the table where the food was laid out, and cast about, wondering whether to serve the man's food on a plate, or find some disposable receptacle for the man to take with him.

Around the table, people were exchanging embarrassed looks, unsure how to react, when Bärbel suddenly piped up.

"But a contribution towards the costs would be appreciated!"

This was unexpected, Bärbel was as much a visitor as this man, and as far as I knew she hadn't brought a dish, nor vegetables or any other kind of donation. At Bärbel's pronouncement Dirk dithered even more, he had been about to take a plate to serve the food onto, but now looked around the table uncertainly. The stranger's face had hardly changed —he seemed unsurprised by Bärbel's interjection. He still looked hopeful, but the desperation showing around the eyes was now unmistakable.

More looks were exchanged around the table, the old ladies looked slightly shocked, but I couldn't tell whether it was by the man's begging or Bärbel's protest. All conversation had ceased, everyone was looking shifty, uncomfortable.

"Of course you should eat, brother," said Margrit, finally breaking the awkward atmosphere that had settled over us. She gestured at Dirk: *give the stranger some food.*

At this the man moved over towards Dirk, pulling an army mess tin out of his bag. Dirk filled it with soljanka, with some of my potato salad on the side, placing one of the dry bread rolls on the top, so that it soaked up the sloppy stew. Within seconds the beggar had left, murmuring thanks, and wishing us a pleasant Sunday.

When the door swung shut behind him, there was a moment's silence, until Margrit broke it.

"If people are hungry, we feed them. We have to. The revolution doesn't stop at that door," she gestured towards the door through which the stranger had just disappeared.

There were murmurs of agreement from around the table, but Bärbel wasn't cowed by the strength of Margrit's statement.

"But we can't feed everyone. We're still struggling to get enough food for ourselves. And this guy, I mean, if he was part of a work collective then they'd see that he got food, even if he didn't have money."

Most foodstuffs were still subsidised, at least the staples were, meaning that anyone who was in work, or receiving an old age or disability pension could afford to both eat and pay their rent.

"So this guy," Bärbel continued, "he can't be working. He's probably going round begging food from different neighbourhoods and projects. It's not socially acceptable, it's selfish and profiteering behaviour."

"But, obviously, if someone is hungry, we feed them. I don't care where they come from. We don't know why that man's not working, or even whether or not he's working," one of the young men who lived on the floor above me joined in.

Dirk had moved back to the table and sat down. He still seemed uncomfortable, but looked up and began to speak.

"I've seen that guy before. He was at our works canteen a few weeks ago."

He spoke slowly, deliberately, but gave no indication about what he thought about the man who had been begging.

"I agree with your guest," Eli chimed in, looking at Dirk. "Food isn't free. It might be one day, but at the moment we pay for it, we work for it, and we don't have much money, none of us do."

"I've seen him before as well," said Robert. He'd been looking thoughtful the whole time. "He was at our factory too. He was asking around for work, but the co-ordinator turned him down, sent him packing. Apparently he was in the Firm—the co-ordinator recognised him, he said he was one of the guards at Hohenschönhausen prison."

This gave us all food for thought, and there was silence for a while. Bärbel broke that silence.

"So he should go to the Reconciliation Commission. We set up procedures for this, we all know the score. Confess, apologise, work out how to make amends, ask a neighbourhood to take you in."

Things weren't quite as straightforward as this, and Bärbel knew it. I wondered why she was being so hard on the man. The Reconciliation Commission wasn't uncontroversial. It wasn't even universally accepted in this little Republic of ours. There were plenty of people who wanted revenge, not reconciliation, and there were plenty from the ex-security services who felt hard done by. The whole thing was a huge mess, and I for one was worried it may get worse before it got better.

"But he's human. We've all done things we're ashamed of." This came from Dirk, who was looking pensive. That surprised me, not just because I'd had the impression he'd been trying to impress Bärbel, and by disagreeing with her he was probably ruining any chances he had, but also because I knew that Dirk had been in the Stasi prison in Hohenschönhausen, and in Cottbus as well.

"We have to move beyond this, otherwise we've got no chance of succeeding in this revolution of ours." Again, Dirk had surprised me. I hadn't heard him talk about the revolution before at all. He had gained the attention of the Stasi not for opposing the State in any real political sense, but for *Republikflucht*—trying to flee the GDR across the Iron Curtain. Nevertheless he had clearly suffered badly at the hands of the Stasi. We had all seen, but not mentioned, how he limped when the weather was cold or wet.

"It's like 1945 again. We can't just give out Persil certificates, granting clean vest status—these people are dirty. Some of them are downright evil!" Frau Lehne said, cupping her hand behind one ear in order to better follow the discussion.

Another surprise. I had never heard Frau Lehne talk politics either.

"But we can't send them to concentration camps—we can't fill the Stasi jails with Stasi agents. It's a cycle, a cycle of malice, of violence and fear. And it's up to us, it's our responsibility to break it," Dirk was less hesitant now, more sure of his position.

The discussion had slowed; this was an old argument, yet one that still had no answer. It was something that we all had to deal with, one way or another. Too many people had been victims of the Stasi, or working for the Stasi, or informing for the Stasi. Many of the informants were unaware that what they said was going into the Stasi files, and now those files had been rescued from destruction and opened up it was proving virtually impossible to tell who had deliberately informed, of their own free will, who had been blackmailed, and who was innocent of any wrongdoing, despite being named in the files as an informer.

"The Commission may not be fit for purpose, but what else do we have?" asked Margrit. "We have to deal with this. We can't just chuck these people out of the country, send them to the West. We need to clean this shit up by ourselves. We need the skills and the workforce. We can't afford to lose another few hundred thousand people."

The GDR had suffered badly from the exodus of disenchanted citizens in 1989. So many people had left the country, fleeing through Prague and Hungary, and then directly over the border to West Germany once the controls had been relaxed that November. Many had come back, but not all, and the ones who hadn't come back were generally those with specialised skills, such as doctors and engineers— the ones who could find well paid work in the capitalist West. A lot of these sent back money, either to friends and family, or directly to the Round Tables, and this helped to replace some of the financial support that had formerly been provided by West Germany. But Margrit was right, we needed skills and bodies as well as hard currency. We couldn't afford to exclude thousands from the workforce.

"It's got to be up to each neighbourhood, each workplace to work out what they can accept, who they can accept. These people have to be reintegrated into society. If we don't do that then we will be creating a fifth column within our Republic," Dirk again. He was still sounding confident of his case, but looked unsure what we'd think of what he had to say.

"They are already a fifth column!" spat Frau Lehne. I

81

looked at her, trying to work out how old she was, whether she'd already been through a similar process in 1945 when the Communists had imprisoned a few of the Nazi bigwigs and lots of the small fry, but gave the middle ranks new positions in the brave new world that the Stalinists were building in this corner of Germany. I wondered whether she had had any run-ins with the Stasi. I found it hard to believe that this cat-loving old lady would be of any interest to even the most paranoid secret police. But I hadn't known her before Autumn 1989, and even if I had, we certainly wouldn't have talked politics in those days.

Bärbel ignored this latest digression, and came back to the problem of food: "Look, this apple juice," she held up the glass of juice that Dirk had poured for her. "It was you who looked after these trees. Pruned them. Kept an eye on them. It was you who collected the harvest, pressed the juice." She looked around at us all, making sure we knew we were the ones she was talking about. "There are food shortages. We're struggling to grow enough food to feed the country. We're using little corners of our city to grow fruit trees and bushes and to plant cabbages. 'From each according to their ability': that hasn't changed, we still need everyone to join in, to help out. And if we have people just wandering around, begging for food from hard working communities, well, the whole system collapses."

Bärbel sat back, looking down at her fruit juice.

"I don't think I disagree with anything anyone has said," I decided to weigh in. It felt like the conversation was about to start going round in circles. "Bärbel's right, we're all working hard to ensure that everyone has enough to eat, and it's fair to expect that everyone does their bit. But we have a humanist duty to ensure that people don't go hungry. That humanism is why we are still independent. We weren't seduced by the promises the West Germans made. I don't have to tell you what we all signed: the Statement *For Our*

Country. We remember what we signed: 'Peace, Social Justice, Freedom of Movement'. Our material and moral values. Those weren't just words, where they? We believed in them. And I think we still do. And if someone hungry walks through that door, that's our challenge. He was in the Stasi? So what! He's still hungry, and we need to deal with that fact first, regardless of whether or not he was in the Firm. Right now, he's a hungry human, and we have food for him."

Silence. I wondered whether I'd put a lid on the discussion. That hadn't been my intention, but it seemed to have been the effect. I got up and went over to the jugs of apple juice, giving people a bit of space to restart the conversation if they wanted to. When I got back to the table the old ladies were talking about the queues at the *Konsum* co-op shop. Dirk and Bärbel were sitting stiffly next to each other, not talking to each other, nor to anyone else. Dirk gave the impression he was thinking about something, Bärbel was looking a little defiant. I sat back down next to Margrit, who also looked pensive. She looked up as I sank into the chair.

"Did I just shut that discussion down?" I asked her.

She shook her head and gave my hand a squeeze. "It's just hard," she said. "You know that better than any of us. There's so many of these challenges, as you called them, and it's wearing us down. In the old days we could just get on with our lives. We'd moan at home, but we'd go to work, take part in some stupid meetings, you know how it was. Say some set piece—you could practically say the same thing every time, something ideologically correct, maybe a quote from Lenin," a far away, almost nostalgic smile crossed Margrit's face, then she looked back at me. "But we didn't have to think. Work, meetings, queuing up for whatever we needed, family life. But now we're having to think, we're having to work harder than ever. We're not used to it, and it hurts."

She was right, in some ways we had it easy in the old days. So long as you didn't do anything stupid—like apply for an exit visa or make a fuss about whatever you disagreed with—if you kept your head down then you didn't have to worry about anything. You got your wages, that covered food and accommodation, with enough to put aside for holidays. The old men in the *Politbüro* did the thinking and the worrying for us. I wondered whether people realised what they were signing up to when they said they wanted the GDR to remain independent.

"Do you think they have to do all this thinking in the West?" I asked her.

"No. I don't think they do. They're scared, but they don't realise it, because they don't think. They have other worries."

I nodded, my thoughts turning to my daughter in West Berlin. They certainly didn't lack when it came to things to buy. More food than they could possibly eat, more consumer goods than anyone could possibly want. But nobody looked particularly happy. Everyone looked well fed, glowing almost, but tired. And worried. I looked around the table, everyone looked a bit grey, shabby. And tired too. But it was a different kind of tired look from that to be seen on the streets of West Berlin. Over there, it was a sort of emotional exhaustion. Here it was a physical exhaustion, combined with an air of determination.

"Do you think we're more determined? I mean, compared to over there?"

Margrit nodded slowly, thinking it through.

"Yes. If we weren't, if we hadn't been, we would have given up. Sold our values in return for an easy life, agreed to a take-over by West Germany. I don't think it was fear that stopped us from accepting the West German offer, I think it was determination. Yes ..." She paused again, lost in thought for a moment. "I think you were right, just now, when you mentioned the Statement. I think that wasn't just the moment when the old government became irrelevant, but it was the moment when Chancellor Kohl's plans for us became irrelevant too. It lost him his re-election in West Germany, and gave us a sense of ownership over our own country, our own destinies."

In November 1989 the largest independent demonstration in the history of the GDR had taken place, on Alexanderplatz in Berlin. It was there that the *For Our Country* Statement was read out by the author Stefan Heym, a statement calling for an independent GDR, coming out against unification with West Germany. At the time it had felt like an irrelevant call— the Wall hadn't even been opened yet, we were still creating the spaces to feel free in, getting used to our new found power. This was the first non-Party organised mass demonstration in the GDR. From that point on the Party was irrelevant, we had become ungovernable.

It was such an atmosphere, hundreds of thousands of us marching, independently, but together. The banners and placards—spontaneous, witty, joyful. We were the people, and we knew it. When I look back on that day now, I know that was when it all started—a determination to learn the lessons of history, to put our experiences to good use: *bleibe im Lande und wehre dich täglich!* Stay here, resist every day! That's when we knew we'd won.

And anyway, who was thinking of a merger with that other German state? Perhaps the hundreds of thousands heading West?

But that was when the West German Chancellor Helmut Kohl chose to unveil his 10 Point Plan for the re-unification of Germany. His poor timing cost him the goodwill of the East German people, made them suspicious of all that the West had to offer: nothing less than a takeover of the GDR project, a full merging into a Western way of life.

A few days later, Egon Krenz, the newly appointed leader of the Communist Party, and de-facto ruler of the GDR signed the *For Our Country* Statement, an act of breathtaking self-servitude, an attempt to stay on the train of the revolution: the Communist Party was grabbing at every straw in sight.

Rumours circulated that Krenz's move was the first part of an attempt to wrest power back from the people, and a general strike was called. From that moment on, everyone, absolutely everybody knew the GDR government had became practically irrelevant. Even the Communist Party realised it, and they offered a share of power to the opposition: the Round Tables were where the decisions were being made now. The government institutions at every level —from factory floor and local council upwards—were relegated to carrying out the will of the people.

Since then virtually the whole resident population of the GDR had signed the Statement, calling for a socialist alternative to the capitalist West Germany. It was a call for the whole country to reflect on shared anti-fascist and humanist ideals, and to take a conscious decision on a joint future. It was the starting point for a new constitution, a new political system, a new GDR. The Central Round Table wrote the new constitution in just four months, trying to keep up with the revolution happening just beyond their meeting room's doors.

"Can you imagine such a statement being signed by even a simple majority of people in West Germany?" asked Margrit. "That's what sets us apart from them. We share something. We agree that a better society is worth working for. There is still truth in the old saying: 'united we stand'."

What she was saying was by no means new. You could hear the same words, more or less, being said throughout our country. The repetition of these simple, even simplistic ideas gave us hope, resilience. We comforted, bullied, accused and supported each other with such phrases. They replaced the slogans of the dictatorship of the Communist Party. The Marxism-Leninism of yesterday was dead. Our only ideology was independence.

"Being an anarchist is a heavy burden."

I looked at Margrit, surprised. I'd never heard her use the A-word before. From her face I could see she was trying the word out, putting a name to the feelings of justice, respect and mutual aid that filled her.

"A heavy, but wonderful burden!" she smiled.

Her eyes shone as she looked around at our neighbours, chatting and arguing and plotting at the table.

19:37

After getting back from the get-together with my neighbours I pottered around the flat, playing at tidying, the fast guitars and heavy beat of Monokel keeping time. I managed to get the dishes done, but decided to leave the pans soaking in water. I wiped down the cooker and the other surfaces in the kitchen, then brushed all the dust on the floor into the corner, a job for later. By the time the five nice boys from Monokel had got as far as *Bye Bye Lübben City* I'd already decided there was no need to exaggerate the whole tidying up business.

I'd enjoyed the chat this afternoon with Margrit. Since the revolution started, most people had developed an urge to talk about all the secret thoughts they'd had locked up in their souls for so long. But it wasn't the case for everyone: the cautious, the timid, and those who had lived long. I guess that if you'd experienced first the Nazis, then the Soviet Occupation, followed by the Leadership of the Party you might be a bit reticent about opening up. But it felt like we were growing into our dialogue, learning to talk to each other. I think it's the small things, like this afternoon, that get us to open up: Dirk, Frau Lehne, and Margrit—each had surprised me, I'd learnt a bit more about them. It was a good feeling, it gave me a sense of belonging.

By now I'd completely given up on the idea of cleaning

the flat, and I was just settling down in my favourite chair, a slight sense of guilt troubling me: I ought to cook some proper food. I hadn't been eating particularly healthily recently—too many bread rolls, too many potatoes and lentils. In fact I was getting a bit bored of lentils, but the farm that supplied my housing co-op was experimenting with sources of protein that required less oil-based fertilisers and imported animal feed. This year was all about trying out various lentil varieties. Still, I'd had a decent selection of food this afternoon, and not just potato salad, so it wouldn't matter too much if I didn't make myself a proper dinner.

A knock at the door saved me from any further thoughts of cooking, it was Nikolai, a colleague from another division of RS.

"Nik! Long time! You coming in?"

"Beer?" he replied, bringing his fist, closed around an imaginary bottle, to his lips in a mime of drinking.

"Beer? Yeah, beer's good. Let's go!"

I took the needle off the record, and switched the Hi-Fi off, then we headed down the stairs to the front door. It was practically dark already, a cold and damp night, the rain falling lightly but persistently. Behind us a Trabant started up and whined past, its tires making whooshing noises on the wet cobbles, its red rear lights glistening and fracturing in the wet air before leaving us again in dusky gloom. The sharp, oily tang of its exhaust cut the warm scent of the brown coal smoke—winter was on its way.

At the bar on the corner you had to give the door a good shove to get it open. Nik tried, then gave up, looking at me expectantly, as if I might have a key or perhaps a jemmy in my pocket. I reached past him, braced my feet against the wet granite doorstep and gave the handle a sharp push. The warped wood of the door scratched across the threshold, the cracked yellow glass rattling. Behind the door was a heavy velvet curtain. Years ago it might have been deep red, but now it was a greyish pink, and it reeked of cigarette smoke and stale beer. Once we'd fought our way past the smelly, sticky curtain things didn't really improve at all. We were in a dusty, dim room, a bar running down the wall to the right of where we stood. Oblong tables, set in perfect geometric order, ranked through the remaining space, the chairs strewn fairly randomly around them. I'd never noticed the disparity between the regularity of the tables and the untidy chairs, and wondered now whether the tables were actually bolted to the floor.

"Evening," said Nikolai to the man behind the bar, holding up two fingers.

The barman Jens nodded and started topping up two glasses that were sitting on the bar, already half full. Nik picked a table away from the habitual drinkers staring glumly into their evaporating beer. After sitting down and stretching his long legs to the side of the table, nudging another chair out of the way in the process, Nik started rooting around in his jacket pocket, eventually pulling out a damp paper packet of Russian cigarettes. He offered me one, even though he knew I hated the acrid sharpness of the black tobacco. In an attempt at diverting my mind from becoming irritated with Nik and his cigarettes, I mused for a moment on the politics of being polite around people who smoked anti-social brands of tobacco. But Nik had another kind of politeness on his mind.

"See these?" He gestured with an unlit cigarette towards the packet. I couldn't see the point of nodding or making any affirmative noises, so just looked at him and waited.

"You know where I got them? A Russian. Captain he is," Nik had this maddening habit of first posing a question, then answering it himself, which was one reason why I preferred to remain quiet when he asked anything. Stay quiet and let him get on with it in his own way and his own time. Don't get me wrong, I liked the guy, I just preferred to avoid him enough to not get too pissed off with his conversational quirks, or his cigarettes.

"This captain-" he started, but broke off again as Jens came over with the beers.

The barman carefully placed the beers on the stained *sprelakart* surface, slowly straightened up, stroked his palms down the dirty apron he was wearing then very deliberately shook hands with me and Nik.

"Food?" enquired Jens brusquely, his face the whole time immobile, expressionless.

"What's on tonight?" asked Nik, showing hardly any more enthusiasm than the barman.

"Soljanka. Lentil soljanka."

"Lentil soljanka?" I tried to keep the resigned incredulity out of my voice; the same farm that supplied my building obviously made deliveries to Jens' bar. I nodded to Jens, and after a pause, so did Nik.

Jens shrugged, and went back to the bar.

"Where was I?" Nik cast around with his still unlit cigarette, as if that may help him regain the thread of his thoughts.

"The Russian. A captain. Was it Dmitri?" I sipped at my thin beer.

"Yes, dear Dmitri. That was it. The Russian captain. Do you know him?"

"No," I shrugged, "but you've mentioned him before."

"He's one of the good ones. Well, we met up again this week. I'm still not sure how much his commander knows about all of this. Poor Dmitri is either in line for a promotion or a one way trip to Novosibirsk. Where is Novosibirsk, anyway? Is that the one I mean?" Nik looked pensive for a whole second or two, before continuing. "Well maybe they're the same thing in the Glorious Soviet Army," he spoke the words in capitals, in the way we all had, ever since the Victorious Red Army marched into town, back in 1945.

"Yeah, maybe promotion and Novosibirsk is the same thing, nowadays, in the Soviet ranks and cadres," I chipped in. Nik ignored my contribution, and continued along the path his thoughts were taking him.

"So there we were in the middle of some woods on the edge of Berlin. Well the Wuhlheide, you know, next to the Russian tank barracks, but you get the picture. There we were, trying to avoid the columns of Young Pioneers and Thälmann Pioneers in their red and blue scarves, marching around as if 1989 never happened. Do they still own that Pioneer Palace there in the woods? No, they don't do they? Been taken over by the Berlin *Magistrat*, hasn't it?"

Nik trailed off again, looking thoughtful and finally lighting up his acrid, and now rather mangled cigarette. Blowing out his first puff, the dark smoke assaulted his nostrils, his nose and eyes crinkling involuntarily.

"So Dmitri and I, in the woods, with all these red-sock kids. He's telling me that something is up, that the Moscow cadre has turned up. They're all over the show in Karlshorst and Wünsdorf, and they're only taking orders over a direct Moscow radio link. KGB: that's what Dmitri reckons. And he should know. But if it *is* KGB, then there's only one reason why they'd be here in Berlin. OK, maybe two."

So this was why Nik was here. He was worried, wanted to give me an informal heads up. He was right to be worried. Although the Russians were always playing politics—officers would turn up out of the blue and start bossing the troops around—but if large numbers of KGB turned up unannounced at the main HQ of the Soviet Western Group of Troops—that had to be significant, particularly if they weren't talking to any of the KGB officers that were permanently stationed here.

"Did he have any idea about whether they're after us or the Western Allies?"

"No. Dmitri's in well over his head. He's not found

anything out, or if he has he's too scared to pass it on."

The timing was vexing—why now with a coup attempt underway in Moscow?—it was bound to make everyone involved a bit jumpy. If the KGB were planning some high level operation in Berlin that would inevitably lead to serious diplomatic pressure from the American, British and French forces based in West Berlin. And any pressure would probably be directed at us—safer to kick the mangy East German cat than the still powerful Russian bear. The four post-war allies still had nominal control over the whole of Berlin, both Eastern and Western Sectors, and that had never been a comfortable fact for any of the governments of the GDR. Strictly speaking, under international law the GDR did not even have sovereignty over its own capital city. That was fine while we sheltered under the protecting hand of the Soviet Union, but now that particular empire was collapsing, and we were going our own way—against the wishes of both East and West—the problem of sovereignty was becoming very significant. The only comforting factor in this mess was that West Berlin was in the same boat. Any moves to destabilise our country using the uncertain legal status of our capital would affect West Berlin too, something the West Germans would want to avoid. Not to mention the Western Allies, who no doubt still appreciated being able to keep tabs on us courtesy of their listening post deep in the heart of our rogue Republic. They would want to keep an eye on us, make sure our little social experiment wouldn't prove infectious to other countries in the eastern half of Europe, or anywhere else for that matter.

On the other hand, if the KGB had for some reason drawn up plans against us it could be much, much worse. The Russians weren't too happy about the way we were heading, but they were a lot more relaxed about it than the Americans, the British, the West Germans or the ever suspicious French.

I was still chewing on this thought when Nik pulled a crumpled envelope from his pocket and passed it over to me. Yellowish, thin paper, Russian. It was sealed, and there was no name or address written on it.

"From Dmitri," was all Nik had to say about the letter.

I put the envelope in my pocket for later, wondered whether to ask Nik about it, then decided that he would have already told me more if there were more to say. I brought the conversation back to the new KGB contingent that had turned up.

"They might just be in town because of the negotiations around the demilitarisation of Berlin and the GDR?"

"Yeah, they might," Nik drew thoughtfully on his dark cigarette, which was burning unevenly down one side, glowing strands of tobacco were floating down to the table. "And my name might be Erich Honecker."

He was right, a peaceful and honourable KGB mission in our town was about as likely as me sitting in a dingy bar with the former leader of the Communist Party.

"These days I'm feeling more like Erich Mielke than Erich Honecker," I sighed, referring to the general who had been in charge of the Stasi for over 30 years.

Nik looked dubious. "Why's that?"

"Oh, nothing really. Just feels like we're creeping around in shadows, spying on people. This isn't what we worked for years to achieve."

"What's brought this on?"

I told him about what Katrin had said a couple of days before, how she'd called me a spy, no better than the Stasi. Nik was quiet for a moment, and to his credit he didn't try to theorise about Katrin's motives.

"OK. I know what you mean. It's sometimes ... sometimes uncomfortable, isn't it? But we're nothing like the Stasi. Nothing at all. We're worlds apart. Honourable."

"But that's what the Stasi said too, 'we're honourable'. I

mean Mielke, right at the end: 'I'm a humanist, I love you all, I did it for you', wasn't that what he said?"

Nik didn't answer immediately. He was staring into the dark smoke curling upwards from the side of his cigarette. I could tell that this was a subject that had been bothering him too.

"Oh yes, yes. I know what you mean. But the Minister said ..."

"The fucking Minister!" I broke in, "Yes! I've heard it. Exceptional circumstances, social experiment under threat, blah blah blah," I was speaking in a low hiss, but I could tell that the anger in my words was affecting Nik, who was still looking at the smoke.

"And there's stuff happening," I continued. "Like West Silesia, like in Moscow, like what your Dmitri's been telling you about. So maybe the Minister *is* right. But at the same time ... Oh—I don't know! I'm feeling very uneasy about things. It feels like we're crossing a line. And I'm not actually sure exactly where that line is! Or what that line even means. I just know I'm not happy about it."

Now Nik was looking at me instead of his cigarette. His intense face probably mirrored my own.

"Listen—you, me, thousands of others. We worked hard over the years. At the end we were hundreds of thousands, even millions. And each one of us risked our jobs, our homes, our freedom, even our families. All to stand up and say what's what. To say what we believed in.

"Me, you, all of us in RS, even the Minister. All of us. And we know about solidarity. We helped each other out in the old days. OK, we didn't expect the Autumn Revolution. Fine, it took us as much by surprise as it did the Party *Bonzen*. But we kept going, we never stopped. The *Bonzen* tried to jump on our bandwagon. The people threw them off again. The West Germans tried to pinch the wheels off our wagon. But we fought them off with sheer bloody determination. And I'll tell you this now: no bastard Russian or American is going to stop us. Because if they want to stop this ... this piece of humanity that we're creating, this Grassroots Democratic Republic that we're piecing together with our own blood, sweat and tears, if they're stealing our future, Martin, we won't let them." His voice lowered, almost a growl: "*We. Won't. Fucking. Let. Them*! The Russians stole our past. If they get hold of our future, then all we have left is the present. And that's not enough. It's got to feel worth it. All that work, the fear, the worries. All this hard work now. What else have we got left to fight for, if not the future?"

I hadn't experienced this side of Nik before, passionate, determined, caring. But he was right. I looked at him, face lowered over the table, the cigarette burning down between the fingers of his left hand, loosely hanging over the edge. He looked tired, as if it were only his spirit that kept him going. Once we'd had an intoxicating sense of empowerment and optimism, but now there was no longer any fizz. The giddy roller coaster of events in autumn 1989 and spring 1990 had given way to lots of talking, lots of arguing, too much hard work. OK, maybe I no longer felt the heat of the revolution coming off every single person I met on the street. But there was still a sense of can-do. The whole country was rebuilding itself. The economy was getting back on its feet after years of stagnation and alienation in the workforce. People were coming together to organise and run their own workplaces, their own living spaces. Yes, Nik was right, nobody could take this away from us. Not without a fight.

"But you're right, of course," Nik had lifted his head, and was studying the smoke from his cigarette again, his voice almost back to normal. "You're right," he repeated. "There's a line. There has to be. We can't cross that line. If it ever gets critical, meltdown stage, with the Russians, or anyone else for that matter, we have to go public. We can't leave it up to the Minister."

It was good to know that Nik was having doubts about the Minister's abilities too, that I wasn't alone with my vague worries.

"But how?" I knew the answer, but wanted to hear Nik say it anyway.

"The Round Tables. We'd get word to them, get them to spread it out in their areas, so that everyone hears about what's happening."

It was a simple idea. But I wasn't sure how easy it would be in practice. The Round Tables were only as strong as their members—they were made up of representatives of local Neighbourhood and Works Councils—ordinary people. Some were savvy, others inexperienced in dealing with difficult situations, never mind real crises. Some were dominant, seeking power, most wanted to share power, find solutions together. But direct democracy is only ever a step away from dictatorship: it only takes one determined bastard to spoil it all. If just one of us crosses that line we'll be back to where we started.

"Maybe it's us who are stealing the future," I said.

"Then we better fucking hope we get away with it," Nik was growling again, "because this is the only chance we're ever going to get." He looked over to Jens, holding up two fingers, and then pointing at me and himself. Another beer and a glass of *Kornschnaps* each were on their way, and, thankfully, would probably get here before the lentil soljanka did.

DAY 6
Monday
27th September 1993

Görlitz: *Over ten thousand people protested against the exclusion of direct representation in the political process in West Silesia. The demonstration was called by the Regional Round Table yesterday. Meanwhile the West German Federal Ministry of Intra-German Relations has described the death of the WSB politician Maier as 'alarming'. West Silesian police investigating the death are being assisted by officers from Saxony.*

Moscow: *The Russian Orthodox church has offered to mediate between the Soviet President Gorbachev and Boris Yeltsin, President of the Russian Federation. Yeltsin is believed to be behind the Soviet of the Republics' attempts to impeach Gorbachev, who is still under house arrest in the Crimea.*

06:55

I was lying in bed, nursing my hangover, trying to persuade myself there was no need to go into the office today. I needed water, but water was two whole rooms and two narrow doorways away, and I knew that if I moved, the ball bearing that was currently pressing against the inside of my skull would go rattling all the way down to my legs, taking all my soft organs with it. My stomach was already unsteady—it really didn't need an oversized steel marble passing through it. On the whole I felt it was just fine to suffer in bed.

The telephone had other ideas. The phone was still a relative novelty—it had only been installed after I started working for the Ministry—and this was my first encounter with a ringing phone whilst in the first stages of a hangover.

So far I really wasn't pleased with the experience.

I moved, more to shut it up than out of any sense of duty. The ball bearing kindly stayed up high, in my head, pressing against my skull, but upsetting my sense of balance. Two more, smaller, ball bearings had materialised somewhere in the lower body, but still being slightly drunk from my meeting with Nik, I couldn't work out exactly where. I stumbled, crawled and lurched towards the screeching phone in the hall.

"Yeah?" I didn't even answer with my name, no longer sure I could manage to pronounce it.

"Oh Martin! It's you! How lovely to speak to you again!"

It was a soft voice, a northern accent, from somewhere along the coast. Warm, inviting. Flirtatious even. And youthful, lively. Despite the pitiful state I was in I straightened my back, attempting to project a positive image of myself down the phone line, even though I still had no idea who was on the other end. The result wasn't pretty—I slid down the wall, my head feeling like there was riveting work going on inside it. Perhaps someone was busy closing up the hole left behind by the lobotomy I had doubtless acquired the night before.

"Martin, are you OK?" A sensitive voice, again warm. A cuddle on a winter's day sort of warm. I wished I was in a better position to appreciate it.

"Eurch. Long night," I managed.

"Oh, really sorry, dear Martin—I've caught you at a bad time! Look, it's not important, I'll call you later."

This person was causing me to visit new tortures on my brain. I pushed some energy into my shrunken grey cells, asking them to come up with a name to match this gentle voice that seemed to like exclamation marks rather a lot. Come on, a name, any name to fit this voice!

"But I'm glad I spoke to you, speak later!"

"Evelyn ..." I said, but I was too slow. Evelyn had taken her voice and gone.

Feeling strangely better after these painful efforts, I allowed my desiccated tongue to feel its way round the corners and curves of her name: *Evelyn*. I said it again.

Since I'd already got as far as the hall, I decided my bed was now just as far away as the kitchen where the mirage of taps beckoned.

Glass of water in hand, sip, swallow, grimace as the ball bearing banged around my head. Try the soundscape of Evelyn's name out again. The thought of her made me smile, which did something awful to my facial musculature. Grimace again.

Trying not to move my mouth, I concentrated on the magic lantern show provided by my mind. Individual scenes were flickering past my internal eye, Overexposed and crumpled by frequent handling and time, some details in clear focus, others just a suggestive shading. Evelyn's blue dress the first time we met. Her smile, her penetrating but soft blue eyes, her pointed chin.

It had been an outing to the State Opera, on the Unter den Linden, my work-brigade plus husbands and wives. It had been during the interval when I first saw her, holding a tray of drinks for the Party *Bonzen* sitting upstairs. I could see her from the bottom of the stairs, where we'd been hemmed in by the crowd. She glanced over, and that's when I noticed her eyes, framed by a blonde bob, her dress matching their exact, impossible hue. Katrin's mother noticed me looking up the stairs and followed my gaze towards the young woman. She gave her one of those disapproving, assessing and thoughtful looks that wives and girlfriends seem to reserve for other women who might sleep with their men.

I took the cue from my wife's reaction to the existence of this waitress, and sheepishly looked away. Knowing me, I probably blushed, even though there had been absolutely nothing significant in the fact that I had noticed Evelyn.

In fact, had it not been for the way my wife had assessed the situation, I probably wouldn't even have recognised the woman the next time I saw her. It was winter: I remember picking my way across the snowy yard in front of the factory, trudging through the wet sawdust put down over the grey snow when I noticed her at the gatehouse talking to the works security. She glanced towards me as I passed, and waved me over. I changed direction to see what she wanted, still not sure who was beckoning to me. I was concentrating so much on not slipping on the slush that I didn't pay any attention to the figures at the gate. When I got close enough, I looked up and saw her eyes. The woman from the opera house. She was wearing a red parka—she must have dyed it somehow, because I hadn't seen one in that colour before, even though it was obviously made here in the GDR. The bright colour lent the cheap fabric an elegance it didn't deserve. Under the parka she had on a brown woollen skirt or dress, woollen stockings and decent brown boots, stained by the snow.

"How nice to see you again! It's all right comrade, this Gentleman will see me to the BPO offices." She said the word Gentleman in English: *Tschändlmann*, and even though I had no idea how the word ought to be pronounced, the soft G, the feel of the word rolling over the high T and the low M and N gave her such an air of charm and grace that even the surly security guard was confused, and let her go with me.

"So it's the Works Party Organisation you're needing?" I asked, using the familiar form of you, as if we were both Party comrades or close friends, but I was neither a Party member, nor a close friend of this intriguing woman. Even as

I said it I realised my mistake, and blushed. I hoped she would put my red face down to the cold wind blowing over the yard, but then realised that she too had used the familiar form, *du*, when she'd greeted me just now. By this time we were halfway across the yard, and the security guard was still standing there, staring after us. He shouldn't have given this woman access without a reliable chaperone, and I certainly wasn't counted as reliable.

"Thank you for saving me from waiting in this cold," she said, still using the familiar *du*, "I believe that guard wasn't even going to let me into the gatehouse: the brute would have made me wait out here!" She threw a deprecative look backwards. "And may I ask you your name? I'm Evelyn," she held her hand out before adding her surname: "Hagenow."

"Martin, Martin Grobe. Pleased to meet you."

I showed her my right hand, hardened and dirty from the workshop. She looked at the hand, raised an eyebrow slightly, bit her bottom lip, then gave me a broad grin while she firmly took my dirty paw. Taken together, all of these actions were enough to make me blush again.

"Where do you work?"

"Over in building B4, in the assembly hall," I gestured with my chin, so that I wouldn't have to look at her while my blushes subsided.

"Well I do hope to meet you again! It's a shame—we're like ships passing in the night!"

"Well, Evelyn, your ship is brightly lit," I heard myself saying. As the words came out of my mouth and reached my ears, my neck and cheeks reddened yet again. Even by my poor standards of flirting, that was a clumsy attempt at a compliment. In my embarrassment I turned brusquely away, mumbling a short *Tschüss*. But I still caught Evelyn's answer a split second later.

"How sweet! Well, I look forward to seeing you again, Martin!"

101

After Katrin's mother had gone, Evelyn turned up again. One day she appeared at the church where we were holding our meetings, down in the crypt. She quickly became involved in our work, bringing supplies of paper, stationary and even a newish typewriter. On one occasion she managed to get access to an Ormig copier—not at all easy in those days when all reproduction and printing was strictly controlled by the state.

Despite our semi-flirtatious early acquaintance, nothing had ever happened between us. No doubt she was as charming and attractive as ever, but I was stressed and exhausted—working all day, queueing up outside shops every lunch break, trying to buy enough food to feed myself and the young Katrin. At home I was cooking, cleaning, trying to sort out coal deliveries in the winter. The daily grind of life in a broken economy was tedious and tiring. A dirty, dusty and depressing business, even without a child to look after, not to mention the involvement in the group that met in the crypt. And I was still hurting over my wife's absence. I doubt I would have noticed if Evelyn had danced for me, naked, on the rickety tables of the cold church hall.

And here she was again. Evelyn. I had no idea how she had got hold of my number, or what she wanted. I hadn't seen her for about five years—I think she must have disappeared after the mass arrests in the wake of the Rosa Luxemburg demonstration in January 1988. It was a depressing time, we were all disheartened, and a lot of people dropped out. Although I'd seen pretty much everyone from the old group at irregular intervals, Evelyn never came into my life again. I hadn't really noticed it until now, even though I'd heard all sorts of rumours: she'd moved south, to Saxony, or to West Berlin, perhaps even to the Federal Republic. But now she was phoning me up.

Despite my hangover, the lingering memory of Evelyn's

voice made the whole day seem a little brighter.

Now that I was on my feet and had a litre of tap water inside me I decided to keep moving. A painkiller, swigged down with strong coffee and I began to feel like I could possibly function again. As the throbbing in my head eased, a feeling of disquiet grew in my belly. I was excited about Annette, and all the promise, the possibilities and hopes that she represented, but suddenly there was Evelyn on the scene again. Evelyn belonged to another time, a very different time: the old days.

By now I was back in my bedroom. I picked out my trousers from the heap of clothes in the corner, held them up and sniffed the crotch. They'll do for another day at least. Pulling them on, I did them up, then looked at myself in the mirror. Grey skin, large pores. Bags under the eyes. I pulled in my paunch, trying to persuade myself that I looked OK for my age, and stood there, studying the reflection. Then I let my shoulders drop, and my tummy sag, pushing my hands into my pockets. My left hand crumpled some paper. Rough, scratchy. Soviet paper. I pulled out the envelope that Nik had given me, and ripped it open. It was empty. Pushing my forefinger in, I poked around. No, completely empty. Squeezing it open, I peered inside. There was faint writing in there, lightly written with a soft pencil. I tore the envelope and folded it out to read the words: *Tue. 17.00h Woltersdorf Lock.*

Was all this really necessary? I had no idea, but I wasn't exactly reassured by the thought that a KGB captain clearly felt a need for such discreet messages. Would I meet him? Again, no idea. I decided that was a question that could wait a bit longer, at least until I was feeling a bit more human. For now it was enough to get to the office.

It was a cold, clear morning, golden sunshine feeling its way uncertainly over the rooftops, leaving the deep streets in damp shade. I walked unsteadily, meandering along the pavement. Stopping only at the baker's to fill my shopping bag with bread rolls, I made my way to the offices.

The stairs nearly finished me off, and I stood on the landing for a moment, getting my breath back before opening the door and going in. Bärbel was already at her desk, and she gave me a slight nod. I wasn't sure whether to say anything about what had happened at the potluck, and decided it might be simpler to keep quiet. Bärbel seemed to see things the same way—by the time I'd pondered this minor problem of social etiquette, standing in the middle of the front office, she had inserted several pieces of paper and carbon sheets into her typewriter and had begun pecking away. More than anything else, the hammering of the keys drove me into my office. I shut the door, knowing I'd only have a few minutes of peace before the others came in for the morning meeting, and I sat down with a heavy sigh. Feet up on the desk, move some paperwork out of the way: the report on Maier's death, due at the Ministry this afternoon, and currently minus any references to both the British major's curious comments and the police report from Saxony.

I tossed the papers back onto the desk just as Erika and Laura came in, talking about the demo on Saturday. Klaus followed, thankfully without a cigar, holding instead a cucumber in one hand and a stack of plates clutched to his chest. Bärbel brought up the rear, holding a pot of coffee.

"You look like you've been up all night! Was it that Wessi?" Erika's opening shot.

I didn't bother to reply, just groaned, and carefully moved

my feet off the desk and onto the floor. The others didn't comment, Klaus just clattered the plates onto my desk, placing the cucumber on top before going to his usual chair in the corner, Bärbel was already sitting, pencil poised over paper, and Laura deposited a tub of *Marella* margarine and a jar of home-made lentil spread before moving a chair fussily into position and sitting down, back as straight as a Prussian general's. They all sat there, staring expectantly at me.

"What?"

"It's your turn to facilitate," Klaus helped me out. "But if you don't feel up to it then I can do it." He didn't smile, just chewed on one corner of his moustache while looking at Laura's chair leg.

I nodded while rummaging around in my drawer for another painkiller, then swallowed the pill. I put my bag of bread rolls on the table, and there was a moment of minor chaos as everyone scrambled for a plate and a roll. Everyone except me, I didn't feel hungry.

"Right, so what's on the agenda today?" Klaus asked.

"I could do with a second opinion on this fascist case I'm working on," Erika mumbled around a mouthful of bread and cucumber.

"Nothing new from me,"—Laura.

"More on Maier, and I wanted to ask you about this report I have to pass on to the Minister today," I contributed. "Oh, and I should tell you about Major Tom too."

We started with my points, and I described my visit to West Berlin. My colleagues were suitably amused by my account, perhaps I even did an impression of the British major for them, despite the hangover.

"Did the Englishman not give you any more hints?" Klaus wanted to know.

"No, and I'm not even sure it was meant particularly seriously, either. Maybe he was just pulling my leg. Who knows?"

Nobody had any more questions, so I moved on to the Maier case. I told them that I'd completed a fuller report and was going to head off to the Mauerstrasse at midday to hand it in. I was just about to explain about the evidence that had come from the Saxon cops when Laura jumped up.

"A wasp!"

We all watched the wasp lazily checking out the corners of the office, flying in and out of the folds of the dusty net curtains. Laura was standing by the door, anxiously following the wasp's progress. It was unexpected, seeing Laura like this—she was normally so efficient and on top of things—but now she clearly wanted nothing more than to get far away from this flying insect.

"Is that it, can I go?" she asked, eyes still fixed on the wasp.

We all murmured assent, and Bärbel and Klaus followed Laura out, while Erika climbed up on to my desk, a piece of paper in one hand and an empty coffee cup in the other.

"Can I talk to you about this case I'm working on?" she asked. "I meant to talk to you about it on Saturday, but we got sidetracked."

"Yeah, no problem. Your place or mine?"

"Let's go over to mine, I have all the paperwork there," Erika leant out of the window and released the wasp from the cup. It flew off in the chill breeze as if nothing had happened.

I grabbed my coffee and we went over to Erika's office. It was much smaller than mine, but lighter—she'd taken down the net curtains and cleaned the window.

"The police have been watching a nest of fascists at the other end of Lichtenberg," she began, opening a file on her desk, and flicking through the papers, looking for something.

There was nothing new about Nazis in Lichtenberg, the GDR had always had problems with fascists and neo-Nazis, but until 1989 the Party simply pretended they didn't exist, going so far as to persecute anti-fascist groups that tried to do something about the problem. Now the fascists were taking advantage of the freedoms we'd fought for in order to spread their poison.

"They opened up a squat last year, and first of all it was used as a base for the usual stuff—getting pissed, listening to violent music, going out and beating up foreigners. But then, six months ago something changed. Things seemed to have quietened down. No more late nights, no more blood on the pavement outside. Men in suits are going in and out, rather than just young lads in bomber jackets and para-boots."

She showed me a photo, big men with shaved skulls in wide, shiny suits, bull necks showing the edges of prison tattoos over collars.

"The police got someone to talk. He said there's a proper office there now, with a telephone and even a fax machine. There's boxes and boxes of propaganda, piled high, everywhere in the squat. Leaflets, newspapers, West German flags. And this."

She pushed another photograph towards me. Large placards were piled up on a wooden pallet, maybe a few hundred of them. In bold letters, black, red and gold, they read *Wir sind ein Volk!* We are one people—the battle cry of those who wanted unification with West Germany—just one word different from our motto: *Wir sind das Volk!*, but so different in meaning, aspirations and politics.

"So where's all this coming from?" I asked Erika.

"We don't know, and that's why the police asked us to get involved. It certainly looks like a political-ideological diversion: they think there are links with the West German *Republikaner*, and possibly the West-CDU."

The *Reps* were a West German far right party, the CDU on the other hand was a mainstream centre-right party, represented in both East and West. They had held power in West Germany under Chancellor Kohl—at least until he failed to persuade us to join his free-market paradise, at which point he was unceremoniously voted out of office by the West German voters.

"They've seen some of the *Rep* big shots visit the squat. As for the West-CDU, no concrete evidence so far, I think it's just based on those rumours of co-operation between the *Reps* and the CDU during the Autumn Revolution."

We know that the *Reps* came over in force during the first stages of our revolution, back in autumn '89, distributing West German flags and placards, trying to get the public mood to swing in favour of unification. We were almost certain that the campaign had been paid for by the West German CDU. Now it looked like they could be preparing a second attempt at counter-revolution.

"So what do you need me for?"

"Just wanted to check in with you. You see, the police don't know whether it's money or the materials that are being brought into the country, so they've given the customs authorities the registration numbers of all known fascists' vehicles, West and East, and they'll be checked on the borders. They're looking at the bank accounts of East-fascists for any suspicious transfers from the West."

I nodded, and sighed. "Sounds like the kind of thing they used to do to us, doesn't it?"

Erika nodded too. "But back then they didn't do that to the fascists, which may be why we're having such a problem with them now."

I considered what Erika had told me. It all seemed sensible, legal, and considering the stakes, proportionate.

"Sounds OK to me. Could it be one for the 96-15 debate?"

"Yeah," she replied, "that's what I was thinking. I just wanted to get a second opinion on it—might be a useful example, provided we embargo it until we get results."

Paragraph 96, section 15 of the 1990 Constitution allows the government to set up a counter-espionage service—my own outfit, the *Republikschutz* was just a stop-gap, crewed by amateurs. One of the many national discussions we were having was whether we should have a professional intelligence service. People were justifiably sceptical of the need for any kind of secret service—to many people they were just an excuse for macho, militaristic games of James Bond, and I couldn't disagree. For the time being the RS had only an accountability and advisory role, and no actual police powers to investigate, arrest or prosecute anyone. Whatever the nation decided to do, this case was a perfect example of how real the threat of foreign interference was. If this fascist squat really was part of a bigger scheme to undermine the revolution, financed by the West, then a competent foreign intelligence body could have given us earlier notice that something was up, and it would have been able to trace the money trail inside West Germany.

"Thanks, Martin."

"No problem. Thanks for working on this, it doesn't look like fun." I smiled encouragingly at Erika, who pulled a face at me.

Back in my office I went over to the filing cabinet to pull out the case that I was working on before I was sent down to West Silesia—the speculation in housing stock that I had told Annette about. I'd hardly opened it when the phone rang. It was the Minister's secretary. I was expecting her to send me on some wild goose chase, maybe to the French garrison in Tegel in West Berlin. But instead she wanted to send me to Ruschestrasse—the old Stasi headquarters—to fetch some files. She said they'd be waiting for me, all I had to do was pick them up from the porter. Files for Maier and Fremdiswalde, she said.

I put the phone down without saying goodbye, I wasn't happy about being asked to play messenger boy. I'd had the feeling right from the start that the Minister was playing games with me, power games. That's not the way it was meant to work any more. I sat there for a moment, feeling peeved, then picked up the phone again.

A couple of minutes later I had the latest from Schadowski, the police officer in charge of the Murder Investigation Commission in Dresden. They'd found evidence of a struggle near the site where the body had been discovered, along with two pairs of footprints leading there, but only one set going away again. Even though it had never been considered a serious possibility, suicide was now firmly crossed off the list. Schadowski had also attempted to interview some senior WSB members, trying to establish Maier's movements in the days before he was murdered, but he'd been warned off. The policeman had sounded resigned at this development, as if familiar with the situation from a time not too long past.

The news I had just received from Schadowski didn't help improve my mood, and I picked up my Maier report and banged my way out of the office. Once outside though, the cool, fresh air eased my thick head, and I had calmed down by the time I had walked as far as the concrete tower blocks which start just this side of the Frankfurter Allee. I crossed the Allee at the traffic lights by the underground station and started up the slight incline of Ruschestrasse, going past the faded graffito *Freedom for my files!* I showed the guard my RS pass, and went into the large courtyard of the old Stasi headquarters. Concrete tower blocks surrounded the whole complex, making it impossible to see in from the outside. Opposite me was the main building where Erich Mielke, the general in charge of the Stasi, had once had his offices. I headed over the yard and went in, asking the porter if a package was waiting for me.

"Here you are, comrade *Oberleutnant*, ready and waiting for you," was the answer.

I took the large envelope she held out to me, and signed

the receipt that had been thrust over the counter.

I didn't look at the envelope until I was in the underground. It was standard A4 size, made of rough, grey paper with high wood-content. Not particularly fat, and most interestingly, not even sealed. To me that was as good as an invitation.

I pulled out the files. Maier's first: not much in there, the F 16 and F 22 index cards that I'd already seen copies of, and a few sheets of paper listing his career at the Stasi, starting in 1964, informing on his fellow recruits in a Border Troops regiment. It looked like he stayed in touch with the Stasi once he'd finished his military service, reporting on colleagues all the way through his work life: starting in a factory, candidature of the Party, full Party membership, conferences. All the people he'd reported on were of course hidden behind codenames, but there were a fair few of them. It was neither particularly interesting, nor particularly unusual. There were tens of thousands of these ordinary IMs, everyday informants for the Stasi, watching everyday people do everyday things. There were no citations or medals mentioned, no particular rewards or criticisms, all very middle of the road.

We were pulling in to Alexanderplatz station now, and I got off with everyone else and changed on to the underground line to Otto-Grotewohl-Strasse. I flicked through Fremdiswalde's file while the train squealed around the tight curves, making flashes of light scratch across the inside of my still tender skull. Again, nothing interesting—he was known under the codename WERTHER and was listed as an offender, not an IM, and the details matched those the police had given me.

I put all the papers back in the envelope, and put that in my bag, next to the report I'd written for the Minister. Maybe the answer to Maier's death wasn't in the past. Perhaps it was a straightforward murder, a criminal action, rather than a political one. If that were the case then there was no job for me or the rest of RS here—only for the police.

I got off at the final stop, and walked up the Mauerstrasse to the Ministry, right at the far end. A sand-beige coloured Wartburg Kombi was parked opposite with a couple of goons sat in it. They looked bored, as if they'd been waiting a while —probably chauffeuring some *Bonze* around, poor sods. I ignored their stares and went into the Ministry and up to the first floor. This time I wasn't kept waiting, but ushered straight in to see the Minister.

"Ah! Martin!" The Minister rose, shaking my hand, and gesturing over to the armchairs grouped around a coffee table.

I made my way over to the informal seating cluster while the Minister pressed a button on his desk and ordered coffee to be brought. He joined me, slowly lowering himself into the chair with a sigh.

"Martin, I wanted to apologise for my behaviour last Wednesday. You wouldn't believe how busy it is round here at the moment—ah! The coffee! Yes, just put it down there please—right, where were we? Yes, I've got the Round Table breathing down my neck about the Maier death, demanding I come to their meetings at all hours of the day and night, asking awkward questions, making demands. As if I haven't got enough on my plate! I told them: 'As Minister of the Interior I am responsible for security matters, and my forces are investigating the case.' But why, they ask me, are RS involved?" He paused, and looked at me meaningfully.

"But why are we involved?" I asked straight back.

"Well, the duty officer that night must have got confused. Made assumptions. And he decided it might be a matter for RS. Presumably you were on call that night? So you got sent

112

down. Unfortunate mistake. But you have that report I asked for, thank you. And the files from Ruschestrasse?"

I handed over the grey envelope and the file with my report in. He put my report on the table then absent-mindedly flicked the open flap of the envelope while I sipped my coffee. Too hot, I blew gently on it, trying to cool it down.

"Strictly speaking, that's the end of your involvement now, but since you've been dragged into this sad business already, I thought you might want to take part in a little jaunt tomorrow. As an observer, if you will. We're going to tie it all up in the morning." He leaned forward conspiratorially, then, in a loud whisper: "We've identified the murderer, here in Berlin. A lovers' tiff, apparently."

The Minister leaned back again, and gave another sigh. Satisfied.

"Tomorrow morning at 0600 hours you're to report to *Volkspolizeidirektion* 52—that's Marchlewskistrasse police station to you and me. Ask for *Hauptmann* Weber. You'll be there at the arrest, you'll be my eyes and ears. Make sure there are no loose ends, we want it all done and dusted. No mistakes." Again he gave me that odd look.

I was surprised: the murderer must have been identified in the last few minutes—Schadowski hadn't told me that they were so close to having a firm suspect when I spoke to him just an hour ago.

"Officially you'll be there in your accountability status, make sure things are done according to the book, considering how sensitive the situation is with the WSB right now.

"Right," he continued brusquely, before I had a chance to ask any questions. "The other thing I wanted to talk to you about is the national debate on the inner-German border." He stared up at the corner of the ceiling, elbows on his desk, steepling his fingers. "The Central Round Table and the

Volkskammer are scheduling the national debate, getting all the materials together for people to think about and discuss, the usual. The Ministry for Foreign Trade is dealing with customs and trade, the Ministry for Family and Social Affairs is dealing with the social questions, and we need to come up with a summary of the security aspects of the border and the Berlin Wall. I'd like you to take that on, come up with a structure for the report, and a quick overview of positive and negative impacts. Make a start on collecting data and statistics, see which way the evidence is pointing. You can liaise directly with the Round Table Committee for Internal Affairs, but keep me posted.

"And finally ..." the Minister got up and moved over to his desk, rifling through some papers in a tray. He grunted, and came back, holding a form out to me. "Here you are, this is for you."

I took the paper, turning it round so that I could read it. It was a confirmation of my promotion to the rank of captain, signed this morning by the Minister.

"*Hauptmann* Grobe!" The Minister said, with an oily voice. Until that moment I'd never been sure what was meant by 'oily voice'—but this was definitely oily. A tone of voice that called hair pomade to mind: slick, greasy, and shiny.

"We decided that your new roles necessitated a higher rank. Take the paperwork along to the secretariat and they'll issue you with a new pass, and a chit for the extra pips for your dress uniform."

The promotion to captain didn't really mean anything to me personally, except for the increase in pay and pension entitlements. In fact it was rather embarrassing. I'd never worn my dress uniform, and I had no intention of changing that particular habit. Apart from that, my promotion meant that I now held the senior rank in the office—until now we had all been at the same level, and that had suited our way of working. But there were other messages here, too many to keep track of. I wasn't keeping up—I needed to find a quiet corner and have a think, but the Minister kept on talking.

"Why don't you organise a little party? Celebrate with your colleagues, I'm sure we'll be able to pick up the tab."

The Minister had stayed on his feet, and he held out his hand for me to take. I got up, swapped my promotion confirmation to my left hand, and proffered the right one.

"And remember, the rank of captain is a very real privilege —and privileges bring responsibilities," the Minister peered at me over his wire glasses, in a way that he probably thought was significant. "Let me know when it happens, your party, and I'll do my best to come along," he said, as he steered me to the door. "Congratulations, again!"

I was standing back in the corridor, and the Minister had disappeared behind his closed door.

12:57

Straight back to the office to try and clear some of the backlog that had been piling up since last Thursday, not to mention this new task that the Minister had given me. Strictly speaking, I ought to wait before starting work on it— we'd sort out who was doing it at tomorrow's morning meeting. Nevertheless I started looking through the paperwork I'd been given—I liked this kind of thing, it felt worthwhile. A series of structured debates were to be organised throughout the country, information materials provided—available at town halls and community centres, summaries printed in newspapers—all to encourage people to think about the various aspects of the question, 'what should we do about the Wall?' The results from neighbourhood meetings would be fed up through the Round Table system, and using that, the *Volkskammer* would work out one or more questions for the referendum, to be held sometime in spring. It was a lot of work, and it was essential that the information materials were clearly written, and above all, fair to all sides of the argument. I didn't object to the task being given to us, quite the contrary, but it really didn't fall within our remit. However, since we didn't have a particularly clear remit we often got saddled with the tasks nobody else in the Ministry wanted.

I went out to the front office and added a note to the agenda for tomorrow's meeting, then came back into my room, pulling the file on housing speculation out of the pile of papers breeding on my desk. Opening it up and flicking through the pages I found I couldn't concentrate. My mind kept returning to the Minister—his behaviour really niggled. I sat back with a sigh, and tried to put my finger on what was bothering me. First of all, Wednesday, he seemed pissed off that I'd been to see Maier's body in West Silesia, and he clearly wasn't comfortable with me working the case: "No need to prioritise it," he'd said. Not exactly warning me off, but nervous, trying to divert me with lots of extra duties—the liaison with the Russians and the British, which he'd somehow hastily organised, making sure my time was taken up for most of Thursday and Friday. Now more work, this report on the Wall—thinking about it again, it struck me that the Minister had said "I want *you* to take it on," using the singular *du*, not the plural *ihr*. He hadn't asked me to bring it back to RS2 for us to decide who should work on it, he wanted *me* to get tied up with the research and report. But what about the arrest tomorrow, and the promotion? I guess the promotion was meant as a carrot, behave myself and I'll do all right. By ordering me to be present at the arrest, he could show me that everything was being taken care of. In his words: all done and dusted.

The person that was to be arrested tomorrow morning is here in Berlin, according to the Minister. I had no idea who it was, the Minister hadn't seen fit to let me in on that particular secret. That brought another train of thought to mind—the West Silesian crisis had been brewing for months now, and had serious implications for the Republic. Yet, as far as I knew, no-one from any of the RS units had been involved in keeping an eye on things, despite the fact that this falls exactly within our remit. Here we were, scuttling around, checking out minor criminal cases, such as unscrupulous Westerners trying to cash in on our naïvety, when the elephant in the room is that the West Silesian League were about to bankrupt the whole country.

I considered what had been happening in West Silesia, the unexpected rise of the West Silesian League, coming from nowhere, somehow well resourced, able to produce good quality leaflets and posters and get them widely distributed. The apparent ease with which they succeeded in gaining autonomy from Saxony, setting up their own *Land* in a very short space of time. Then suddenly there was talk of secession from the GDR itself, joining the West Germans under article 23 of their constitution. An agreement had been signed with West Germany to allow the transit of goods between West Germany and West Silesia, without any inspection by our customs officers. And we were hearing rumours of military hardware and even military forces being brought from West Germany into Silesia. Now there was Maier's death, and the Minister was unhappy about me having any involvement in the investigation.

Back to the Minister, no matter what I was thinking about, my mind always returned to Benno Hartmann. If I was right, that he was gently warning me off the Maier case—then why? And even if I was wrong, why hadn't he assigned either us or our colleagues to look at the West Silesian crisis? Even if he hadn't done so before, now would be the time—Maier's death was sensitive.

The only conclusion I could come up with was that the Minister knew it was being taken care of by someone else. But who? We didn't have any other central organ responsible for security—the Criminal Police departments were all focussing on local and regional criminality, and the Stasi had been disbanded over three and a half years ago. Was there a new, secret security operation that I hadn't heard about? That hardly seemed plausible.

My thoughts were interrupted by the shrill demands of the phone.

"Grobe," I said into the receiver.

No response. They didn't hang up, there was just no-one saying anything. I could hear the faint rumble of traffic in the background, but no voice, not even breathing.

"Hello, hello! Can you hear me?"

Now they hung up. Just a soft click, then the dialling tone. If it was important then they'd phone back. A mental shrug, and I got up to make some coffee. Enough thinking, time to get down to some work.

19:45

It's a wonderful thing about being in love that you seem to glow. It's not like I'd fallen in love with Annette or anything, certainly not yet. But I had a second date with her, and so far I was enjoying her company. It felt good. She'd made a very positive impression on me, and I hoped I had done so on her too. In fact, I hadn't felt this positive about a relationship since Katrin's mother. I suppose Evelyn had always been there, a vague and unconfirmed possibility floating on the horizon, static charge deflecting the light around the idea of her. But she'd been gone for a long time too.

When I met Annette at Friedrichstrasse station, and we walked along the Spree, arm in arm, we had that lovers' glow around us. I could tell because people smiled at us as we went past. This is Berlin, people never smile. But there they were, basking in our luminescence. We weren't the only ones glowing—on the other side of the road a couple were stood in a doorway, locked in a kiss; on our side of the road a man stopped in front of us, his arms widespread, forming a roadblock. I was puzzled by this for a moment, until a woman sped past us, riding her bike on the pavement, head down, legs pumping, pretending to show determination to mow down the obstruction. With a squeal of brakes she stopped, and man, woman and bike collapsed into a heap of giggles. An older woman went past, holding a toddler by the hand. The kid was shooting pigeons with his forefinger, cocking back his thumb before each blast.

"Leave them alone Mario, the pigeons are our comrades too!"

Annette and I grinned at each other.

"That's what I like about this place—even the birds are your equals!" She joked.

"The state and every citizen has the duty to protect the natural environment as the foundation of life for present and future generations."

Annette just looked at me as if I'd gone mad.

"It's in our constitution. Saving the pigeons is the constitutional duty of all citizens of the GDR. Visitors too," I joked.

"Ah, a lawyer as well, I see! And I suppose you know which paragraph and section it is?"

I did, but I also didn't want to appear too geeky, so I just gave her a hug, which somehow turned into a kiss. It was just a brief one, lips touching, then moving away, shocked by the electricity discharged between us. We looked at each other in surprise and delight, still in each others' arms, until I got embarrassed and moved away slightly. Annette took the hint, and we carried on walking, but this time holding hands. We'd reached the Monbijou bridge, and the setting sun was glinting off the Bode Museum. It was a bright evening, and the autumn leaves on the trees in the park were glowing pink in the dying light.

"Have we got any plans for this evening?" I asked.

I had some ideas of my own, but I thought that Annette would have too, so it felt like a good idea to check in with her. She smiled, the toothy grin that made me laugh.

"Yes, you'll love this, Martin, a bit of cutting edge multimedia entertainment."

"What's multimedia?" I asked. I must have looked sceptical because she laughed at me, grabbing my hand and running through the park.

"Come on, we can get the tram from here—where's the stop?"

We got to the tram stop, and she looked around, unsure which side of the road to stand on.

"Where are we going?"

"Prenzlauer Allee."

The number 71 rolled in, headed for Heinersdorf, and we jumped on. I stamped tickets for both of us and we sat down as the orange Tatra shuddered and keened over the points into the Rosenthaler Strasse. We were sat near the back, and we could see people getting on and off. In silly voices Annette made up conversations for the other passengers we could see, trying to make her words match the movement of their lips. She wasn't saying anything particularly funny, but the childishness of it, and the excitement from our brief kiss gave us an enjoyable levity. I felt like I was sitting in a bubble of light, even though outside the tram windows the town was turning dark, the street lights were winking on and the tram itself was ill lit by underpowered and dirty bulbs.

As the Immanuel Church loomed out of the dusk Annette jumped up.

"This is our stop, here we go!"

We jumped down from the tram, and went into one of the side streets.

"How was your day?" she asked, "I'm sorry, I should have asked hours ago, but I was so pleased to see you that I forgot my manners!"

"Crazy. Really weird. And stressful."

"Do you want to talk about it?" Annette sounded concerned, but had slowed down, and was peering at each house in turn, trying to find the numbers in the dusk.

"Something rotten in the State of West Silesia," I murmured.

Annette had found what she was looking for, and I'm not sure she heard me. She was heaving open the heavy door, before ushering me into the hallway and up the stairs. It was a normal house, grey-brown rendering, grey-brown lino on the stairs, and the ubiquitous smell of floor polish, brown coal and cabbage. We stopped on the second floor, a note pinned to the frame of the door: *Event in the cellar!* Back down the stairs we went, looking for the steps down to the cellar: a stunted door, cowering beneath the staircase. It was wedged open, and we could hear distorted music coming from below.

We made our way down the steps, feeling our way with our heels in the darkness. The steps felt gritty underfoot, as did the floor of the cellar when we got there. Heads bent to avoid the pipes crossing the low ceiling we stumbled through the grey darkness—there wasn't much light here, the flicker of a film projector showing us the way. We sat at the back of a small crowd, on cushions on the floor. Before us Fritz Lang's *Metropolis* was playing against the side of the cellar, and in front of that a young man, wearing dark clothes and sunglasses sat on a beer crate, hunched over a guitar. His long dark hair obscured his face and fingers as he plucked the strings, his feet were stretched out, and before them an array of pedals. As I watched, his right foot darted out, and tapped a pedal, then again just a few seconds later. The reverberating guitar chord was joined by another one an octave lower, and both stretched on while Lang's fantasy world was built up on the wall behind.

The chords continued reverberating, joined by another

one whenever the foot tapped a pedal. Without warning, a scratchy voice, a Saxon accent, began talking slowly. The measured, reverent tones suggested poetry, and it took me a couple of lines before I recognised it through his mangled vowels: Dante's *Inferno*. I shared a quick look with Annette, who was biting her fingers in an effort not to giggle, and we returned our full concentration to the performer.

I couldn't tell you how long it went on for—Dante's words had a lulling effect, and the music wasn't actually that bad, drawing me in, taking my mind off the events of the day.

"The contrast of the decayed context with the superior cultural experience provides a dramatic frame of reference suited to ..." began Annette as soon as we'd escaped. One of her silly voices, Saxon this time, same as the performer.

We laughed, and I pointed out that the interchangeability of both nouns and adjectives made her assessment as meaningful as a speech by the Party leadership on May day.

"A bit experimental for my taste, but, I don't know, there was a sense of preparation, practice and ability that won my respect," was my contribution, said in a low voice, for I knew I was talking bollocks, and there were still quite a few people about. It embarrassed me to think that these strangers might overhear.

This made Annette laugh again, and she told me that it was I who was taking it all too seriously.

"What was that place anyway?" I wanted to know.

"Oh one of those squats. An Ossi one, which is why the culture was so good!"

"Do you know many squatters?"

"Yeah, used to live in a squat myself, in Kreuzberg. Ancient history, but I still know a few people in the scene. I know some of the squatters who came over in '90, down in Friedrichshain, and through them I've met a few of the squatters up here in Prenzlauer Berg too."

Shortly after the Wall opened, a stream of squatters came in from West Berlin. Feeling the pinch from hardline police tactics over there, full of youthful arrogance and convinced that they were the ones to show us in the East how to do this revolution thing properly. A series of squats were opened up, the Wessis mostly concentrated round Friedrichshain, the Easterners taking over derelict buildings in Prenzlauer Berg, and, to an extent, in Mitte and Friedrichshain too. Interestingly the two scenes didn't mix too well—even though they had a squatters' Round Table, and the West-squats were twinned with the East-squats. You didn't find many Easterners wanting to live in a Wessi-squat. I didn't blame them, the Wessi-squats sounded quite stressful. They tended to annoy their neighbours more with raucous parties and fly-tipping, and I'd heard that they had all sorts of alternative-living experiments going on—toilet doors were considered bourgeois, as was exclusive use of underwear.

The Ossi-squats seemed much more civilised to me—sure, they annoyed their neighbours too, with loud parties, graffiti art and flags, and below average awareness of hygiene—but they were, on the whole, well integrated into their neighbourhoods, providing support and labour to whoever needed it, whether it was doing the shopping or taking empty bottles to the SERO for the elderly, or carrying out structural repairs to one of the many semi-derelict buildings.

But despite all that, it looked like they couldn't put on a decent cultural event.

"Do you know anywhere round here? A bar? A place to go dancing?" Annette wanted more of me, and I wasn't exactly ready to go to bed yet either.

"I'm sorry, I should have said before ... I've got a really stupidly early start in the morning—I can't stop out too long."

Her face fell, but a smile sprang back into position before I had time to react.

"That's a shame, but never mind—Monday's not really the

day to go dancing, is it? What's happening in the morning?"

"I've got to be there when the police make an arrest. Nothing particularly exciting–"

Annette patted my arm, reassuring me that it was OK.

We walked back to the tram stop, it was still rather early, and I hoped that Annette wouldn't think I was giving her the brush off, but if we went to a bar or something now, who knew what might happen between Annette and me. That was a really nice thought, but I wasn't sure I was ready for it yet.

We sat on the tram, silent, but still holding each other's hands. When we got off, I walked her back to the Friedrichstrasse station. We said goodbye with a hug, and another brief kiss. This wasn't so unexpected, it didn't have the same electric shock effect as before, a mere brush of soft lips against mine. I found myself responding, leaning in for another kiss, but Annette had moved away. I opened my eyes, she was already halfway down the steps to the U-Bahn.

"Bye Martin—thank you for the lovely evening!" She blew me a kiss, and was gone.

DAY 7
Tuesday
28th September 1993

Moscow: The Soviet President Mikhail Gorbachev is no longer under house arrest. The news comes as Internal Military units, under the command of the Soviet Interior Ministry, move against the barricades erected by the KGB around the parliament building, which was occupied last week by members of the dissolved Soviet of the Republics. President Gorbachev is returning to Moscow to take command of the Internal Military, but it is unclear how he can survive the crisis without the support of the KGB.

Görlitz: The West Silesian government has ended the co-operation between Silesian and Saxon police in the matter of the invest-igation into the death of the WSB politician, Johannes Maier. The West Silesian Interior Minister, Jakob Schröter, stated last night that his police force can deal with the murder inquiry without what he referred to as: 'outside interference'. As yet there has been no official response to the offer of assistance made yesterday by the West German Federal Criminal Police Agency.

05:54

I showed my pass to the policeman sitting at the front desk, asking for Captain Weber. He didn't answer, just pointed up to the first floor. It was the first time I'd been in the Marchlewskistrasse police station, and I was curious.

Apprehensive too. The cops from this station had a reputation: the hard lads of the Berlin police force, happy to take matters into their own hands. They were the ones who made sure suspects stumbled down stairs and walked into fists. Before the revolution a friend of mine had his flat turned over by Marchlewskistrasse officers. No reason, no excuse given, and despite the fact that he lived in Prenzlauer Berg, a long way off their beat.

Up the granite steps, hand trailing the steel balustrade. The corridor at the top was busy—mostly cops in uniform, holding plastic shields and helmets, heading towards double doors about halfway down. I followed them into a large room. Red, black and state flags adorning one wall, opposite a notice board covered with press and magazine clippings, declarations and hand written headings: some kind of wall newspaper for the brigade. The police officers were falling into ranks, facing the flags and an officer, who was conferring with a woman in mufti. The officer was a captain: that'd be my man. I waited for him to finish talking to the woman, then went to introduce myself.

"Grobe. The Minister requested my presence during this arrest."

"Weber. Take a seat," he shook my hand firmly but briefly, then turned away.

I looked around for a chair, the only ones available were against the back wall, below the wall newspaper. I decided to remain standing but moved a little to one side, next to the doorway.

Silence had fallen, and the cops were all facing their captain. Shields resting on the floor, held steady with the left hand, helmets clipped to belts, right hands pressed against legs, fingers parallel to trouser seams. All very correct and commendable, if a little intimidating to a civilian such as myself.

"Comrades, your task is to effect the arrest of a suspect.

According to the ABV Officer of the area, the suspect is in the squatted building on the Thaerstrasse. Disembarkation on the Mühsamstrasse beginning at X minus 7, mustering on the Bersarinstrasse, 100 metres north of Bersarinplatz at X minus 3. At time X *Kommando* B will effect entry and secure the front of the building. *Kommando* C will effect entry to buildings to the rear, on Bersarinstrasse," here Weber walked over to a detailed map, pinned to the wall next to a blackboard. "They will secure access to and from the rear of the squat. *Kommando* C will follow *Kommando* A and will provide support in locating and detaining the suspect. The suspect is using the flat on the second floor, right hand side."

The captain paused, then walked back to the front of the ranked policemen. "Remember, this is a squat. We should be prepared for disrespectful behaviour, including violence. Use of reasonable force in self-defence is acceptable."

A murmur rose from the assembly, the men at the back digging their elbows into their neighbour's sides and grinning. The captain waited, face immobile, then pointed towards me.

"First Lieutenant Grobe here will be coming along to observe the operation. He is from the *Republikschutz*. Take note of his appearance—since he has chosen not to come in uniform you will need to be able to tell him apart from our clients."

Given the reputation of these bulls, the captain's order had a disquieting affect on me. Thirty faces looked my way, assessing me, but giving no clue to what they thought. I decided that this was not the time to tell the captain that I'd been promoted, that I was now his equal in rank. But it might be judicious to let him know before zero hour, and if I could, somehow to give the impression that I had the ear of the Minister.

"Right, men! Time X is at ..." Weber looked at his watch, comparing it to the clock on the wall above the door, "06.35.

Embark in the yard immediately. Transport is waiting. Dismiss!"

The cops filed out, talking in excited whispers, clearly relishing the prospect of raiding a squat.

"You can come with me, no need to go on a truck," with a brisk half-smile Weber strode out of the room, the squad parting to let him through, with me in his wake.

"Why don't you wait in the yard, we'll be taking the Volga. I'm just going to pick up the paperwork."

I made my way down the stairs, surrounded by cops telling each other stories of previous raids, pumping each other up, preparing for violence. The Minister hadn't mentioned the fact that the arrest was to take place in a squat. He hadn't told me who we were supposed to arrest either. Presumably the snatch squad, *Kommando* A, had been briefed on his identity before I got here.

The cops were talking as if 1989 had never happened, I could overhear snippets of conversation:

"We'll show these arseholes!"

"They'll wish they'd been gassed when we've finished with them!"

"If any of them tries to resist ... just let them try!"

And here I was, on their side of the barricades. I was part of the system now, alongside these men who took pleasure in violence and who hated anyone who didn't fit into the meat-veg-and-potatoes, wife-and-two-kids model of how life should be.

Weber had come out into the yard now, holding a clipboard with several pieces of paper on it. All of his men were sitting on the back of the W50 trucks, the engines growling as they waited for the signal to depart. A driver held the front passenger door open for Weber, and before getting in he nodded to the nearest truck driver. With a roar and billowing exhausts, the trucks moved out of the yard and on to the street. I got in the back of the black Volga car, and we followed the convoy.

It was a short drive up to the Frankfurter Allee, the convoy heading up the Strasse der Pariser Kommune rather than going by the more direct route via the Frankfurter Tor, presumably to avoid passing too close to the squat on the Thaerstrasse. It was all going according to plan: park on the Mühsamstrasse, cops sprinting along to the junction and forming into three squads, one squad entering a couple of buildings on that street, the other two running around the corner into the Thaerstrasse.

Weber was sitting patiently in the front seat, and I sat behind him, watching the uniforms disappear into the early morning gloom.

"We'll wait here a moment, let the dust settle," said Weber, half turning towards me.

I pushed my door open and got out.

"Grobe! Wait here!" Weber wasn't playing nice guy any more, he too had opened his door, and was half out of it before I had even thought of a reply.

"I have my orders."

"I order you to stay here," Weber's face was turning dangerously red.

"Fuck you, I'm a captain, too!" I shouted back over my shoulder as I broke into a jog.

I ran across the road, skipping over the tram tracks and holding my hand up to ward off the sparse traffic. Round the corner, into the Thaerstrasse. A small knot of cops stood around a doorway a bit further up the road. I shouldered my way through, getting an elbow in the kidneys for my efforts, although at least none of them seriously tried to stop me. Past a heavy wooden door, the lock smashed, and into the hall. Up the stairs: second floor right, Weber had said. I was going up as fast as I could, feeling the pain in my left kidney, but not responding to it, concentrating on getting up those stairs, blocking out the shouts and the screams around me. A helmeted policeman, wooden truncheon ready in his hand, was standing at the entrance to the flat. He was peering in through the open door when I reached the top of the stairs, but he must have heard my laboured breathing, turning to look at me. I held my palm out towards him, moving past, into the flat. There were two doors in front of me, and the corridor bent round to the right. Both doors were open—one room looked empty except for a cop swiping at a shelf of LPs with his truncheon. In the other room two bulls were shouting at a form huddled in a sleeping bag on a mattress. One bent down, pulling the sleeping bag from the bottom end, the other grabbing an arm that had come into sight. Between them they pulled the slim figure off the bed, screaming at her to kneel down, face the wall, hands behind the head. Only when she had complied did the cops turn to me, a satisfied grin on each of their faces as they stood either side of the naked woman.

"Is this who we're looking for?" I asked them.

They smirked at each other before one of them answered.

"No, it's not," then, as an afterthought, "sir."

I looked at the young woman, slim, not too tall, broad mohican, vaguely coloured red: Karo.

"You two—out! Now!"

The cops glanced at each other and shrugged, one looked down—devouring the image of Karo, naked and shivering on her knees, breasts lifted up by her raised arms, nipples and goose pimples standing out in cold and fear—then gently trailed his truncheon over Karo's chest, deliberately catching a nipple, then up, over her shoulders as he moved out of the room.

As soon as the two cops had moved away, Karo turned to see who was in the room with her, hands still clasped behind her head. I could see the fear in her eyes give way to bewilderment, soon hardening to hate.

"You," she spat, "wanker!"

I didn't say anything. What was there to say? I just turned and closed the door behind me, moving further into the flat. Shelves ran the length of the corridor, the contents lying smashed on the floor below. More shouting ahead. Doorway left: bathroom, empty—looking untidy, but so far untouched by fist or truncheon. Doorway right: kitchen. Young man, also naked, lying on his belly on the floor, four cops: the pair from the first room stood by and looked on as the other two did the work, one with a boot on the boy's head, pressing it hard into the bare wooden boards. The last cop had a knee on the boy's lower back and was shouting directly into his ear.

"Where is he, you shitty communist? Speak up, can't hear you! Where the fuck is he?"

The kid was hysterical, shouting and crying, snot and blood running from his nose.

"Silence!" I shouted, in my best parade ground voice. It worked. The only sounds were the background crashing and screaming from the rest of the house, and the snivelling of the figure on the floor.

The four cops looked at me, expectantly. It was obvious they didn't appreciate my interruption, but I hoped they would appreciate my rank.

"Is this the suspect?"

The four shuffled a bit, looking down at the mess of humanity lying on the floor. They shook their heads like naughty schoolchildren accused of stealing apples.

"Right, out. Now! Exit this flat, now!" I grabbed one by the arm, the one with the most braid on his shoulder boards. "*Oberwachtmeister*, I want all the residents of this building gathered in the backyard. No need for any more searching of the premises, just the people. Out there, now."

"Yes, comrade first lieutenant!" he snarled, roughly pulling his arm free from my grasp.

"Move! Oh, and *Oberwachtmeister*? It's Captain now."

The cop didn't look back, just moved down the corridor at

a fast pace, already bawling orders. He stopped, shuffled around in the mess on the floor with his boot, then stooped and picked up some papers. He turned, and came back to me. I was still at the end of the corridor, watching him.

"Herr *Oberwachtmeister*," I started, deliberately not calling him comrade. "What's the name of the person we're looking for?"

"Fremdiswalde, comrade captain."

I'd been too slow. Fremdiswalde was registered at this address—I'd even seen it in his files. And there was obviously some connection between Fremdiswalde and Maier—Fremdiswalde had been to school in Hoyerswerda, which is where Maier was based before the revolution. Then there was the fingerprints on the papers from Maier's pockets. What had the Minister said? *A lovers' tiff.*

"Dismiss!"

Before he turned and went, he pressed the bundle of papers into my hand. Without looking I rolled them up and put them in my jacket pocket, then turned my attention to the boy on the floor. His nose was still dripping, but the snivelling had turned into a heavy panting. I looked round the kitchen, found a paper bag with some dried bread crusts in it. Tipping them out I held it to the boy's mouth, being careful to avoid the blood and snot. His breathing calmed, and he turned himself onto his back. A look of fear, then hostility crept into his eyes, the same hard look that I'd just been given by Karo.

"What's your name?"

There was no answer. It didn't feel like I was going to get far with my questioning, but I tried again anyway.

"Where's Fremdiswalde?"

The kid's face screwed itself into a grimace, and he spat blood out onto the floor. He was sitting up now, leaning against a kitchen cupboard.

"Gone. Not here. You won't find him here."

"When did he go?"

"Cleared out last night, in a bit of a hurry. He's gone."

I left him to it, and went back to the front of the flat. The door was open again, and Karo was crouched down in the corner, now wearing a pair of jeans and a pullover. She looked up at me as I came in.

"Do you know where Fremdiswalde is?"

No answer.

"Come on Karo, this is important, he's wanted for murder!"

"Wanker!" she spat.

"I think you've overstepped your authority, Herr Grobe," said a voice from behind me: calm, collected, measured. Captain Weber had caught up with me.

I turned to look at him. He was standing on the threshold of the flat, not yet inside. With two quick steps I was out of Karo's room, another step and I was in Weber's face. He stood his ground for a moment, then stepped back. I moved forward, taking care to remain in his space, pulling the flat door shut behind me. It didn't close properly, it had been kicked in, but it was now more shut than open. Pushing past Weber, I went down the stairs, looking out the back door into the yard as I reached the bottom. About a dozen punks were stood against the back wall, hands behind their heads, legs spread wide apart, some were naked, none had enough clothes on for the early morning chill. I considered going out there, issuing more orders in an attempt to improve the situation for the squatters, but a glance over my shoulder told me that Weber was on his way down. I'd probably done all I could, and I'd definitely outstayed my welcome.

07:13

The number 13 tram was rattling down the hill as I reached the corner, and I sprinted over the road to the stop. It was fairly empty, the early shift at the factories along the river would already be at their machines, the office and shop workers still at home having their breakfast. I slumped down into a seat, keeping half an eye on the world around me, but most of my brain and body just switched off. I got off at Marktstrasse, and swayed for a moment. I ought to go to the office, report back at the morning meeting. But my flat was closer, and the thought of a dark room and a cup of coffee was too comforting. Time to go home.

I put the pan of water on the hob as soon as I got in, and stared out of the window as I waited for it to boil. Clouds of steam brought me back, and I hurriedly spooned some ground coffee into a mug, pouring water over it. The round smell of coffee rose to my nostrils, familiar, soothing. I absently stirred the grounds which were still floating on the top of the water. Going through to the living room, I sank into my chair, putting the coffee on the floor. The curtains were open, but the sun was low and hazy, I didn't need to get up and close them.

The doorbell woke me. Not a great way to wake up, and certainly not after this morning's experiences. I put my hands on the chair arms and pushed myself up, pulling my feet back so that I could stand up, knocking the mug of cold coffee over in the process.

"Shit!"

The doorbell rang again: loud, long and insistent. I left the coffee, and went to the door, opening it.

"Katrin!"

"Papa, hi! God, what's happened to you? Have you been drinking?"

"What time is it?"

"It's about eleven. You have been drinking, haven't you?"

I trailed back to the living room, picked up the cup, then

went to get a cloth from the kitchen. No harm done, just a bit of coffee on the wooden floor. I wiped it up, aware that Katrin was making more coffee.

"Are you OK, Papa?"

"Yeah, yeah. Fine. All the better for seeing you."

She grinned, but it was true: a couple of hours sleep, and the smiling face of my daughter—that's what good medicine is all about.

"So what's up? You look awful."

I thought about our last conversation, and the chat I'd had the other night with Nik, and I decided to tell Katrin about my morning. The edited version, no need to go into the gory details.

"The guy you were looking for wasn't even there? So this whole raid was for nothing, barging in on people while they're asleep, shouting at them—"

"Yes—"

"It's no better than the bad old days, is it?" Katrin was on a roll.

"It wasn't my idea, and anyway, these things happen in the West too, don't they?"

Katrin softened, "Yes, suppose so. Doesn't make it right though. Anyway, how do you know this guy is the one you want?"

"I don't. That's just what I was told, by the Minister."

"What? No evidence, just his word. Do you believe him?"

"Of course. I'm sure it's all right." But was I? "But to what do I owe the pleasure?" I asked, trying to change the subject.

Katrin blushed, then, in a mischievous way: "How are you getting on with Annette?"

I grinned back. "I ought to be cross with you—interfering in my life like that! But, it was ... interesting."

"Mm-hm?"

"Yeah, we seem to get on well. It's been nice. It was good to think about something different for a while. I doubt anything will happen."

"But you've met her twice already—of course something might happen!" Then, more quietly: "Thanks for not being pissed off with me."

"Well, like I said, I ought to be. But it's good to know someone cares enough to do something like that."

"I thought you'd blow a gasket—that's what I wanted to talk to you about last Friday, but we didn't get round to it. And I hadn't expected Annette to respond so quickly to the advert. In fact, she'd spotted it even before I told her about you. But she's great, I really like her—she'll be good for you."

"I don't know if it'll get that far. And just because I'm not too annoyed with you doesn't mean you can carry on interfering in my life!"

"Yeah—sorry," Katrin did at least manage to look a little contrite. "But I hate to think of life passing you by."

"It isn't. And it's not as if there's never been any others, you know?"

Her eyes widened: "I didn't know—I never noticed."

"No, you wouldn't have—it was after you went. I was here, alone, it was a crazy time, that autumn. Everyone had so much energy, we were all so frantic, busy, tired, excited ... things happened."

"But nothing lasted? I mean, was there anything serious?"

"I'm always serious when it comes to things like that. But, no, nothing lasted. It was like ... nothing could ever come close to what I had with her." I didn't say her name, I rarely do, but we both knew who I meant. "When the cuddling ended, when whoever it was had left, or when I came home again afterwards ... that was it. Then I'd feel so alone. More than before. You hold someone, and you feel safe. Your thoughts are quiet, you can feel your heart beating. For a change it's not hurting. But then afterwards, I knew that I was by myself, and it just hurt all the more."

I'd never had this kind of conversation with my daughter

before. In the time that Katrin was gone she had grown up. The few short weeks between her going and the Wall opening, when we could see each other again; they had changed her. She was no longer my little girl, but an adult. Our relationship had been redefined, and we were still working out how to communicate with each other, these two new people. It felt good to talk to her about these things; as grown ups, as equals.

"What was it like, y'know. When Mum ..." Katrin didn't finish the sentence.

"It was ..." I looked at her, my mouth spelt the word: *terrible*, but my breath wasn't strong enough to say it. Her eyes glanced off mine, then slid down towards the table, her hands cupping the mug of coffee, her face wreathed in the rising steam. My own eyes slipped down to the table too. My hands were mirroring Katrin's, cupping my own mug of coffee. "Just ..."

Silence overtook us.

"I was so young. I don't know if I was too young to remember, or just blocked it out somehow," she whispered.

My lips shaped that word again: terrible. My mind wandered back to those awful days. I don't think about it too much now, it still hurts. But I couldn't forget that time, even if I wanted to. How could I forget how, in the morning, I'd get up, functioning without being. I'd put a pan of water on to boil and go and wake up Katrin, make sure she got out of bed and got dressed. I'd take her halfway to the school where she'd meet up with friends. We would hardly exchange a word, both lost in our individual battles for survival. I must have been a grim sight in those days. I wasn't sleeping. Wasn't eating. Just tired, running on empty.

After dropping Katrin off I should have gone to work. But I didn't. I don't know how long that phase lasted: days, maybe weeks. I couldn't be around people. Instead of getting on the tram to the factory, I'd head back to the flat. As soon as Katrin was out of sight I could feel tears drip down my cheeks, gathering in the corners between nose and upper lip. I'd stumble along, head bowed so that passers-by, hurrying to work or waiting at the tram stop in the grey, slushy snow wouldn't see my tears. Letting myself back into the flat, the tears would flow freely. I hated Katrin's mum. Loved her. I missed her so much, and felt betrayed by her absence. I was imploding with the weight of the love I still felt for her, that I could no longer give her. The years we would no longer share. The times we'd no longer laugh together, argue together, make love together. She was no longer there to hug, so I'd hit the walls with my bare fists. I had to feel a different pain. The bloody knuckles gave me a physical pain that I could deal with. It wasn't long before I'd open another bottle of schnapps. It would dull the pain in the knuckles but not the agony of my corroding soul. It didn't stop me from thinking either. All the times together, the three of us. All the good times, all the fights. All the times when we had enough to be happy, and the times when we struggled to keep our little family going. I'd stare out of the window, the snow flying past, landing in dark heaps on the road, blocking the pavements. The flat would steadily cool down as the morning's ration of coal burnt up, the wind would whine while I sat and shivered, making not a sound. I'd used up all the chances this life was going to give me. There was nothing left, no other reason to continue the struggle of this life. Except Katrin. For her I'd sober up, light the stove, wash the coal dust off my hands, wash the tears off my face, wash the blood off the wall, try to make things OK for when she got back from school.

"I'm sorry Katrin, it must have been really hard for you. I did my best, but I know it wasn't enough. It must have been really shit for you." I was still looking at my hands, clasped around the mug, the fine tracing of scars, picked out by coal dust under the skin of the knuckles. I'd slid off into the past, my mind tracing the contours of years-old pain. I looked up at Katrin. On the other side of the kitchen table a cold mug sat in front of an empty chair.

A tune wavered through the open door from the living room. Low and reedy, sonorous. Familiar. My heart stopped, the whole world froze in a moment of ecstasy and anguish, the notes summoning an imprint of memory that faded away at the edges, leaving a silhouette of the woman I had lost.

I followed the traces of vibrating air into the hall. Katrin was standing in the living room, her back to me, swaying with the music that she was playing.

I stood in the doorway for a moment, washed by the sounds. "That was your mum's."

The music stopped, and Katrin turned around, holding the alto recorder in both hands.

"Of course ... you knew that," I added.

Katrin smiled, a gentle figure, solid and real, taking the place of a memory. She carefully put the recorder back on the bookshelf, taking her time to line the instrument up with the pattern of dust that outlined its home.

"I didn't know you'd learned to play," I said to her back. She slowly turned around, and stepped towards me.

"Yes," she looked up into my face, her mother's eyes gazing at me. "It's one of the few things I remember about her. A friend is teaching me how to play." She came closer, and with her index finger stroked a tear off my cheek. She put her arms around me, ignoring my stiffness. "Isn't it time to move on, Papa?"

"What do you mean?"

"It's been years. You don't need to stay here, all alone. Life can offer more than this." She let go of me, took a step back, and tried to look me in the eye.

"I've got my work. And you." I looked at the recorder on the shelf. Easier to look anywhere than at my daughter. I wanted to tell her that my heart is just too big, I can't let go, can't just forget. There was no way to prise that pain out of my chest.

I continued staring at the recorder, the dusty shelf, the books, as Katrin picked up her coat, patted my arm, kissed my wet cheek and left.

13:23

I sat at home for another hour or so, not doing much, just trying to motivate myself to get on with the day. Finally I got my coat on and went to the office. When I arrived, only Bärbel and Klaus were there.

"Laura and Erika have gone over to RS1 to talk about the Nazi nest," Klaus told me.

"Who's handling it at the RS1 end of things?"

"Nik's co-ordinating it I think. In fact, RS1 have been doing most of the work on it. What are you up to now?"

"Dunno. Thought I'd better come in, though. Guess I've got a load of stuff I could be getting on with."

I told Klaus about the raid, leaving nothing out. He was clearly shocked, but didn't say anything for a while, just sat there, smoking a cigar. Finally, he stirred.

"Wasn't the state prosecutor there? Or independent witnesses?"

"No, there was no need because it wasn't a search: they intended to arrest him. But you can be sure they had a good look around while they smashed the place up."

"You kind of hoped those days were gone, don't you? But here we are, three years in, and the cops are still bastards," he said.

"Still the same people wearing the same uniform. I guess it's naïve to think that things can change that fast."

Klaus nodded, and chewed on his cigar for a bit.

"Maybe we need to think about taking this to the Round Table. We could suggest some kind of oversight body to be present whenever things are controversial or might get violent," was what he came up with after a while.

I didn't disagree with Klaus, just didn't want to think about it right now, so I cut him off.

"Yeah, sounds good, but let's talk about it with the others."

He didn't reply, just jotted down a few notes on his notepad, then looked up as my phone rang. I was already on my way to the toilet so I asked him to answer it for me.

"Who was it?" I asked when I got back.

"No-one there," he shrugged. "Bad line. Look, I've got to go to my old workplace, get some employment records stamped for the tax office. Why don't you come with me—it doesn't look like you're going to get much done here."

Erika and Laura had taken the Trabant, but a police patrol car was parked next to a colourful sign advertising a neighbourhood meeting. I admired the vehicle's green and white two-tone paint job, blue lights and loudspeakers on the roof. Klaus jangled the keys before unlocking the doors.

"How did you get hold of this?"

"You know the Wartburg we have?"

"The one that never works?"

"The only one we have, yes. Well, the cops came down here last week, when you were tootling around in Silesia. They just wanted to drop off some paperwork or something. They drove straight into the back of it. Laura gave them a right talking to, so they towed the Wartburg away and a police mechanic is going to sort it out. Meanwhile, we get to use this mean, green machine," Klaus grinned.

We got in, and headed off towards Schöneweide. If I'd been in better condition I would have been tempted to play around with the lights and the sirens, but as it was we just sat there in silence while Klaus filled the car with cigar fumes.

141

We drove down the Wilhelminenhofstrasse. On the left the usual soot stained brown-grey buildings—flats, and some shops on the ground floor. On the right were tracks, a diesel locomotive, stationary, engine hammering out greasy, black smoke. Attached to it, a train, a long line of empty flat-bed wagons.

"Transformer works," said Klaus, nodding towards the factory beyond the goods train. It too was stained and sooty, but behind all the dirt were yellow bricks, and an elaborate industrial gothic design. It must have been beautiful once.

"Just a bit further down—that's the cable works, KWO. Designed by the same architect for Emil Rathenau last century. And that, on the corner at the end is the TV factory, where I ended up working in '89."

I nodded, concentrating on the road ahead of us, tyres rumbling over the broken concrete flags lining the tram tracks we were following.

"There's the main gate, over there. Can you see somewhere safe to park?"

I looked round for a parking spot. On the left the road broadened out as a side road entered, making a triangle with a pedestrian island in it. As we slowed down to park I saw someone come out of the factory gates opposite. He turned to go to the tram stop, and as he came closer I realised who it was.

"Stop! That's him! Fremdiswalde!"

Klaus looked over to where I was pointing, at the same time braking to a sharp stop, and before I'd a chance to get out he'd already gone, leaving the door swinging open. I ran after him. Fremdiswalde had already headed back into the cable factory. Klaus was at the factory gates before I was even halfway across the railway tracks, but someone jumped out from the gatehouse, tackling him round the legs. He crunched into the side of the gatepost, tangled up with a security guard. I took a short detour, avoiding the pedestrian gate, hurdling the slack chain hanging across the vehicle entrance.

"Left!" shouted Klaus from behind me, and I headed round that way, leaving behind the string of curses Klaus was raining down on the guard who'd grabbed him. Ahead of me I could see in the lee of the factory wall dozens and dozens of cable drums, some just over a meter in diameter, others more like two metres wide. Next to the drums, covered in chalk, and dusted in soot, men were winding up a cable as thick as my forearm. To my right there was a three storey building, built in the same yellow brick as the transformer works down the road. A door led into this building, and I was about to go in when I noticed that the men in chalk and soot were looking further down the way, towards another block perpendicular to this one. I ran down to the corner of the long high building. A door at the foot of a staircase slammed shut. In through the door, I saw another to my right heading onto the ground floor, and a staircase snaking upwards. Brown art deco tiles covered the walls to elbow height, climbing up with the stairs. They were greasy, threads of soot lining the grain. The steps were concrete, with steel runners, and although not steep, they were high. I ran up, following the echoing footsteps. Sometime around the third or fourth landing I lost track of how many levels I'd gone up, just concentrating on the pounding steps echoing from somewhere above me. My heart ready to pop, my head banging, I'd already tripped over once, catching my right knee on a steel edge. Why am I doing this to myself? I'm not a cop—I can't even arrest this guy if I catch up with him! Some part of my brain kept feeding me reasons to stop, but still I continued up this nightmare of a staircase.

A crash of a heavy steel door falling into the frame: Fremdiswalde had exited the stairwell. It didn't sound too close, so I passed the next floor and carried on upwards. A large number 6 was painted on the wall where the staircase ended. The steel doors were to the right. I aimed for these, trying to shoulder them open, pulling down the handle as I hit the brown metal. A dull impact, a sharp pain. Ignoring shoulder and knee, I tried it the other way, pulling the door open, using my weight leveraged against my heels. Behind the door the light was dim, the air filled with desultory dripping. What light there was came from skylights, but they were cracked, broken, and hadn't been cleaned for years. Shadows danced in the corners. As I stood there letting my eyes adjust, some of the shadows materialised into workbenches, bits of machinery, and, at the other end of a long room, a human shape. It was turned towards me, as far as I could see, and swaying around. I stood there, trying to work it out, my eyes struggling with the grey light. As my surroundings come into focus, I realised that the workshop was a lot longer than I thought: the figure wasn't swaying, but running down the length of the floor, jumping across gaps in the floorboards, and dodging drips from above. I didn't fancy following him, and while I dithered, the door behind me slammed. This was nearly too much for me, my knee and shoulder were killing me, my lungs felt like they were about to rip. I swivelled around to see Klaus, face red, panting. I pointed towards the fleeing figure, now nearly at the far end, and Klaus nodded, setting off, jumping from one safe looking part of the floor to another. Meanwhile, I tried to use my head. I could go down a level, see if I could head Fremdiswalde off at the next staircase along. I turned back to the door, headed down to the floor below, and went in, turning left onto a corridor that looked about twice as long as the workshop above. I passed office doors and frosted glass panels. A scream reverberated down the corridor, but there was no-one in sight, no sign of who had made this sound, and nothing to suggest that anyone else was in the building: nobody came to their door to look out into the corridor. I stopped, and over my own gasps I could hear a whimpering, a ticking sound, and Klaus swearing. He didn't sound hurt, so it must have been Fremdiswalde that had screamed.

I picked up the pace again, and skidded on the polished lino as I turned into a wider part of the corridor. Our fugitive was on the floor, holding his leg, face contorted in agony. Klaus stood above him, looking down, obviously unsure what to do.

"What happened?"

Klaus gestured towards the wall, where a paternoster lift clicked its way past an opening, a loop of chain running from the top floor to the basement and back again, from which boxes hang. You get in a box on one floor, and jump out when you've reached the floor you want. The lift doesn't stop, just goes round in an endless, slow loop.

"He ran down the stairs and jumped to get on the lift. He tripped, missed it—trapped his leg. I had to pull him out," he shrugged. "But it looks like you've got your man after all."

I nodded, bent double, trying to get my breath back. After a while I straightened up to see Klaus examining Fremdiswalde's left leg.

"You'll be all right, Sonny Jim, no blood. You'll probably just have a big bruise in the morning."

Fremdiswalde didn't seem impressed, he was still on the floor groaning.

"Why don't you find a phone and call the cops, I'll stay here with him. Make sure he doesn't leg it again," grinned Klaus, taking a cigar out of his pocket.

17:06

It took quite a while for the bulls to show up and take Fremdiswalde into custody. I considered going with him, make sure he'd be treated right, but guessed that I probably wouldn't be of much use. Besides, I had a mysterious appointment with Dmitri. Woltersdorf Lock, he'd said. I knew it was somewhere on the eastern edge of Berlin, but wasn't quite sure where, so I'd looked it up. Strange place. Get the S-Bahn to Rahnsdorf, a station in the middle of the forests around Berlin-Köpenick, then change to a tram that went through the woods until it got to a little village just outside the city limits. I was lucky, Klaus gave me a lift to the nearest S-Bahn station and the tram was waiting when I got off the train, so I climbed aboard, pushing my ticket into the stamping machine and pressing on the handle on the top to punch a hole. I sat down at the back, thinking about the tram ride with Annette last night.

Only one other person got on, a middle aged man in a long brown coat and a trilby. He sat down in the front seat without looking around, content to stare out of the window, watching the people at the S-Bahn station.

With a jerk the tram moved off. It was a rattly old thing. After a few metres it left the road and swerved into the trees, grumbling over track joints, jolting and shaking the whole while. I wanted to have a think, try to process the day so far. There was so much to think about, but the lurching tram made it hard to do anything but look out of the window. After about a kilometre of trees the tram banged over some points, the track making a small loop next to an abandoned hut. The man sitting near the front seemed to take this as a cue, knocking at the driver's window—a knock like a policeman's, a hard triple-rap. The driver clicked open the door, and the man leant in, saying a few words. The tram was rattling too much for me to make out any of the short conversation, but the man seemed happy. With large, confident strides he came down the carriage, pulling open the rear door.

"You, this is your stop. Out, now!" The tram had slowed a bit, it was going about walking pace. "Quick, out here, go down that path and you'll be met there!"

He spoke with a Slavic accent, and I think it was this combined with his confidence that made me follow his orders. I jumped down, my right knee almost giving way as I landed on the forest floor, the tram door slamming shut behind me as it hastened off, leaving the forest and disappearing round a bend.

I looked around me. Nothing but the tram rails, the hut about fifty metres behind me and a track going off into the gloom. I followed the path, back the way I'd come, past the abandoned hut.

"Grobe!"

I looked around. No-one to be seen.

"Grobe!"

A closer look, the voice had come from the other side of the rails. I stepped over them, and found myself face to face with a Russian NCO. She didn't say anything else, just beckoned me to follow. At this point I wasn't seeing many alternatives, so I followed her for a few hundred metres. We headed directly into the forest, until, on a wider track we came upon a Soviet Army UAZ jeep, well disguised in its olive drab. Beside the passenger door stood a man wearing fatigues. And an eye patch. The KGB officer who had been watching me the other day at the Karlshorst HQ. A military haircut—short and greying, skin like parchment, shiny and without any wrinkles—somehow it gave him a youthful look, even though he was about my age. Without smiling he held out his hand for me to shake.

"Dmitri Alexandrovich."

I took his hand, but didn't say anything.

"You must forgive me for these little games, but you were being followed. Here, take these, put them on. We don't have much time."

He handed me a Soviet Army greatcoat and cap, and held the back door of the UAZ open for me. I shrugged into the coat, put the forage cap on, and climbed in. My guide got into the driver's seat, and Dmitri climbed in beside her. The jeep made easy work of the rough logging track, and the three of us sat in silence as we sped through the woods. Anyone we passed would only have seen a Soviet vehicle with three Soviet Army soldiers in it—with the cap and coat I would be unrecognisable.

We must have been on the go for about twenty minutes before we stopped. At first we had stuck to forest tracks, but then we crossed a railway line and sped through the centre of the small town of Erkner. Out the other end we headed east. After that I lost track, but now we'd stopped in a clearing. The NCO ran round the front of the jeep, holding Dmitri's door open for him. I managed to get out under my own steam, by which time Dmitri was already heading down a narrow path. I followed, noticing that the NCO had got back behind the wheel, and was sitting there, eyes straight ahead, not looking towards me or her officer.

I caught up with Dmitri, who had stopped and was waiting for me.

"Once again, apologies, my friend, for all the silly games. But I have to be careful." His one good eye assessed me: "And so do you, it seems."

"Why was I being followed? Is it because of you?"

"Maybe. But I think it is fair to assume that you grew a tail some time ago, and not just today." He'd started walking again, and I fell into step beside him. "After all, you are looking into the Maier affair. Think back. You know how this is done: remember! Think!"

Dmitri was right. I hadn't noticed, maybe I hadn't wanted to notice, but there had been clues. The Trabant that started up and drove off when Nik and I came out of my house on the way to the bar on Sunday. The couple kissing in a doorway, too many people on the quiet, residential streets near the squat last night, all heading the same way as us.

"You may be right," I admitted.

"Yes. You must think, observe. They will not just be following where you go, but also following what you do. The Maier case is very interesting to a lot of people."

"Is it related to what you told Nik about the operation run from Moscow?"

"Martin, listen. You do not know if you can trust me. You do not know me. But I know you. I know your files, I know what you've done, what you do now, the way you think. So I can talk to you, but you? Do you listen to me? That is what you must decide. Trust no-one. Only the people closest to you, and do not trust even them with anything."

I laughed. It was too absurd, all too dramatic. I'd been given a secret note, practically been thrown off a moving tram, then abducted in a Soviet jeep, to be taken to a secret location: all to be told not to trust anyone.

Dmitri didn't respond, he just carried on walking. I watched him for a moment, considering whether to go back to the jeep, demand to be returned to civilisation. But Dmitri was right, I should trust no-one. Nevertheless, I needed to know more. I caught up with Dmitri again.

"OK, let's play it your way Dmitri Alexandrovich. What's your interest in Maier?"

We'd reached a lake, and Dmitri stared out over it before answering. It wasn't a huge lake, but big enough to take a rowing boat out on to. We were surrounded by dark forest and no sounds could be heard, not even birds.

"I do not know, Martin. I wish I did. But the West Silesian problem ties in with the KGB, and what is happening in Moscow right now. So that makes it my problem too."

"But you're KGB, surely you should know what's going on?"

"Not my area, but I'm trying to find out. And now this detachment from Moscow ... I cannot use the normal channels. No *drushba* with these officers from the Third Directorate. No drinks and shared secrets," Dmitri sighed, and turned away from the water, his eye pointing towards me again. "And you know even less, but perhaps we can help each other, I think.

"So, in the KGB," he continued in his low, slow voice, the Slavic accent hardly affecting his German pronunciation, "there are two factions. There are those who say the time is not yet right, we should support Gorbachev because with him we have the best chance of keeping the USSR together. But there are many more who say, it is now, it is time to remove Gorbachev, to move ahead with the plan."

"Do you think Gorbachev will survive this second crisis? And what's this plan?"

Dmitri considered his answer for a moment.

"No, maybe he won't survive. It all depends on my colleagues in Moscow, whether the right people support him. It's difficult to say what will happen. We have the same problem as you. Agents have been put into key decision-making positions throughout the government—it's their job to keep control of power, whichever way it goes. At the moment it looks like the power will be in the economy, rather than the Party apparatus. If Gorbachev doesn't survive then Yeltsin will sell off land and industry, and my colleagues will be there with the cash, waiting to buy it all up."

"And if Gorbachev stays?"

"If he stays then his attempts to roll out perestroika will meet further resistance and more coup attempts. The problem is, Gorbachev doesn't understand economics. He's not in control of his perestroika any more."

"But if Gorbachev doesn't survive, how can we? We depend on Gorbachev to protect us from the West."

"That is why I am talking to you. Your little experiment here in the GDR depends on what happens to old Mikhail Sergeyevich Gorbachev." Dmitri looked at the lake for a moment, then picked up a small stone and threw it into the water.

"See those ripples? The circles get larger and larger the further away from the centre they are. Gorbachev is at the centre—a small, insignificant pebble, and the GDR is a long way away from him. By the time the ripples get to you they make big circles, they seem quite significant. By the time they get to Bonn or London or Washington those ripples are part of a huge wash of water moving outwards from Moscow. It's his reputation that is saving you, making the West think twice about moving in."

"Do you mean that if Gorbachev stops making ripples—"

"I'm not sure what I mean," Dmitri was still staring out at the water. The ripples were getting fainter and fainter. "Perhaps that you shouldn't rely on Gorbachev. He has troubles of his own, and if you ask me, he'd be glad to be rid of what he sees as an unnecessary burden. I think he gave up on you years ago."

We stood together like that, Dmitri lost in his own world, while I thought about his words.

"You mentioned that the KGB has officers in place in the Soviet government—are they here too? Is that the plan?"

I had the Russian's attention now. He gazed at me with his one good eye, a look of mild surprise crossing his features.

"You don't know? Mmm, I keep forgetting—you've not been directly briefed in these matters, you RS officers are just amateurs."

I tried not to feel nettled by what Dmitri said—after all, he wasn't wrong. I concentrated on what he was saying.

"But I know your minister has been briefed on the situation, I had hoped that the information had been passed down. No, the KGB isn't involved any more, we left it all to the Stasi to run, even though the plan was developed by one of our officers based in Dresden, and the Stasi set it up with our help.

"About six or seven years ago the Stasi began to put

officers—*Offiziere im besonderen Einsatz*, OibE—into strategic political and industrial positions. There was a meeting in June 1989, all the socialist secret services were there—Egon Krenz represented the GDR—and they agreed the overall policy. If the economy begins to fail, or the political situation changes dramatically, they will be in place to steer decisions and policy. Their aim is to remain in control of the country no matter what happens. In Moscow they are still waiting and ready, we call them the Oligarchs—a few men with a lot of power. It doesn't seem to be happening in other countries. But here in the GDR? Who knows? I think the general strike in November 1989 came as a surprise to them, maybe Mischa Wolf didn't get the activation signal out in time. If they're still in position then they're still dangerous, they could take over at any time, and nobody would even notice until it was too late."

This was all news to me. It sounded like a conspiracy theory, but Dmitri seemed serious, and most importantly, believable. Markus Wolf—who liked to accentuate his Russian connections by calling himself Mischa—was until 1987 the head of the head of the HVA: the part of the Stasi that was responsible for foreign operations. He'd since fled to the West. Egon Krenz, the Crown Prince of the Party with a reputation as a hardliner had also gone West. Did they still have control of these OibE agents?

"What would make them act? Are there any triggers other than this activation signal from Wolf?"

"Could be anything," Dmitri tossed another stone into the lake and watched the ripples until they lapped at his boots. "I think it would have to be some kind of major crisis. You've decentralised so much of your decision making; that will make it hard for them to exert too much influence here. But if there were a major crisis then they could engineer the re-centralisation of power structures, a state of emergency perhaps—that would give them back control, allow a task

152

force to take power."

"And they could even organise that crisis? Is that what they're doing in West Silesia?"

"Precisely," Dmitri looked up, pleased with his pupil.

"So West Silesia is like a test run, to see how easy it is to sideline the Round Tables? And at the same time they can destabilise the whole of the Republic, setting the scene for a bigger crisis? But haven't they gone a bit too far? I mean, by involving the West Germans? Surely that's not part of the KGB plan?"

"Yes." Dmitri was staring out over the water again, thinking, "I doubt the West German involvement was part of the plan. But now that they are on the scene they'll be turning the situation to their own advantage. Something went wrong, somebody went off the rails, is my guess. Perhaps that's why some of the KGB are here at the moment, perhaps they've been sent by Moscow to try to sort out the mess."

"Why are you telling me this? It's your colleagues that are involved."

"As I said, some of us think the time is not yet right. We do not want the Oligarchs to control our country. Or yours." His tone of voice changed, the rolling R and the alien vowels of his Slavic accent became more pronounced.

"For over 70 years we've made it our business to take people's dreams, to make them our own. Then crush them without mercy. We told the world that we were a paradise, created and maintained by the iron discipline of the workers and peasants. We exported our revolutions, invited others to share our utopia at the barrel of a gun. We have failed. Our revolution was already doomed in 1917. The reforms are failing too. If Gorbachev loses his gamble then it is over for us. It will be your turn to carry the flag."

I didn't know how to react. When a KGB officer is this lyrical and this critical you have to pinch yourself, check you're still awake.

"You're a socialist?"

"Something like that. Perhaps something stuck, from school or *Komsomol*," Dmitri answered. "And I think the same happened to you, no?"

"Perhaps. Perhaps you're right, Dmitri Alexandrovich."

We turned away from the lake and walked on through the woods in silence, only the cracking of the twigs underfoot measured time.

20:24

It was dark by the time we drove back into Berlin, and I was glad that we didn't take the route through the woods—Dmitri must have thought I was adequately disguised in the gloom, and they dropped me off a few hundred metres from the S-Bahn station in Grünau. I got off the train at Ostkreuz and wandered home, wondering what my next move should be. Dmitri was uncanny, the way he never smiled and seemed to know me and my feelings far better than I did myself. Then there was the way that Dmitri told me so much, yet somehow so little of it seemed concrete or useful. Nor had he given me any actual advice, any indicators as to how I should proceed. Except to be careful, and to trust no-one.

"Thanks a bunch, Dmitri Alexandrovich," I muttered to myself, walking down the street. As I passed the bakery I glanced into the darkened window, using it as a mirror, looking to see if I was being followed. I couldn't see anyone, but that didn't have to mean much—they knew where I lived, they didn't have to accompany me to my door.

Trust no-one. Only the people closest to you, and do not trust even them with anything—Dmitri's words swirled around my head, but I had to trust someone, it would be good to talk through the events of the last few days, throw ideas around, try to get some perspective on what was happening, and what we should do about it.

Right now, though, I needed a drink and an early night. Too much had happened today, and I needed a bit of downtime. I stumbled up the stairs, and was standing outside my flat door, fumbling with the key when I noticed I had a new message on the notepad: *In the bar, come and find me when you get back, Nik.*

The idea of sitting in Jen's smoky bar, having a conversation with Nik didn't exactly re-energise me, but at least he was someone I could trust. Probably. At least he'd be a start.

I pushed open the heavy door of the bar, and parted the curtain, looking for Nik. He was sitting at the same table as last time. I went over, he didn't notice me coming until I was at his shoulder, holding my hand out for him to shake.

"Christ, I was expecting you hours ago! How was it?" he asked me.

"He's a bit cryptic, isn't he?"

"Yeah, he is too. But he's an interesting fellow," Nik laughed.

I nodded, thinking that *interesting* didn't do Dmitri justice, he was much more than that.

"What did he tell you? Or shouldn't I ask, just say if I should shut up," Nik was looking into his beer, waiting for me to tell him to mind his own business.

"You know, honestly, I don't know. I'm knackered—it's been the longest day I've had since 1989. I need to think about what he told me, try and get it straight in my head. He was telling me about what's happening in Moscow, and how it might affect us. He talked about some very scary things." Nik was nodding, encouraging me to carry on. "But he was very clear that I needed to be careful about who I talk to about the Maier case."

"Yes, you mentioned you'd been down to Weisswasser, to see the body. But are you still involved?"

"Officially, not really. We arrested the suspect today, but I'm not actually working on it—we're not the police after all."

"You make it sound like you still want to be involved?" He watched me nod before continuing. "It's good if you're looking into it: somebody needs to. One of us—not an apparatchik—it should be somebody who cares. Are you by yourself? You shouldn't be—it's complicated. Why don't you involve your work team?"

"Dunno, I don't really know them that well, I guess. Plus, I'm really not sure I'm going to do anything about it."

"Look, they're good people. They're like you and me, they care. If I were you, I'd start with them. Talk to them. And Martin? You can rely on me. Whenever you need me—just shout."

He looked very earnest, pretty much the same as on Sunday night, but livelier, more animated. I nodded agreement and made my excuses, heading back out into the dark street. A quick look both ways, nobody in sight. Back into my own house, up the stairs and into my armchair.

Just as I was making myself comfortable the phone rang. I was beginning to regret having a phone at home, it only ever seemed to ring when I wanted to have a bit of peace and quiet, and if felt like these days there often wasn't even anyone on the other end. I picked up, and sure enough, a couple of clicks and a vague hissing came down the line. I was just about to hang up again when finally a voice came from the receiver.

"Martin! Martin? Is that you?" It was Evelyn.

"Evelyn, yes, it's me—sorry I couldn't speak to you yesterday, I was in a bit of a state."

"Oh, poor you! I hope you're OK? But Martin, I'm so glad I've finally caught up with you! I'm so excited, a friend who works in the Ministry of the Interior gave me your number, I hope you don't mind, but it's been so long!"

"Evelyn, it's good to hear from you, where have you been

all these years? What are you doing these days?"

"Oh, you know, just scraping by, doing the usual—I'm working at the Kosmos cinema at the moment, so let me know if you need free tickets! What are you up to? Oh, listen, talking on the phone isn't any fun—why don't we meet up? I mean right now—we could go to the cinema right now! That would be so much fun, do say yes, dear Martin, it's been so long!"

I was completely knackered, and wanted nothing more than to doze off in my own chair in my own flat. But Evelyn's enthusiasm was infectious, and she was right—it had been so long. Why not? A film didn't sound too strenuous, and I was curious about what had happened to Evelyn since I last saw her.

21:37

Half an hour later I was standing on the Karl-Marx-Allee, in front of the Kosmos, waiting for Evelyn. Behind me lights beckoned warmly through the glass façade of the cinema, but it was getting cold standing in the late September evening without a jacket on. After twenty minutes I was ready to give up and go back to the tram stop. I turned to gaze ruefully at the glow of the foyer when I saw Evelyn, just inside the entrance, waving at me.

"Silly you! I thought you'd never see me," she grinned at me, not at all bothered about being late. "We'll have to go straight in, it's about to start." Evelyn was simply and elegantly dressed, as ever, and looked exactly the same as I remembered her—the years had taken no toll from her.

We went through the foyer, and past the ticket collector— Evelyn just beamed at him as we went by into the auditorium. The trailers were playing, and we slid into the back row, the ranks of white seats before us a dusky grey in the gloom.

"It's *Paul and Paula*—have you seen it before?" Evelyn whispered in my ear, her breath tickling me and making me twitch. I hadn't seen *The Legend of Paul and Paula* for years, I probably saw it last with Katrin sitting between her mum and me on the couch at home. Because of its fairy tale escapism and its rejection of the cultural demands of Socialist Realism it had been a popular film in the 1970s. But then it had been banished to late night television and finally dropped after the main actors both went into exile in the West. Since the revolution the film had become popular again, a trend for nostalgia and an appreciation of the film's celebration of love made it a favourite among young people.

It's an enjoyable film, not demanding much attention or thought from its viewers, and the easy pace of the unfolding story suited my mood perfectly. We'd already got to the bit when Paul unexpectedly comes to Paula in the middle of the night, and is surprised that she has prepared a feast for him. The scene, playing on her prescience and his confusion, is touching, and I smiled at the memories it brought back.

It was at this point that Evelyn decided to slip her hand into mine. I froze, caught between the two-dimensional memories of a long dead past, and the heat making its way up my arm. I slowly melted into the warmth from the body close beside me, and my fingers slipped through Evelyn's as we tightened our clasp. We explored each other's hands, tracing outlines of fingers and palms, our heads moved towards each other until they were resting together. Things didn't go any further, we just sat in a warm fuzziness as the story played towards its tragic conclusion on the screen before us.

After the film we sat in the foyer, Evelyn sipping a glass of *Rotkäppchen* sparkling wine while I confined myself to water. I was tired, and the memory of yesterday's hangover was still too fresh to ignore. We chatted about the film and the cinema, and how Katrin's *Jugendweihe* ceremony had been held here at the Kosmos.

"Do you remember: *Are you ready?*" laughed Evelyn.

"Yes, and then they had to swear to defend socialism, and to be led by the revolutionary Party!" I added, but Evelyn didn't find that bit nearly as funny as I did.

She looked away, and there was silence for a second or two until suddenly she turned back to me, her eyes fixed on mine. "Martin, let's go, right now! Let's just go to mine," she laid a hand on my knee, and tipped her face down so that she could look up at me through her eyelashes. "Martin, it's been too long, say you'll come!"

I sat there stiffly, looking at her, not knowing what to say or do. I could still feel the outline of her hand in mine, and that had awakened a need for human warmth that I had all but forgotten. The idea of holding Evelyn in my arms, sharing her bed, feeling close to her, to anyone—it was almost overwhelming. But I was tired, so tired. I could feel every muscle in my arm as I lifted Evelyn's hand, sliding it off my knee, and putting it on the armrest of her chair.

"I'm sorry Evelyn, you've no idea how much I'd like to, but I think it would be better if I just went."

Evelyn lifted her chin, and looked at me directly again. As an equal this time, not attempting to pull me in with her charm. Her eyes flickered, and I couldn't tell whether what I read there was hurt, scorn or cold indifference.

DAY 8
Wednesday
29th September 1993

Moscow: Hostilities continued on the streets of Moscow last night as Interior Ministry and KGB forces clashed. So far, the conflict has been focussed on the centre of the city, but there are fears that it may spread to residential areas.

Görlitz: Further marches in support of the Round Table were held in many towns in West Silesia last night. An estimated ten thousand people participated in the latest protest in the capital, Görlitz. The marchers have called for a full re-integration of the Round Tables at all levels of government in the Region. The West Silesian League condemned the marches, denouncing what they described as: 'incendiary attempts by foreign agents to interfere in the internal affairs of West Silesia'.

08:15

It was good to be sitting in the office, surrounded by the team. I'd had a crap start to the morning—I felt guilty about Evelyn, the alarm clock went off an hour early, and I was clean out of coffee, even though I'm pretty sure I bought a packet last week. In the end I'd settled for a cup of *Presto* instant coffee, it didn't taste particularly good, and it certainly didn't give me the jolt I needed to start the day. But I was in the office now. Outside, the sun was shining, and in here I had a steaming mug in hand and my colleagues were with me. They all looked pretty sympathetic—I assumed Klaus had told them about the squat raid yesterday morning —nevertheless, when we got started Laura had a go at me about not sticking to agreements.

"I know we agreed on Friday that I'd write the report, hand it in, then walk away from it. But we got some more information from Saxony, and I think it's fair to say we all had doubts, even last week." I picked up the envelope from the Saxon police, passing it to Laura, who was sitting to my right. "I was going to tell you at the meeting on Monday but the wasp thing happened."

Laura subsided visibly at the mention of the wasp, but rallied again. "What are you saying, Martin?" she asked.

"Well, I did a report for the Minister, but I left out the new information from Saxony. I wasn't sure whether that was the right thing to do, and to be honest I'm not sure why I didn't put it in either. In the end it didn't matter, he knew about it anyway. Basically, the whole thing is weird, it doesn't add up at all." I started listing all the things that had happened this last week that I was unhappy about, ticking the points off on my fingers as I went. When I got to the last finger I tapped it on the table, pausing for a moment: "Finally, he sends me to witness an arrest and he looks like some fat cat, satisfied that he's tied up all the loose ends, and gives me a promotion. It's all very odd, but I got the distinct feeling he was trying to buy me off. And if that's the case, maybe we should ask ourselves, why?"

There was silence in the room, everyone looking at me, weighing up my words. For some reason I hadn't told them about Dmitri. I didn't have any good reasons not to, in fact I should have told them—we were a team, we were meant to be working together. But it just didn't feel like the right moment.

"Martin's been under a lot of strain this last week, maybe

he didn't handle it as well as he could, but I think we might have done more to support him too. And if Martin's got a strong feeling about this then we should listen to what he has to say."

I was thankful for Klaus's contribution, and was ready for his question.

"What do you think we should be doing, Martin?"

"I think we should be careful not to rock the boat too much at this stage: if I'm wrong then there's no need for all of us to be making trouble for ourselves. But I'd like to go and interview Fremdiswalde. I don't think he murdered Maier."

"Martin! Why can't you leave that to the police? Surely that's their job!" Laura was running out of patience.

"What are we here for if we're not trying to spot dangers to our society? So, strictly speaking, interviewing Fremdiswalde isn't part of our job, but it doesn't mean we shouldn't take an interest! We didn't ask ourselves whether it was our job when we shut down the Stasi! That was the police's job too, and they weren't doing it, so we turned up mob handed and took over the Stasi offices. Remember that? You were there too!"

"OK, OK, you two! Play nicely!" interrupted Klaus, leaning forward to attract Laura's and my attention, "I know that last Thursday I was all for following it up, but I think Laura's made a really good point: it's just not our job. Martin—those were different times, we can't work in those ways now."

"I'm not sure. I think Martin may have a point," Erika spoke up, edging into the conversation for the first time. "We can't just sit back and let the state expand again, taking over responsibility for all areas of our lives. Yes, we're RS, and criminal investigation is outside our remit, but we're also citizens, and we have a responsibility towards our country. I think we should support Martin, give him another couple of days, and if he doesn't come up with anything by then we can just try to keep it unofficial—try to minimise any fallout."

I smiled a 'thank you' at her, while Klaus and Laura shared a glance before nodding a reluctant agreement.

We ran through the rest of the meeting, no surprises, nothing particularly exciting. I told them that the Minister had asked me to prepare the security report for the Wall debate. We agreed to leave it a couple of days before deciding who should take that task on, give me a bit of space to carry on nosing around the Maier case.

The others filed out of my office, and I pulled the telephone towards me, poking around on my desk for the letter from the Saxon police. Finding it, I punched in the number and asked for *Unterleutnant* Schadowski. A couple of minutes' conversation, and I had all I needed: Schadowski confirmed that the theory was that Maier had been having an affair with the much younger Fremdiswalde, who was now the chief suspect. Maier had broken off the affair, and Fremdiswalde had lost it, killing Maier during a final liaison at the edge of the coal mine, then dragging the body down to where work was taking place. The Saxon police had prepared a report, and were sending someone up to interview Fremdiswalde tomorrow morning. I asked Schadowski to send me a copy.

"One other thing, comrade *Hauptmann*," continued Schadowski, "I thought you should know: I've been ordered to report to the Ministry of the Interior if I have any contact with RS."

I thanked Schadowski, and hung up. His final words were hardly reassuring. Why the hell should I not be talking to Schadowski, and who exactly at the Ministry was keeping tabs on me?

Sitting on the S-Bahn on the way to the Ministry I thought about last night. On the way home after the cinema I'd felt physical regret: it would have been so nice to cuddle up to someone in bed, to lie spooning another warm body. And there was a feeling that after all these years—years of being aware of that flirtatious tingle whenever we saw each other—something was inevitable. A feeling that by avoiding that inevitability I had somehow cheated fate, and fate would come back for revenge.

But this morning I just had a sense of vague guilt. I felt guilty that I'd refused Evelyn, even though it wasn't something that I'd actually wanted; guilty that I hadn't thought once about Annette last night, even though what was developing between us was something that didn't just feel good—it felt like it had a future.

I swept my thoughts to one side as I got off the train at Friedrichstrasse, and my mind turned to work matters. I'd had a phone call, been asked to report to the Ministry by some minor civil servant, so here I was. As I turned into the Mauerstrasse I saw the same goons that were there yesterday, but today they were in a dark blue Lada. Feeling their stares I pointedly ignored them, and went up the steps into the building.

I reported to the Minister's secretary, expecting to be directed to Frau Demnitz again, but instead of which I was told to go upstairs to one of the tiny offices where the worker bees administered their paperwork. I was seen by a young man in a brown suit, no tie, just an open collar. He sat behind a desk that filled the space between the walls, and I wondered how he got out from behind it—did he crawl underneath, or climb over the top? His window looked over the courtyard below, but faced south, so I couldn't see much more of him than a dark shape silhouetted against the bright window.

"Captain Grobe, you have been asked here today because it has come to our attention that you have not surrendered the paperwork attendant on your promotion for correct processing." This guy had obviously been taking lessons from Frau Demnitz, and I wondered how long I'd be kept here, listening to his bureaucratic declamations.

I concentrated on the blue sky behind his left shoulder, feeling absurdly pleased when a fluffy cloud, high up in the sky, started a slow journey across the window. When I next tuned into what the drone was saying he'd moved on to the responsibilities of a higher rank. I wished now that I had paid more attention, because if I understood what I was hearing, this suit here was actually threatening me. Of course, he made use of bureaucratic phrases, but the gist of it was that if I didn't pull my socks up, start behaving like a captain and doing what I was told instead of phoning Dresden at every opportunity, well, what? Unfortunately I'd missed the bit where the implicit threats might have been outlined, but I certainly wasn't going to give him the satisfaction of asking him to repeat the juicy bits.

The civil servant hadn't even begun winding down when I got up. As I left I asked him over my shoulder whether he was finished, but didn't bother hanging around for an answer. I closed the door on him and wondered whether to just go back to Lichtenberg without dealing with all the promotion crap. But I thought that since I was here anyway, I might as well go and sort out the paperwork at the secretariat—if I didn't they'd just haul me back again tomorrow. I followed the corridor round to the back of the building, and used the stairs there to go down to the ground floor. The front desk at the secretariat wasn't occupied, and all the other staff were busy typing away, steadfastly ignoring me. I looked around the room while I waited, the sound of typewriter keys and the pinging carriage bells echoed round the bare room. In the corner a dusty cheese plant was about to give up the fight for life, and next to it a door stood slightly ajar. Not enough to see into it, but over the clackety-clack of the typewriters, and the more regular chatter of the telex I could hear a woman's voice spilling out from the room beyond. I couldn't make out what was being said, but I could hear the accent: gentle, Mecklenburg, quite a high voice. I'd heard it recently, very recently. But when?

"Can I help you, comrade?" The secretary whose job it was to deal with enquiries had returned to her post.

I handed the Minister's commission papers over to the secretary without a word, still staring at the door. The secretary drew a new pass out of a locked drawer, along with a form. She stamped the form, then handed that and the pass to me, along with some more papers for me to scribble my signature on.

"Here you are comrade captain—your new papers and a requisition slip for the dress uniform. You can get that at the Police *Präsidium*."

I took the papers, but I was still staring at that door, the one with the sign, *Archiv* on it, thinking about the voice coming from behind it, because now I'd recognised it. The context had thrown me, but I knew whose voice it was. Now the question was: what was Evelyn doing here, at the Ministry?

13:57

When I came out of the station at Ostkreuz, the first thing I saw, on the corner of Simplonstrasse and Sonntagstrasse, was a dark blue Lada. The same two goons were sat there, watching people come out of the station. They hadn't seen me yet, I'd stopped just under the shadow of the overhead track, and hesitating only for a moment, I turned around, crossing over the tracks by the bridge, headed for the far exit.

As I came down the steps off the pedestrian bridge I could see the Tram 82 just go round its turning loop. A quick sprint, and I caught it just as it was about to leave.

I have an unfortunate character defect. At least, the Marxist-Leninists were always telling me that it was a defect, but I keep hoping that in these new times it may be seen as a positive trait. Whenever someone tells me to do something I have the urge to do the exact opposite—particularly if what they're telling me to do seems unreasonable. And that's probably the reason why, a few minutes later, I found myself in front of the prison in Rummelsburg.

I went to the administrative block at the front of the prison, and after identifying myself asked first to see Fremdiswalde's belongings. A guard took me to an office on the first floor where he barked an order at a secretary. I was handed a box containing a grubby handkerchief, a small bottle of *Aminat* shampoo, a red penknife, a black and white check cotton Arabic scarf, a partly squashed *Fetzer* chocolate bar, a KWO works pass, an empty *Forum* cigarette packet, twenty Marks plus small change, a set of keys and an envelope with Fremdiswalde's name on it. The envelope was addressed to a flat in Berlin-Friedrichsfelde.

"Is that it?"

"Yes, sir. Accused 264721 didn't have any further items on his person at the time of his arrest."

I took the keys and the envelope, put them in my pocket, and signed a receipt that the protesting secretary pushed over to me.

I had been left alone, standing in front of a grey steel gate, five meters high. It rattled as it ground open, just wide enough to let me slip through. A prison guard in green uniform and peaked cap sat in a metal sentry box, staring at me, no smile or acknowledgement touching his face. I stood in a non-space, a space that didn't exist—neither the outside world, nor the prison—the gate rattled shut again behind me. Looking at the steel plates of the second gate in front of me, waiting for them to open, I ignored the guard to my right as well as the watchtower that looked down on me. In my mind I was elsewhere, or rather, in another time. The last time I'd been through these gates I was lying on the floor in the back of a truck, with police boots resting on my head, neck, back and legs. So often I find myself having to forcefully remind myself of the changes this country has gone through. Just a few years, but already I take so many of our new freedoms for granted, feel resentful of the burdens we have willingly taken upon ourselves as individuals and as a society. In the old days we were expected to go to meetings and official demonstrations, but to be there in body only. Now we demanded of ourselves that we give our whole presence to meetings: *No revolution without participation*, the clumsy slogan to be seen daubed on walls throughout our Republic. No matter how inconvenient it may be, active participation is our guarantee that no longer will people be dragged into this prison for daring to think for themselves. And, as I reminded myself, active participation was the reason I was here now.

The clang of the gate opening again behind me shook me out of my thoughts. Another guard came in, gesturing back through the gate to the outside world.

"Accused 264721 is on police remand in Block B," he announced.

I followed the guard back out through the gate onto the Rummelsburger Hauptstrasse and around to the left, to another set of buildings outside the prison walls. We went through another grey gate, this time a mere two metres high, with iron spikes along the top, and then past some garages and up some steps into a red-brick house. Once inside we passed through several locked gates, some backed with reinforced safety glass, and down the stairs into the cellar.

"Wait," I said to the guard. "How long have you been

here?"

The guard and I were looking at each other. It was difficult to read his face or thoughts, the peak of his cap was pulled low to hide his eyebrows, hide his expressions. He was about the same age as me, perhaps he had been there when I was last here? Perhaps he recognised me. But he must have dealt with hundreds, thousands of politicals in his time. He knew that someone like me must have been somewhere like this at some point in the not too distant past. He continued to look at me, a reserved look, evaluating.

"Fifteen years," he said, just when I'd given up on getting an answer.

So he had been here when I was bundled through those gates. I ran through a short catalogue of all the injustices, the indignities, the physical and mental cruelty I had experienced and seen here. What are we going to do with people like him? Our new way of doing things requires respect for each other, but how could I respect him? Inside myself I could feel hate, a desire for revenge gnawing away.

The guard marched off, opening another barred gate to a long corridor, expecting me to follow. A quiet *fuck you* directed at his back, and I decided, for the moment, to put it all to one side. I wasn't here to reopen old wounds, but to talk to Chris Fremdiswalde, see if I could bolster my doubts with some information, some real evidence. I entered the corridor, lit by dull bulbs, no natural light, cells lining one wall.

Fremdiswalde was in one of these cells, barely two metres wide and not quite as deep. A rough wooden bench was built onto the back wall, and the front of the cell was made up of bars. The tiger cages. I'd heard of these cells from friends who had been arrested and held here by the police. Although there was a bench you weren't allowed to lie down during the day, and even sitting on it was discouraged by the guards. Maybe that was why Fremdiswalde was hunched up against the wall, hardly noticing me and the guard standing on the other side of the bars.

"Stand back! Announce yourself!" the guard barked.

But Fremidswalde didn't even flinch. He was nursing his right hand, his left eye was so swollen that it was almost shut, surrounded by tender bruising. He was putting most of his weight on his right leg.

"Chris?" I said gently, trying to attract his attention while I moved between the guard and the bars.

Still no reaction. Chris remained hunched against the wall. The guard, standing slightly behind me, shifted, leaning back against the brickwork behind.

"Chris?" I tried again, "Chris, my name is Martin Grobe. I'm from the *Republikschutz*. I need to ask you a few questions about Hans Maier. Did you know Maier?"

Still no reaction.

"What was your relationship with Maier? Did you work with him? Were you friends?"

Nothing, not even a slight movement.

"Chris, you do know that Hans Maier is dead? I saw his body myself."

I thought that Fremdiswalde still hadn't reacted, but then I caught the shine of tears gathering in his eyes. I looked over my shoulder to the guard.

"Get this man a cup of water."

The guard shifted his gaze from Fremdiswalde to me, his eyes hard underneath his visored cap, a satisfied set to his mouth.

"It is forbidden to leave accused persons in the presence of civilians," he smirked.

I drew myself up to my full height, turning to face the man directly, and with the hardest voice I could manage: "What is your name?"

"Nagel."

"*Unterwachtmeister* Nagel—go and get some water for this

prisoner. Now!"

The guard hesitated for a moment, considering his options, then: "*Jawohl,* comrade Captain!" before marching off down the corridor.

I waited until he had turned the corner before looking at Fremdiswalde again.

"Chris, you've got to tell me, I'm the only one who can help you in here."

I wasn't holding out much hope for an answer, but then, shaking with sobs, his eyes moved to meet mine.

"I can't," he stammered. "They'll kill me–"

"Who? Who will kill you?"

But by now the guard was coming back, pacing along the corridor, and Fremdiswalde was sliding down the wall. I waited long enough to make sure that he got his water, then left. There seemed little point in asking any more questions. Fremdiswalde was already half-scared to death.

I was let out through the front gate, and with a deep sigh I found myself back in the real world, on the Hauptstrasse. In the middle of the road the tram tracks stretched off in both directions. No traffic, no parked vehicles, nobody to be seen. No tail. I looked again to my right, towards the twin chimneys of the power station, I couldn't see them over the top of the prison wall, just the white plume from one of the tall chimneys, hanging motionless in the blue sky, pointing north towards Lichtenberg. Turning left, I followed the wall of the police compound, trying to find the end of the prison complex. Where the wall of the cells turned away from the road there was a gap, then the army barracks began. I walked as far as the gate, and showing my RS papers I passed the guard and walked through the military base, down to the river.

The camp was practically empty. Compulsory military service had been ended, professional soldiers had been drafted into the factories—only the disarmament corps and the *Grenzer*, the Border Police, still used the site. At the jetty a launch was casting off, about to patrol the border between Kreuzberg and Friedrichshain, on the lookout for smugglers crossing the river between West and East. I watched the launch steadily make way down the Rummelsburg Lake to the river Spree, the new GDR flag fluttering at its stern. Ahead of them, beyond the prison, barges and lighters were tied up along the bank, all empty, all waiting to go and fetch a new load of Silesian brown coal for the power station. Some of the barges were dead or dying, slowly collapsing into the water, timbers rotting, water stains seeping up the lifeless sides. A sapling had rooted in a wheelhouse, and was growing directly up to the sky, but it looked like it was growing sideways out of the listing vessel. It was a clear day, the sun hanging fairly low over the *Kulturpark* hiding in the woods of the Plänterwald off to the left. The bright light shaded the trees in their autumnal livery: more yellows and golds, less reds and bronzes now, hardly any greens.

I sat on a bollard, looking out over the water, watching autumn emerge, trying to let the lapping water wash away the fear, the anger, the shock that I had felt in that prison. I felt somehow powerless in the face of that institution.

Accompanied by the sound of the water licking the bank I could feel how my own fears from the past were gradually separating out from how appalled I felt at Chris's treatment. No matter what Chris might have done, there was no way he should have been abused like that.

In our enthusiasm for building a different society had we neglected the question of criminality and punishment? It couldn't be denied that we were concentrating more on economic survival and changing the everyday lives of the majority of the population. Beyond an amnesty for political prisoners we'd hardly spared a thought for all those left behind in the cells. It was understandable, we couldn't deal with everything at once, we'd actually come a long way in less than three years. But seeing Chris just now ... Were things still really that bad? Had nothing changed? Or had Chris for some reason been given special treatment? I had seen no other prisoners, Chris had been held alone in the underground cells and I had no way of comparing their welfare with his.

15:06

I left the waterside and walked back to the main road. On the way I pulled Fremdiswalde's keys and envelope out of my pocket. The envelope was empty—the police had probably kept whatever letter had been in it. I didn't recognise the address, it wasn't his registered address at the *Thaeri* squat, nor was it any of the ones listed in his Stasi files, although they'd be a few years out of date by now. The keys were normal, a mortice key and a four sided key, together on a ring. Looked like the keys to a flat, maybe I should go and have a look?

A tram and a bus later and I was in Friedrichsfelde. I could have taken the scenic route, tried to shake off anyone that might be following me. But I guessed it was pretty obvious that I was still taking an interest in Fremdiswalde, and I was sure the prison in Rummelsburg would pass on word of my visit. Nevertheless I looked around as the bus belched off, leaving the heavy taste of singed diesel in my nostrils. I couldn't see anyone, I was there all by myself.

It didn't feel like Berlin, not the Berlin I knew. Low rise houses, plenty of gardens, some of the side streets unmade, just beaten sand marked by car and bike tracks. Turning into a side street I could see that the residents had blocked it off, making raised beds to grow vegetables on what had been the road. A sign, decorated with rainbow swirls, read *Colour from below*, a huge pile of pumpkins grew from a single plant, surrounded by peppers, herbs and flowers.

The house I was looking for was three storeys high, and had two front doors. I tried the mortice key in the lock of the nearest door, but the door was already unlocked, so the key stopped after just half a twist. Good to know I was on the right track, though. I went up the stairs, checking each doorbell as I went. Up two flights, and past a toilet on the half-landing, and there he was: C.Fremdiswalde. I let myself in using the four sided key and stood just inside the hallway, quietly closing the door behind me. No sound. Just that dead feeling you get from an empty flat. Stale cigarette smoke, and another smell over the top of that. I sniffed, trying to identify it, similar to the cigarette smoke, but vaguer, and sharper.

It wasn't a big flat: a tiny hall, just a couple of paces long, a small cupboard, and behind that a bedsit with a kitchen-niche taking up the wall opposite the window. I stood in the middle of the bed-sitting room and looked around me. What was I looking for? I decided to look over the place briefly, then do a second, more thorough search.

There wasn't much here, a few clothes, a pile of papers on the table. No books, no posters or pictures decorating the walls. The kitchen area looked like it had only been used for making tea and coffee, mouldy coffee grains were to be found in a few mugs, but no evidence of any food. I started with the table in the corner: lots of notes, scribbled, scratched out, pretty much illegible. Newspapers, piled up. I flicked through the papers, in each one articles had been cut out. I checked the dates: all from the last few days, the earlier ones had holes in the front pages, more recent papers were cut up inside, the articles steadily getting shorter. He'd cut out the reports about Maier's death, but where were they? I looked in the steel bin by the side of his desk, here they were, mixed up with letters, written on expensive Western paper, but someone had tried to burn them. There was my unidentified smell: burnt paper. Whoever did it must have been in a rush, just setting light to them in the bin. Soot marks streaked up the inside of the grey steel bucket, but here and there legible bits remained: *My dearest Chri ...* was on one charred remnant, another corner of a letter: *Görlitz, d. 13 Juli 1993* the date and place written at the top of a letter, in the same handwriting. And here again on another fragment: *Your ever loving Hansi.* I found an envelope, and carefully filled it with the scraps of paper, the ones that still had some handwriting on. When I got back to the office I'd compare it with Maier's handwritten statement from when he was recruited as a Stasi IM, but it certainly looked like love letters from Maier to Fremdiswalde.

I surveyed the room, poking into corners, feeling under socks, patting down pullovers. But it was hopeless, I didn't know what I was looking for, I'd probably found the most useful stuff already.

From Friedrichsfelde I decided to return home. My team had given me two days to come up with something concrete, but so far I had nothing. The idea of going back to the office empty handed was hardly appealing. Sitting on the underground train, rattling through the darkness, my mind raced through all the material it had been collecting since last Wednesday. I looked at the reflections of other passengers in the dark window. The tunnel wall speeding past was just a few centimetres away, but was invisible, more felt than seen.

When I got to my flat I rolled out some old wallpaper on the table, anchoring it with a shoe at one end and the English major's bottle of whisky at the other. Looking at the expanse of paper before me I started a mind map of everything I could possibly connect to Maier: Maier's involvement with West Germany, Fremdiswalde as Maier's killer, the brown coal industry, the Minister's extraordinary behaviour, the

KGB detachment that had arrived from Moscow, Major Tom's cryptic hints, and finally, Dmitri's conspiracy theory of a Stasi task force centred around an experienced and well trained OibE.

But why was Fremdiswalde so scared? Who did he think would kill him if he talked? The guards? Maier's colleagues in the WSB? Or Dmitri's task force of Stasi ghosts?

I looked at the branch that concerned the Minister and added a few more notes. Why was the Minister behaving so oddly? Tying me up in work, keeping tabs on me? Who was following me? Were they connected to the Ministry? After all, I'd first seen those thugs in the car outside the Ministry on the Mauerstrasse. Or was I just being paranoid, fed by Dmitri's conspiracy theories?

I looked at the untidy diagram I'd scrawled and I wasn't particularly impressed with my own efforts. But even this had to be better than just reacting. The whole of this last week I'd been a mere chess piece, moved around the board by the Minister, the police, the prison service, a KGB officer and even by my own daughter.

But I had to be honest with myself, I wasn't getting anywhere. I wasn't uncovering clues or putting together a theory about the whole case. I looked at each of the points I'd jotted down—searching for anything I could pull on, make the whole thing unravel; some aspect I could check out, some lead to follow. There wasn't anything. The investigation into Maier's death was being followed up by Schadowski and his team in Dresden. And I couldn't see how I could just march up to the Minister and ask him what the hell he was up to. The only gap I could see, the only point where I could find any room for manoeuvre was Dmitri's conspiracy theory. If I were to accept Dmitri's ideas then I needed to check them out first. It would be next to impossible to find out whether there were any Stasi sleepers posted at the Ministry. I had even less chance of finding out why the KGB had sent a detachment from Moscow. The only thing I could check was whether I was in fact being followed or not. This morning I'd nearly told my colleagues that I thought I was being followed, but was I really certain? The Lada at Ostkreuz station had brought back bad memories, but were they really there for me? I couldn't shake the idea that I was just being paranoid, encouraged by Dmitri.

Time for a little test.

17:06

"Thanks, Nik, I'm glad you could help."

Nik didn't say anything, he was too busy peering over the top of a book, making a mental note of a battered old Citroën that was parked about twenty metres up the other side of the Karl-Marx-Allee.

"I'd say it feels like the good old days," Nik replied eventually, "except it's not, is it? No, in those days we knew why we were doing it. But now? Shouldn't we have got past all this bullshit?"

I waited for Nik to answer his own question, but for once he didn't seem inclined to do so. He closed the book, and slotted it back into the gap on the shelf, stepping away from the plate glass window to join me in the shadows at the back of the shop.

"You spotted the green Citroën? I didn't see any others, but they could just be driving around the block, waiting for you to go out again." He looked me up and down—beige raincoat, slouch-hat, "I see why you wanted me to wear my coat and hat. So that's your plan. How long do you need to get rid of them for?"

"We should swap hats, yours is a bit different," I answered. For the rest, we matched up pretty well: similar size, age and build, same vintage raincoats. If Nik kept his head down then he could easily be mistaken for me.

"I don't actually need any time—it's enough for the moment just to check whether I am actually being watched, and if so, how serious they are about it. It's enough if you take them round the corner—but if you feel like taking them on a tour then please, be my guest!"

Nik chuckled, pulled out a newspaper, unfolding it as he stepped out the door on to the street, then walked off, head buried in the paper. I stood by the window and waited to see what would happen. The Citroën drove off, did a U-turn further up, then slowed down just past the bookshop, picking up a grey woman wearing an anorak and carrying a shopping bag. I leaned out of the shop and watched as the Citroën turned off around the corner, following Nik.

20:32

I couldn't get comfortable, sitting at home. The roll of wallpaper was still spread out on the table. I stood up and looked at it, shaking my head. So now I'd confirmed that I was being followed. So what? It didn't get me that much further.

I picked up the whisky bottle and the wallpaper rolled itself up, slowly at first, but gaining enough momentum to knock the shoe onto the floor before sliding down after it. Pouring myself a measure of scotch, I stood by the window, looking down at the shadowy S-Bahn tracks below. I was too restless to stand here drinking whisky, waiting for trains to pass. I put my jacket on and left the flat.

I walked around the streets near my house, no destination in mind, no purpose to my journey. Just movement. A block or two away there's a site where a house had collapsed. It was, I thought, a sort of representation of what has happened to our country. For 40 years the Communists had simply ignored the need to maintain buildings all over the GDR, all their hopes, dreams and money had gone into building prefabricated concrete flats. By the 1980s the pre-war housing stock was literally crumbling: whole streets like the Mainzerstrasse, whole quarters like Prenzlauer Berg, even whole towns like Görlitz were falling into rubble. This tenement block here in my neighbourhood had given up the fight against gravity by the end of 1989, and the neighbours shifted the debris, putting huge timber beams into place to shore up their buildings on either side, then turning the empty space into a park. A play area for the kids at the front, a rose garden with seating at the back.

The garden was unlit, the orange semi-darkness of street lamps not quite penetrating as far as what had once been the back yard. I wandered the narrow, curved paths between the rose-beds for a while, imagining rather than seeing the dark green and brown of the mottled leaves. Reaching one of the sturdy wooden props against the side of the house next to the park I turned towards the front. A figure was standing on the empty street, but from the silhouette I couldn't tell whether it was looking towards me or the other way. As I watched the shadow it slipped away along the street. It was time for me to be getting home too, it was getting cold.

I left the park and turned back, heading home. I could never understand why the streets were so empty in the evenings—thousands of people lived in this neighbourhood, the lights in all the windows were some kind of proof of their existence. But once people had come home from work, once the shops were shut, the only signs of life were from the old-fashioned pubs on the corners. I turned onto another road, the pavements here were narrow, hemmed in by concrete street lights and parked cars. A man, tall, wide, wearing raincoat and tweed hat was coming the other way. As he came close I drew aside, standing on the kerb to give him enough room to pass. But he must have felt that I wasn't giving him enough space, shouldering me into the gutter as he drew level. I spun as I stumbled down onto the cobbled road, trying to keep myself from falling. By the time I'd found my balance he'd disappeared around a corner.

In my agitation the minor incident affected me more than it should have. A drunk, weaving his way home, nothing more. But I had begun questioning my own ability to gauge distance, trajectory, movement. I was beginning to question my own judgement.

I was just walking up the stairs to my flat when Margrit came down.

"Hi Martin! I'm glad I bumped into you—the neighbourhood Round Table has just told us that our allocation of paint has come in. I've called a house meeting so that we can decide what colour we want. Can you manage the weekend?"

This was good news, for years our country had drowned in greys and browns, the Communists never seemed to plan for the production of bright paint, and it was only now, after three years, that we were in a position to start livening up our towns and cities with splashes of colour. It didn't really improve the standard of accommodation, but it did make us feel better about the places we lived in.

Pleased as I was by this piece of minor good news, I wasn't really in the mood to have a chat in the stairwell about it. I told Margrit that Sunday would be fine by me, and was about to carry on up to my flat.

"Are you doing anything now? I thought we could have dinner together, or a drink later?" Margrit asked.

"I don't know, it's been a heavy week. I was thinking of having an early night."

"Why? What's been happening?"

Until that moment I'd felt pleased that Margrit was taking an interest, but now the dark cloak of mistrust cast its shade over me again: why did everyone want to know what was going on at work? Could she know I was interested in

Maier's death? I tried to clear my head, this was crazy; I was becoming paranoid.

"Sorry Margrit, just too tired to be good company tonight. Maybe next week?"

I carried on up the stairs, reproaching myself for being unfriendly and too wary, the whole time hearing Dmitri's voice playing in a loop: *trust no-one!*

As I opened the door to my flat the telephone started ringing.

"Grobe?" I said into the receiver.

"Martin! It's me!" Evelyn. The last person I wanted on the end of the phone right now. "Martin, I wanted to apologise for dragging you out last night! It was very naughty of me to do that, but I hope you'll give me another chance?"

Completely lacking in the energy required for decent conversation I just grunted. I wasn't sure what to say, and I distrusted my ability to navigate the difficult emotional waters surrounding Evelyn.

"Why don't we have a proper date, maybe next week, or what about the weekend? Oh that would be lovely! Say you will, Martin—you have to because I've had the worst day ever!"

My ears pricked up at this, I knew that Evelyn had been in the Ministry this morning, in the archives. I'd thought about it on and off all day, but could come up with no reason why she would have been there.

"I spent the *whole* day following the District Secretary of the *Kulturbund* around the cinema. He wants to put art on the walls of the auditorium! Imagine that, Martin! 'It's a cinema!' I told him-"

"I'm sorry Evelyn, I have to go—I'm meeting someone. I'll phone you back." I put the phone down on her, and stood there in the hall, looking at the grey apparatus, wondering why I'd been so pleased to get one in the first place.

Dmitri's voice was still echoing around my skull.

DAY 9
Thursday
30th September 1993

Görlitz: Boxberg power station in West Silesia is to be privatised. A spokesperson for the West Silesian Union announced this morning that the power station and all coal fields in the region are to be transferred to a Trust Company and that proposals from the international markets are being solicited. The Berlin Ministry for Coal and Energy said they had not been consulted on the plans.

Moscow: Clashes between KGB and Interior Ministry troops have continued throughout the night. Reports of fighting have also been received from the capitals of other Soviet Republics, including Kiev, Minsk and Tbilisi.

08:12

Morning meeting, again. Normally they were slow and gentle, easing us into the workday. The only one who worked hard at these meetings was Bärbel, keeping minutes for us. The rest of us used it as a chance to make contact with each other, keep up to date on what was happening in our lives, inside and outside of work. But I wasn't looking forward to this one. Once again I'd got out of the wrong side of bed—my alarm clock went off early again, even though I could swear that I'd reset it. The weather was foul, all the worse after the last few days of sunshine. But to cap it all, I couldn't find my shoes—I'd ended up splashing through the rain and puddles in an old pair with cracked soles.

All of this rather put me on edge, and made me worry that Laura might criticise me again—it wasn't much of a fear, I know, but I had wet feet, hadn't any coffee inside me, and I'm always a lot happier when we get along at work.

As it was, it wasn't too bad. I wouldn't say it was a harmonious atmosphere, but everyone listened attentively when I reported back on yesterday's events. Laura kept her peace, and Klaus snorted when I got to the bit when Nik helped me to spot my tail. I had their attention now.

"You need to tread carefully, Martin. Somebody out there isn't happy about you sniffing around," was Klaus's response.

"I think they've been following me all week, even before I started actively looking into the Maier case. They're just keeping an eye on me, I'm not in any personal danger."

They looked sceptical about my reassurances, and, thinking about the state Chris was in, I wasn't particularly convinced myself. But they didn't make any more of a fuss, agreeing to my suggestion that I try to talk to Chris again.

We finished up and Erika asked Bärbel to go and fetch more coffee from the *Konsum* shop in the next street, then asked me to go over to her office with her.

"Are you OK?" she asked once we'd got there.

"Yeah, fine. It's all a bit surreal, and I can't shake the feeling that I'm wasting everyone's time. On the other hand, Chris has been really badly beaten up. It's like nothing has changed. When you go inside those prison walls it's like you've stepped back in time."

"Have we changed anything at all about the prison system?" she replied, thinking aloud. "We've broken down the walls of the prison-state that we lived in, but we haven't touched the walls of the physical prisons. Why aren't we coming up with other ways to see justice done?"

Since my visit to Rummelsburg yesterday I'd been asking

myself much the same question. Murder and other violent crime was still being committed—and prison was the traditional remedy for such ills. But even if most prisoners weren't treated as badly as Chris had been, it was still inhuman to simply lock people up. Where were the second chances, the opportunities to make good any damage done, the option of living a life?

"I think this is something we should talk to the Round Table about—we're part of the Ministry of the Interior, so in a sense this is our area. Let's find out what's being done about it, let's get involved. I mean, we're already involved—we've got some responsibility already: Chris is there because we found him." I noted that Erika had said *we*, accepting a collective responsibility for his capture. "And he's not the only one we've dealt with that has ended up in jail. We need to be coming up with alternatives to the current system."

"Yes, let's talk to the others about it, I agree."

Erika nodded before staring into space, tapping her pencil against a pad of paper. Finally she turned her attention back to me:

"But Martin, what I wanted to talk to you about—I've been thinking about what you said about the Minister. Let's say, just for the moment, that Maier was involved in negotiating with West Germany about coal and electricity. And if that's the case then maybe he was the one who negotiated the money, arms and BGS troops too? What if the Minister is involved in Maier's murder—because he wanted to stop the *Diversant*. He could be involved because he wants to protect the GDR."

Erika's face was flushed, she was quite excited about her theory. It wasn't an impossible scenario that she'd painted, it just seemed very improbable. But then again, there were no reasonable explanations for what was going on.

I thanked Erika, and went to the door, turning back to look at her just as I opened it. Erika was staring back at me, her eyes troubled.

Sidling out of the door I could see Bärbel had got back from the shop, the packet of coffee was on her desk next to the typewriter. Erika's office was behind Bärbel's desk, so she couldn't see me in the doorway—her eyes were fixed on the door to my office, on the other side of the reception area. She had the telephone receiver cupped in her hand and was talking quietly into it:

"Yes, he said he was going to the prison again ... that's right, bye," she said softly before putting the phone down.

"Bärbel, who were you talking to?"

She jumped, and looked around at me, shaking her head.

"Bärbel, tell me—who were you talking to on the phone?"

"Martin, I was talking to a friend about dinner—as if it has anything to do with you!"

How sure was I that I'd heard her right? And even if I had, she could have been talking about anyone—it didn't have to be me. I stood there looking at Bärbel, she'd just shrugged and turned her back on me, shifting files around her desk. The more I thought about it, the more uncertain I became. I couldn't shake the feeling that I was misjudging everything at the moment, I should probably just leave it, after all, maybe I was just being paranoid.

I went into my office and phoned the director at the power plant. "Do you know who was negotiating the power-line deal with the West Germans?" I asked him.

"Oh, didn't I mention it? Until last week that would have been Hans Maier, you know, the guy who was found dead in the mine."

14:12

Here I was again, for the second day running: Rummelsburg prison. I checked in at the guardhouse by the gate, and was asked to wait. After a few minutes a prison officer marched up to me.

"I'm to take the comrade captain to the director's office," he reported to me, as if he were talking about someone who wasn't present.

Before I had a chance to reply, he did a smart about turn, and headed back the way he'd come. I followed him across to the red brick administration block, up some steps into the hall, then up more steps to the first floor. He knocked on the door of the office, and we entered.

"I regret to inform you, comrade captain, that Accused 264721 was found dead in his cell an hour ago," said the director without looking up. He was a tall man, wearing civilian clothes and a narrow, clipped moustache. He didn't bother rising from his chair to greet me, merely extended a hand over the paperwork he was still perusing.

"I'm sorry you've had a wasted journey," he added distractedly.

"How was he killed?"

"Not killed, comrade captain. Suicide. Now if you'll excuse me–"

"I want to see his body."

Finally the director looked up at me, a faintly surprised and indignant look.

"Very well, if you wish." He gestured at the guard to take me away, and we left without another word.

The guard and I headed back into the main body of the prison, through a gate in the fence that ran across the centre of the site, then past the huge three storey cell blocks and some modern concrete buildings, under a mesh of steam and heating pipes. Finally we came to a more human sized red-brick house, with a low concrete wing added to the right of it. A plaque by the entrance marked it as *Haus 8, Prison Hospital Wing*. The basement served as a basic morgue, Fremdiswalde lying on a steel table. His left knee was still noticeably swollen under his trouser leg, and some fresh bruising could be seen around his right eye and cheek. He was wearing only the standard issue blue nylon jogging trousers and socks, and two long, parallel welts could be seen running diagonally across his left breast.

"How did this happen?" I asked the nervous orderly, although the answer was obvious to anyone looking at the body. Tongue protruding from blue lips, red marks around the neck, eyes bulging and bloodshot.

"He was found just over an hour ago, when they came to take his breakfast tray away. He'd hung himself from the bars, using his tracksuit top."

I stared at the orderly until he turned away, taking a form from the desk behind him. It was the custody record. An entry had been made late last night advising that force had been used to subdue Accused 264721. That was it, nothing else.

"Tell the director that I want a report on Fremdiswalde's death, on my desk by tomorrow morning," I snapped at the guard, and marched out of the hospital wing, letting him follow me for a change.

I stood at the tram-stop in the rain. Water was leaking through my shoes, but in my anger and agitation at Chris's death I hardly noticed the dampness. I hadn't expected this. Chris had been frightened yesterday, but I hadn't taken him seriously. If I'd listened to him, maybe I could have done something, got him out of there. He'd still be alive.

I turned my back on the biting wind blowing down the Hauptstrasse, hunching my shoulders against the cold and burrowing my hands deeper into my jacket pockets. The fingers of my right hand closed around a thick wad of papers, and I pulled them out. That cop had handed them to me on Tuesday, during the raid. I unrolled the bundle, and looked at the first page. It was Chris Fremdiswalde's Stasi files. I'd seen them before, there wasn't anything useful in there. Except, perhaps there were more than the few pages I'd already seen. The first page listed Fremdiswalde as an IM working for the Stasi, not just someone with a criminal record—that too was different from the version of the files I'd seen.

I shuffled through the pages, rain spotting the paper, wind ruffling the edges. What I read didn't make too much sense to me, wrapped up in Stasi jargon, codenames for groups, handlers and operational processes. But from what I understood, Fremdiswalde had been recruited when he was lifted for stealing at school—they'd signed him up when he was still a kid, under the codename WERTHER. The Stasi seemed to have had him reporting on youth subculture groups until late 1988, when he was given the new codename FELD and used in operations against individual targets, his handler named as IMF MILCHMÄDCHEN. That was Maier.

So Maier had been handling Fremdiswalde. That was a turn up for the books, although on consideration it wasn't too much of a surprise considering the close contact between the two men. Reading between the lines I could see that Maier was also in charge of several other IMs—the name TRAKTOR came up a lot in that last period, and it seemed odd: from what I'd seen, codenames of IMs were usually proper nouns, mostly first-names, but just like FELD, this TRAKTOR was a thing, not a person's name. I looked through again, checking the references to TRAKTOR. The first time he was mentioned there was a note added by hand in the margin: DÄ GOTTFRIED. Meaning *Decknamenänderung*—the code-name had been changed from GOTTFRIED. I'd seen the old codename before, I'd noticed it because GOTTFRIED was Bishop Forck's first name—until recently the protestant bishop of Berlin-Brandenburg. That particular codename had cropped up several times in the file the Stasi had kept on me. Maybe I needed to pull the file on GOTTFRIED/TRAKTOR, see how significant he or she was.

At that point the tram rattled up, and I got on. I folded up Chris's papers, and wiped away the condensation on the window to see outside. It had stopped raining, and the grey cloud was lifting. My eyes drifted down from the sky to the road running either side of the tram tracks. To our right I noticed a Trabant spluttering along next to us. I was too high up to see who was inside, but I didn't like the way the car was keeping pace with the tram. It looked like the watchers had picked up my scent again. I thought fast: the next stop was Rummelsburg S-Bahn station, if I got off there then I'd have two choices—get on a train, or just go through the station to the other side. The tram stopped and I climbed down the steps, crossing the road behind the little grey car, passing between the row of workshops and huts that lined the entrance to the station. I didn't look back, but I could hear the tram move off. The cyclical whining of the Trabant's engine remained at a constant pitch, telling me that the car was still stationary, watching my movements. In the station I turned round the corner, ignoring the steps that lead up to the platform, continuing instead through the tunnel towards the Nöldnerstrasse exit on the far side. A moment's hesitation as a train rumbled in overhead, and then I ran out on to the street and turned right. I'd intended to hide round the back of the church further up the road, but as soon as I made it out of the station I could see that it was too far away. A scrubby patch of grass and several mature trees were right next to the station, I quickly slid behind the damp trunk of a chestnut.

A moment later I hear footsteps and panting. Peeking round the bole of my tree I could see a small, bald man run out of the station. He leant forward, hands supported on his thighs, taking a few deep breaths before going to the phone box. He spoke for a few moments, in which time the Trabant whined up, having taken the long way round by the road. It splashed up next to the phone box, and the small man got in, the car starting up and going past me as I edged around the broad tree to stay out of sight.

The Trabant would be cruising around, looking for me, so I thought it might be better to avoid going directly to my flat. I got the bus to Lichtenberg station, before changing on to the underground for one stop, as far as Magdalenenstrasse. I walked into the old Stasi complex and entered the main building. I asked the porter for the GOTTFRIED, TRAKTOR and FELD files, and as he went away I walked into the reading room to wait for him there. After about five minutes he returned.

"I'm sorry, comrade captain, the FELD overview has been signed out to the Ministry, and I can't find any files for TRAKTOR or GOTTFRIED."

"Are there no library copies in the registry?" I asked, but the porter shook his head.

"If you could tell us which departments and district they were registered in then I could have the F 77 lists checked, but it might take a few weeks."

"No need."

I left the Stasi headquarters. FELD's background files would presumably be the same as the ones I had in my pocket, Chris's personal copy that had been found during the raid on the *Thaeri* squat. Far more interesting was the fact that the library copies of the GOTTFRIED/TRAKTOR overview files were missing. The library copies of files should never leave the archives—that way they couldn't be misplaced or lost, and there would always be a copy of a file available. Had they been shredded in the last days of the Stasi, or removed more recently?

Maybe if I looked at the references to GOTTFRIED in my own Stasi files I could work out who it was? Copies of my Stasi files were at home, so that should be my next stop.

I walked straight back towards my flat, keeping half an eye open for anyone following me. The only vehicles I saw were on the Frankfurter Allee, and there were very few people on the streets. A couple of *babushkas* carrying shopping bags, a few kids on the way home from school, if I was still being followed then they were too good for me to spot.

I was halfway home when I heard the door to a tenement block open just as I went past. I glanced into the hallway, and there stood Laura, ushering me in. A quick look up and down the street: empty. I went in, the heavy door swinging shut behind me.

"Martin, they're waiting for you—some plainclothes cops came to the office asking for you, they went away and now they're sitting in a car outside the offices. They said you sexually assaulted a girl. During the raid on the squat," Laura glared at me, accusing me, waiting for an answer.

"What-" I started, but was cut off by her.

"Well? Did you?"

"Shit! Shit-shit-shit!" I hit the wall with the palm of my hand. Laura took a step back, but her face stayed hard.

Things were moving much faster than I'd expected. "Laura —now this is important. When they came to the office, where was everyone, how did they react?"

"Martin, what does that matter? We want you to come to a meeting, tell us what happened. And we want to know the name of the young woman so that we can talk to her too-"

"For fuck's sake!" I was almost shouting, "this is a fucking set-up! Do you really think I'd assault someone? Do you? Come on, it's classic Stasi tactics! Did those cops show any ID? Or did you just take their word for it?"

"You know what? I'm not interested in your excuses, come with me and we'll talk it through—you need to tell us what happened during the raid."

I could just shove Laura out of the way, keep moving, keep

191

following the lead I'd found. But instead I tried to swallow my anger—I needed my colleagues, and I needed Laura to believe that I hadn't done anything wrong—it mattered to me what my colleagues thought of me. Another deep breath, pushing down my sense of urgency. I tried to get through to Laura again.

"Look, Laura: Chris—Fremdiswalde—he's dead. They killed him," I looked into Laura's shocked face and pushed on. "And as for that assault story, it's classic Stasi attrition tactics. Text book. You know how it works! I'm being followed, they've been in my flat trying to mess with my head, all those phone calls—and now this. They're trying to make me doubt my own sanity! They're turning you against me, isolating me. We've seen all of this too many times!" I was getting agitated again, yet another deep breath, trying to calm down. "Those men that came—they're involved in the Maier case, they're probably not even cops. What did they look like, remember the old days when they used to follow us? They looked like that didn't they? They had *that* look, didn't they? Laura?"

Laura nodded hesitantly, her arms crossed in front of her. She took another step back, and her eyes flicked upwards, away from my face. She wasn't happy. I'd taken control of the conversation, was putting her under pressure. And she was shocked at the news of Chris's death.

"So, come with me, we're going to meet somewhere away from the office, then you can explain it all, and we'll work out what to do. Together." She wasn't really taking in the information I'd given her, she was still trying to steer me back to the accusation of assault.

"Laura, I can't. They're on the lookout for me, and they probably followed you here. There's not much time, we haven't got much time. They know I'm on to them, they'll be cleaning up, covering their traces. I think that's why they killed Chris. Laura, I need your help: I can't do this by myself. Tell me, what was everyone doing when those men came to the office?"

Laura bit her lip, thinking, wondering whether to give me the benefit of the doubt. I could see the thoughts as they went through her mind—the serious accusation competing with the picture she had of me, the trust she had in me. I could imagine her thinking about the Stasi, not wanting to admit that there may still be people doing this kind of thing.

"And this, whatever it is you're doing right now, it's really urgent?" she asked.

I nodded.

"And when you've sorted this out then you'll answer our questions about the accusation?"

I swallowed the indignation that was welling up—how they could still play us off against one another! I nodded, agreeing to what she wanted.

"I was in the front office doing some photocopying—they talked to me first—"

"So where was Bärbel? Why didn't they talk to her first?"

"Well, the photocopier is right by the front door, no, that's it: Bärbel went to the toilet just as they came in."

"What—did she get up when she saw them coming?"

"Really, Martin! Does it matt—"

"Yes! Come on, tell me!"

Laura hesitated, her eyes closed, concentrating.

"A moment after, yes. The door to the stairwell was open, she must have seen them coming up the stairs."

"And the others?"

"They came out of their offices just as the cops went. I think they heard our voices, realised something was up."

"How did they react?"

"Shocked, I think. Well, Erika sat down and Klaus looked grim."

"And Bärbel, when she came back from the toilet?"

"I didn't say anything to her, but she must have overheard what I said to the others. She just sat down at her desk and carried on typing."

I paced up and down the tenement hallway, trying to process the information, fitting it in, slotting it this way and that like a jigsaw piece.

"Laura, get back to the office—have you got your personal Stasi files there? Really it's mine I need, but they're at home. So get your–"

"No they're not—you photocopied them at the office, then left them in the copier. I put them on your desk and watched how over time you piled more and more paperwork on top of them."

"You are a star! Great—get them for me. Get your own too, ask Erika and Klaus for theirs. Look through for someone called either GOTTFRIED or TRAKTOR. They're both the same person, and we need to work out who it is. Then meet me on the Grosser Bunkerberg in the Friedrichshain park, at half past six. Bring the other two, but not Bärbel—don't tell her anything. Make sure to watch out for any tails. And call my daughter—tell her to get in touch with Annette. I need to meet Annette on the spooky bridge at eight. Katrin will know what I mean. But make sure to tell her it's important— that I need her help."

She nodded: "And where are you going now?"

"I'm going to the police headquarters," I told her.

16:30

The police *Präsidium* in East Berlin is on the Keibelstrasse near Alexanderplatz, and going there was a bit of a gamble. I couldn't be sure that the men who had come for me weren't actually cops, but even if they were I suspected they wouldn't have put out an alert for me just yet. And who would expect me to head straight into the lion's den? Nevertheless I felt nervous as I crossed the Alexanderplatz after leaving the U-Bahn station. There were always police officers here, hanging around, keeping an eye on the tourists and the punks. They didn't take any notice of me as I went to the payphone at the edge of the square. It was a Glasnost phone—no booth, just a payphone with a rain hood over it, anybody could overhear my conversation if they wanted to. But that was fine by me—I wasn't planning on saying anything. I put a couple of 20 Pfennig coins in, watching as two red lights lit up on the payphone, then dialled the number for the KGB headquarters in Karlshorst.

"*Da*," came the voice at the other end.

I didn't answer, just kept an eye on my watch. 10 seconds, then hang up. Redial, hang up after 30 seconds. I'd done the same from a payphone near Ostkreuz before I got the S-Bahn up to Alex. I'd laughed at Dmitri when he told me the procedure, just the other day; but he now knew that I needed to see him urgently. A crash meeting.

No problems getting into the police headquarters, show my pass at the gatehouse, cross the yard and into the equipment house. Down the steps to the basement and show my requisition papers to the cop in charge of handing out uniforms.

"Just the extra pips?" he asked, stamping the paperwork.

"The whole lot."

He looked at me again: "Haven't you already been issued with a uniform?"

"Plain clothes. But now I need a service uniform too—so far I've only had dress."

He shrugged and turned to the shelves, "What size?" he called over his shoulder.

Twenty minutes later I had what I needed and I was out of there. He'd even given me a woven nylon bag to put it in, printed with a brown paisley pattern. I reached into the bag and checked the shoulder boards—they had the usual green piping of the *Volkspolizei* rather than the Bordeaux red of the RS. I grinned and checked the left sleeve of the jacket I'd been given—it had the *Volkspolizei* shield sewn on it.

"Very sloppy" I murmured.

If that cop had been paying attention he would have given me the red RS shoulder boards and removed the police shield from the jacket, but he hadn't checked my paperwork properly—just assumed I was a cop too. That was fine, it suited me and my plans perfectly. For my purposes it would be much better to be seen as a cop than a member of the RS.

17:17

I got off the tram at the planetarium on the Prenzlauer Allee. I'd made sure to look around as I got on the tram, watching who else was getting on, then checking for the same faces when I got off. All clear, didn't look like I was being followed. I walked over to the planetarium entrance and spent a few minutes admiring the notice board, then bent down to tie my shoelace. Plenty of people were walking up and down the Prenzlauer Allee, but I was the only person standing still. Walking around the building with a stick of chalk hidden in my hand I discreetly made a mark on the corner, just a short horizontal line at hand height. I carried on through the park, parallel to the railway tracks, heading towards the Thälmann memorial.

Between the planetarium and the memorial there's a narrow bit, the path edged in by buildings, and at just that point it curves round to the right. I stood close to the bushes just after the bend—it was a good place to spot a tail, from here I couldn't see the planetarium, which meant that anybody who was following me wouldn't see me waiting until they reached the bend. The problem was that this simple trick wouldn't work if I was being boxed: if I had a tail in front and to the sides of me as well as behind then they could simply pick me up again when I exited the park. After a few minutes of waiting I was satisfied that there was nobody behind me, and I left another chalk mark on the corner of the swimming baths.

Crossing through the shrubs I came up behind the huge Thälmann memorial, a bronze sculpture of Ernst Thälmann, the German Communists' hero, fist raised in front of a red flag carved out of stone, flowing in the wind, and the whole lot set on a red granite plinth. It was large enough to hide a squad of cops behind, but there was nobody there. I walked around the whole monument, pretending to admire the stonework, but really looking over the Greifswalder Strasse to see if anyone was coming into the park. All clear, mark on the corner of the plinth, and off again.

A couple of turns around the small pond in the park, then Dmitri was standing there, in civilian clothes.

"Martin, how long do you have? Everything OK?"

"Things have started happening—I need some more information."

"Ah! So, Martin, you have decided to trust me?"

"Perhaps. But it doesn't look like I have many choices. Listen, Dmitri, last time we met you mentioned the Stasi task force, and you said you'd look to see if there were any links with Maier. Have you had a chance to do that? And were they, or even the KGB involved in the death of Maier?"

"Martin, Martin," Dmitri shook his head, almost sadly. "An Englishman once said to me: It's not the questions that are dangerous, it's the answers—think twice before you ask anything, he said. And I think that was good advice. These OibE operatives are not amateurs, and nor are the KGB. No, it was someone else who killed the Maier politician. But, here, I have something for you."

From under his coat he pulled out a file, buff coloured, with a red diagonal stripe, some Cyrillic letters and numbers on the front. I opened it, flicked through the papers. It was all in Russian.

"What does it say?"

"I don't have time now, but it's an internal KGB report on the task force that Maier was part of. Shall we just say someone from the KGB team sent by Moscow was persuaded to hand it over? Maier was being run by an OibE—I don't know whether from here in Berlin or from Moscow, but the OibE is called GÄRTNER, he is leading the group. There is also a list of agents he or she has been running. I believe one of them panicked and killed Maier, then moved the body to the coal mine."

GÄRTNER—gardener, another agricultural codename to go with Milkmaid, Field and Tractor.

"Why did they panic?" I asked Dmitri. "Was it perhaps because Maier was getting too cosy with West Germany?"

"That is what I am thinking too, they had to ensure that Maier didn't get too close to the West. Maybe Maier was becoming too much of a loose cannon, couldn't be trusted any more. Perhaps GÄRTNER didn't intend to have Maier silenced, just wanted him scared so that he'd do what he was told."

This was at odds with the police investigation's findings—did Fremdiswalde kill Maier because of an argument, or because he was ordered to by the OibE, or Moscow?

I flicked through the file again, this time a little more slowly. Codenames were written in Latin characters, and I could see now that TRAKTOR came up a few times, along with both FELD and MILCHMÄDCHEN and some new names: BAUM, ZIEGE, SPATEN—tree, goat, spade. This looked like confirmation that Maier was involved in the Stasi plans.

"Do you know anything about TRAKTOR?"

"I haven't had a chance to analyse the documents, I just looked through, and thought that you probably needed it more than I do. But it looks like TRAKTOR is based in Berlin, he keeps a low profile. BAUM is in Berlin too."

"Can you find out who these people are?"

"I have my staff on it already, although we do have some other priorities."

I thought of the situation in Moscow, what was happening there made my little adventure here look petty.

"Of course, sorry."

"No need to apologise. I think this is all linked. Stay with it Martin, I think you're on the right track, and your timing is perfect."

"How do you know what I'm up to?"

Dmitri didn't answer, he just pointed at the nylon bag that I'd put down between my feet, the police uniform visible inside.

"I wish I could help you, but I think that if I did it may well do more harm than good."

"But there is something you can help me with: can you spare a couple of your people? I need to make sure that a friend doesn't get into any trouble."

I gave him the details, and Dmitri nodded, then held out his hand.

"Martin, when we meet again we shall have a drink together, and make proper toasts—this time not to the great leader Stalin."

"How do you know ... oh, never mind."

It was time for my next appointment.

18:26

I got to the Friedrichshain park and stationed myself in the bushes at the last junction before the footpath winds up to the top of the Grosser Bunkerberg—one of the many hills in Berlin made after the war from the rubble of the bombed-out city. I didn't have long to wait, Erika, Laura and Klaus went up the hill together. I squatted in the foliage for another five minutes, waiting and watching to see if they were followed, then came out of my hiding place and walked up the path to the top of the hill. When I got there Klaus and Laura were deep in conversation, Erika stood off to one side, listening, but with arms folded. She saw me climb the steps, and came towards me.

"Martin, what's going on?"

The other two had turned to face me, Klaus held his eternal cigar, Laura had folded her arms when she saw me.

"It's all got really complicated, and honestly, I don't know exactly what's going on. Fremdiswalde is dead. Allegedly suicide, but he was badly beaten, and conveniently he died before he could be interviewed by Schadowski's murder squad. Here, look: I've got his files, Maier was both his handler and lover. Nevertheless it looks like Fremdiswalde killed him. I spoke to Dmitri—he's KGB, Nik has contact with him, and I think he's OK—this Dmitri thinks that there is a Stasi plot to destabilise West Silesia, maybe the whole of the GDR. It looks like Fremdiswalde and Maier were mixed up in it, and if I'm right, the Minister is too."

The three of them stared at me, Klaus fiddled with his cigar, Laura shook her head, and Erika started massaging her left thumb.

"Yes, we know that Fremdiswalde did it, so surely the case is closed? Oh, and this came for you this afternoon." Laura handed me an envelope, it was from the Saxon police.

It had already been opened, and I slid out a police report on the death of Maier. It was quite thick, full of unnecessary technical particulars that I wasn't in the mood to pore over, but I scanned the summary and leafed through the rest. There wasn't anything new in it, just the details and a catalogue of evidence. On the 22nd of September Maier had been at the Nochten open cast lignite mine for an official meeting about the low availability of the machinery due to frequent breakdowns. Afterwards he said he wanted to inspect the mine by himself. He was told where it was safe to go and issued a hard hat. The body, strangled using a length of soft material, most likely from a scarf, was found at half past one the next morning on the tracks of the transformer cars at the excavating end of the F60 Overburden Conveyor Gantry (*F60 No. 33, built 1972-74; dimensions: 504m long x 82m high x 240m wide, capacity 100,000 tonnes per hour* the report helpfully, if irrelevantly provided). Presumably the original intention was that the body should be left at the other end of the gantry where it would have been quickly covered by the spoil dump. The police theory was that the perpetrator had mistakenly enticed Maier to the wrong end of the gantry, by which time it was too late, since it would have been impossible for one person to carry a dead body 500 metres down into the pit and up the other side. So Maier had been left on the tracks. Signs of a scuffle had been found near the body. Workers at the site hadn't seen or heard anything, which wasn't surprising—although the mine ran all day and night the miners would have been concentrating on watching the machinery, not looking one and a half kilometres further down the mine to where Maier was being throttled. If the police estimate of time of death were correct, it would have taken about three hours for the lumbering F60 to reach Maier's body, and another half an hour to roll over the head and feet as it moved along the rails. Fremdiswalde, who had worked at the mine after leaving school, had been recognised by a works security guard. The guard said that he saw Fremdiswalde leaving the mine at around 20.30 on the 22nd, and had seemed agitated. The guard had assumed that Fremdiswalde had been working and therefore had neither challenged him nor informed the police until Maier's body was found. Two pairs of footprints led to the scene, but only one set led directly from the site of the murder to the edge of the mine were Fremdiswalde was seen. The police had found the draft of a letter at Maier's flat, a dear John letter, ending the relationship with Fremdiswalde, and the police surmised that Maier had asked Fremdiswalde to meet at the mine in order to finish the affair in person.

Skin particles and hairs found on Maier's body matched Fremdiswalde's blood group.

Laura waited until I'd finished flicking through the file, then: "It looks pretty cut and dried to me."

"I'm sure the Minister is very happy with the police conclusions—but he's involved. How else can you explain everything that's been happening over the last few days. It's not just a case of a murder of passion, it's bigger than this!"

"OK, so let's just assume you're right, how long have you suspected the Minister? And do you think he set those goons on you?" Laura demanded.

"I don't know—the suspicion has sort of been growing over the last few days."

"And you didn't tell us? And why couldn't we tell Bärbel about this meeting?"

"I did tell you—several times! I told you how I thought the Minister was behaving extremely oddly, that I was being followed. And as for Bärbel, well, think about it, somehow the Minister knew I wasn't happy about the Maier situation —how? And why wasn't she shocked, or even surprised when the cops—if they were even cops—turned up to fetch me today? She's not one of us, she was an official under the old regime, and we inherited her—what do we know about her, really? I didn't tell you about Dmitri, that was wrong, I'm sorry. But it was good that I didn't, because otherwise Bärbel would have just told the Minister."

"Martin, are you sure about this Maier connection to the Minister?" Klaus interjected before things could get even worse between Laura and me.

I looked at him, held my hands palm outwards, the police report and Dmitri's papers stuffed under my arm.

"Look, I'm not a hundred percent sure, it's all pretty circumstantial—I want to cross reference my own Stasi files. I think we might find something there. Did you bring your files too?"

We stood there for a few moments, all looking at each other, then Laura shrugged off the bag that was hung over her shoulder, and pulled out a couple of folders. She handed me one of them—it was my Stasi file. I took it and walked over to the low wall surrounding the area at the top of the hill. I laid the files on it, then looked over my shoulder, encouraging the others to join me. They came over, and watched as I flicked through Fremdiswalde's papers.

"Here, look, Fremdiswalde was an IM—but he was working in a special task force, everyone in that task force has some kind of farming codename. Fremdiswalde was FELD, and Dmitri reckons that there was an OibE, this is him, GÄRTNER." I looked up into three blank faces, "An OibE is a Stasi officer put into some position of power well before the 1989 Revolution so that he can exert influence, usually over a government department or government agency. Dmitri reckons there are still some active OibEs, and that they may be trying to organise a counter-revolution—they have the same set-up in the Soviet Union, and the attempts to depose Gorbachev may be part of the same plan as the secession of West Silesia. GÄRTNER must have been heading up a task force, and Maier was part of it. He was in at the beginning—his codename probably gave them the idea for all the other names—look, they're all agricultural names, and we know that Maier was MILCHMÄDCHEN, and that his codename is older than the OibE plan.

"I reckon that he just got too close to West Germany, started following his own agenda: an independent West Silesia with him at the helm. They needed to discipline him, bring him back into line. But they cocked it up and he ended up dead in an open-cast mine.

"If what Dmitri says is true then there'll be links with the Ministry of the Interior here in Berlin—look," I showed them

203

the part in Fremdiswalde's file that showed TRAKTOR to be the same agent as GOTTFRIED. "I'm sure that name crops up in my files too—maybe we can work out who it is."

I started leafing through my files, looking for any mention of GOTTFRIED. Erika joined me at the wall, getting out her own file and looking through it. Although I had my back to Laura and Klaus I could hear them murmuring, then after a short hesitation they joined us—they'd brought their files too.

"We really need an F 3 for GOTTFRIED or Maier. That's the 'Who Knows Who' file which would show us the links. That is, if there are any," said Laura as she put her file on the wall.

"OK, I've got a GOTTFRIED here—report dated September 1983, the human chain for peace that we formed between the American and Soviet embassies. It says GOTTFRIED was present at the scene, but left before the participants were taken into detention," said Erika.

"That doesn't help us at all! There were hundreds of us there that day," snorted Klaus.

"OK, keep looking, maybe we'll find more, wait, here: *Situation Report on the 1987 Peace Workshop*—the one that the church banned, look: 'GOTTFRIED has made representations to Diocesan *Genaralsuperintendent* Krusche, offering to act as one of a group of guarantors for the groups involved'."

Trouble was, that made it look like GOTTFRIED was on our side, far from being the IM that was set on impeding the work we were doing. But at least it showed that GOTTFRIED had some links with figures high up in the church.

"OK, I think I've got something—Martin, you may be right, listen: *Situation Report on the mood of the opposition groups after the Zion Church affair*. It says that GOTTFRIED has begun discouraging groups from using his church—it's in my file because I was in one of those groups. It was his church, it was the church where the Minister used to be the Pastor!"

It added up—he'd have links to Krusche, and he was there

the day we did the peace chain between the embassies. I remember him staying long enough to get his photo taken by the Western media, then leaving just when the police vans turned up.

"OK, there was another one too, Dmitri said there was another person working from Berlin, what was the name?"

From my bag I pulled out the file that Dmitri had given, and looked through it.

"BAUM! That was it—but I don't know what it says, it's all in Russian. Klaus, do you understand this?"

Klaus took the file, and flicked through, stopping whenever he saw the codename BAUM. After a while he cleared his throat and looked up.

"Hard to say. But from what I understand it looks like BAUM is in the Ministry too. Look: there's orders here regarding police and border guard deployments along the West Silesian border; or here: BAUM is instructed by Moscow to doctor reports on meetings between West Silesian and Berlin officials. Whoever she is, she must be pretty high up in the Ministry."

"She?"

"Yes, definitely a woman, it always refers to BAUM as a female: *yeye, ona, eu,* etc."

"Do you get any sense of her relationship with the Minister?"

"I'd have to look through it more carefully—it's formal language, written using lots of KGB and police jargon."

"Doesn't matter," I said, thinking out loud, "I know who it might be. Someone who was an IM, if she was pulled from the same pool as the others then we probably know her. Someone who just disappeared in 1988 when this new task force was formed, and is now suddenly back on the scene ..."

The four of us stood there, at the top of the Bunkerberg. The leaves of the trees and bushes on the hill around us were turning yellow, bronze and red, whispering in the light wind.

Under different circumstances it would have been pleasant, but I had the feeling that I still had to persuade my colleagues that I was planning to do the right thing.

"What are we going to do about it? Do we have to act now?" Erika asked.

"I think so, the cops were at the office and Martin's house, and we were alarmed enough by that to send Laura out to warn him," Klaus answered.

"Dmitri seems to think that this is the time to act as well," I added.

"Can we trust him?"

That was the big question. If the report Dmitri gave me was true, then Moscow had been running both the Minister and BAUM, who had been manipulating the West Silesian situation. But if Moscow were capable of doing that, then they were certainly capable of scaring me into acting—a few people watching me, a couple of meetings with a KGB officer who would feed me disinformation. Anything was possible.

"I honestly don't know," I concluded. "But it only makes sense if what Dmitri says is true. If he's not on our side, well, what would the Russians gain? They don't care about the future of our country, and they've got their hands full with the coup attempt in Moscow right now. Add to that the fact that the Minister has definitely been trying to tie me up without ever actually ordering me to back off. It all fits in— we need to somehow get to the bottom of this." I could see Laura was about to raise an objection, but carried on talking: "If we had more time we could do some more research, go through the Round Table, but I think if we leave it much longer then I'll be arrested by the police or grabbed by whatever ex-Stasi group is behind this. Either way we'll be tied up and unable to do anything. I think we need to act now and then go to the Round Table afterwards."

Erika and Klaus were nodding, Laura was still thinking it through.

"Erika?" I looked at her, waiting for her answer.

"Yes, let's do it."

I turned to Klaus, he nodded slowly. That left Laura.

"You really think this is the only way?" she asked eventually.

"Yes. I'm not happy about it either, but what else can we do? You got any ideas?"

Laura shook her head. "OK. Have you got a plan already?"

"I most certainly do," I tapped the bag with the police uniform in it. "I think you're going to like this."

20:02

It turned out that my colleagues didn't like my plan, but they couldn't come up with anything better, so they agreed to go along with it. We made our arrangements, then parted. Now I was waiting for Annette on the bridge that ran above the central slaughter yards and the S-Bahn tracks. It's a long bridge, more of a tunnel on stilts, full of shadows and darkness. Even during the day not much light makes its way through the dirty, frosted glass; now at night it was clear why my daughter called this the spooky bridge when she was small.

The echoing clang of footsteps told me that someone was coming up the steps from the S-Bahn station. I was standing further back along the bridge, so I couldn't see who it was, but it sounded like more than one pair of feet. When the figures arrived at the top I saw Annette, but she'd brought someone with her—my daughter.

"Katrin, what are you doing here?"

"Hi Papa. Your colleague said you needed help, so I thought I'd tag along with Annette."

"What's going on, Martin, what's so important? Katrin said it was really important that I come."

I was a bit put out by Katrin's unexpected presence, it had

knocked me off balance. Before I could think of anything to say the sound of a further pair of footsteps echoed down the bridge; rapid and purposeful. I turned to look and was startled at how close the two men were. Both wore hats pulled low over their eyes. One had a *Lederol* fake leather jacket on, the other a short trench coat, much like mine. They glared at us as they came closer, there was no doubt that we were their quarry.

"Shit–"

"What is it, Martin?" Annette had picked up on my stress.

As for my daughter, her eyes met mine but she said nothing, letting her eyes do the talking: accusatory.

As I looked around for an escape route I heard a train grind into the station below us. Our only choices were down the steps onto the platform, or the other exit, further along the bridge. But there might be men in plastic-leather jackets waiting for us there too. I looked towards the two men bearing down on us, gauging how much time we had, when someone brushed past me, I hadn't heard anyone come up the steps, but here was the Russian NCO that had driven the jeep the other day.

"Platform's clear, get on the train!" she hissed as she went past, casually swinging a heavy shopping bag as she went.

I grabbed Katrin and Annette's hands and pulled them towards the steps down to the platform, the last thing I saw before I went around the corner was the Soviet soldier kick one of the men in the crotch while aiming her bag at the other guy's face. We could hear the men's grunts as we ran down the stairs, jumping on the train just as the door buzzer went.

"Martin, what the fuck is going on?" demanded Annette, glaring at me as I slumped down on the floor next to the door.

Katrin was looking back at the station, lit up in the dark.

"Nobody followed us down to the platform. Right, Papa, I

think you have some explaining to do."

"In a minute! The next stop is Lenin Allee. If there's a train on the other side of the platform we're going to run across and get on that, but we need to check if we're being followed. Annette, you check to our right, see if anyone else crosses to the other train. Katrin, check behind us, and I'll look to the left. We need to keep watching until the train pulls out of the station."

Katrin nodded at Annette, who, after some hesitation nodded too. As we drew into the station I saw with relief that there was indeed a train standing on the other side of the platform. I hauled open the doors before we'd even stopped, jumping down, hearing the others follow me, and the shout of the platform attendant.

"Schönefeld: *zurückbleiben!*"

Katrin jumped into the doorway of the other train, just as the red lights lit up, and the buzzer went. She blocked the doors from sliding shut, allowing us to slip in. We were clear —no one had followed us across the platform.

I led the way to some empty seats, and we sat down, Annette and Katrin sitting opposite me, not saying anything, just staring at me, waiting for an explanation.

"Annette, I need your help. There's some stuff I've got to deal with, and I can't do it by myself. I need your contacts, I think some of the squatters could help."

Annette looked suspicious. "What kind of stuff?"

In a low whisper I told her of my suspicions about the Minister, how he was probably connected to the Maier case.

"Are you sure? It sounds a bit far fetched."

"Did you see those two men on the bridge, if it hadn't been for ..." I realised I didn't even know the name of Dmitri's NCO.

"What about them? They were just two dudes on the way to the station—"

"They were Stasi," I sighed, and leant back.

"Come off it! There hasn't been any Stasi for at least three years!"

"Annette, Papa's right. They were Stasi," confirmed Katrin.

Annette looked from Katrin to me, eyes wide. Astonished, and now, finally, a little afraid.

"You better be worth the trouble," she said, not quite under her breath.

Annette suggested we head over to the Squatters' Council—they were meeting that night in Friedrichshain—we'd probably get there in time for the beginning. We got off at Frankfurter Allee then walked to one of the Wessi-squats near by. Annette shouted up to one of the balconies where a couple of punks were hanging out. They chucked a key on a piece of string down to us, and we let ourselves in. The key was hauled back up.

The meeting was in a kitchen on the ground floor, about a dozen young squatters sitting loosely round a table too small for the amount of empty beer bottles and fag butts it was holding. A couple of them looked up as we came in.

"Oh shit! Oh man! Who the fuck are you bringing here this time?" This was directed at Annette, but the question was clearly about me.

"Hey, people," Annette's voice and accent had changed, she sounded like a young punk herself now, drawling the words out. "This is Martin, he needs our help. He's from the *Republikschutz*—"

"Fuck off! Bull-pig! Stasi pig!" The young man who'd first spoken was on his feet, shouting, pointing his finger at me, but staring at Annette, his spit flecking the front of her anorak.

"Wait," Annette tried to get them to listen, "Wait! Martin's been in the opposition for more than 15 years—he was doing actions when you were all in nappies!"

"Yeah, and he's become institutionalised! Just look at

him!"

"Never trust anyone over the age of thirty!"

"Bulls out!"

Pretty much everyone in the room was shouting at Annette now, but only Katrin was looking at me.

"Papa, let's go, come on."

Katrin was pulling me, I grabbed Annette's hand and we went back out onto the street.

There was silence for a couple of minutes, then Annette took my hand again.

"Sorry. That didn't go as planned."

I was shocked. Is that what we'd worked for, what we'd sacrificed so much for, just so that Westerners could come over here, squat our buildings and insult us? Ever since Rudi Dutschke the fucking Wessis had been telling us that we were passive and apolitical, giving us lessons in Marx and Lenin, as if we weren't getting enough of that every day from the Party! And now they were living here in our Berlin with their patronising fucking arrogance. I didn't feel like I had any energy to carry on. Let them sort out this mess if they thought themselves so much better than us!

"Martin? I'm sorry," Annette said again. "I should have thought, the council is meeting in a Wessi-squat tonight."

"I thought the Squatters' Council was for all the squats?" asked Katrin.

"It is, but the local squatters are getting pissed off with the Wessis, so most of them don't go to the meetings if they're being held at a Wessi-squat. The locals say the Wessis are too dogmatic, think only in terms of black and white ... But Martin, you know Karo, why don't we try her?"

"I'm not sure that's such a good idea ..." I tailed off, remembering the last time I'd seen her, huddled in the corner, shaking, probably traumatised.

The three of us were walking slowly back to the Frankfurter Allee, Katrin quiet, probably as shocked as I was by the Wessis' vitriol. Annette tried to be encouraging, which grated hard against my feelings of dejection.

"Why not? What's wrong with Karo?"

"Nothing. At least I hope not ... There was a police raid at her place a few days ago. It was pretty bad, and I was there. With the cops, I mean."

"God, Martin, you don't make things easy, do you? Right, where does she live? OK, you hang around somewhere near by, I'll go and talk to her, see if we can sort this mess out."

We walked along the Rigaer Strasse, and Katrin and I went into the *Fischladen* bar while Annette went round the corner to the Thaerstrasse squat.

Food was still being served and Katrin brought us two plates, overflowing with steaming goulash. We both picked at the stew, neither of us saying anything. All the plans I'd made, they just weren't going to work. I somehow had to get hold of Laura, Erika and Klaus and call off tomorrow's mission. Without more bodies there was no way it could work. But if we didn't do it tomorrow then we may not get another chance. And then what?

I was deep in my thoughts when Katrin patted my arm. Annette was standing in front of us, her eyes and face were hard. She avoided looking at me, speaking only to Katrin.

"Karo wants to talk to you."

Katrin got up and the pair of them left the bar, leaving me behind, brooding over my ruined plan.

"I'm sorry about what I said to you, you know, during the raid on Tuesday."

It was Karo. She was standing in front of my table, looking down at her feet. When she finally looked up I could see a large bruise shading her left eye.

"I think you're the last person who needs to apologise," I answered. "I'm the one who should be apologising to you."

"No, it wasn't you, brother. It was the bulls. Katrin made

me realise—she said you'd never do that, that you'd do whatever you could to stop it. It made me think again, run through what happened. And I guess that's what you did— try to stop it, I mean."

Not sure what to say, I looked down at my goulash, cold, practically untouched.

"Annette says there's something we can do for you."

"Not for me, for all of us," I looked up, meeting Karo's eyes, hope welling up again in my chest. "Fancy another revolution?"

"Hell, yeah! Any day! Do we get to settle up with the bulls?" Karo grinned at me. I was forgiven.

"I think we might find a way. And there's something else I need too."

"What?" Karo looked at me, her eyes bright.

"I need a place to crash tonight."

DAY 10
Friday
1st October 1993

Moscow: The Soviet Army has declared support for the President of the Soviet Union, Mikhail Gorbachev. Broadcasting from Moscow's television complex Marshal of the Soviet Union Gennady Bereskov announced an operation to round up rogue KGB troops in the capital. President Gorbachev is expected to return to Moscow this morning.

09:47

In 1906 an unemployed cobbler put on a second hand captain's uniform then commanded some soldiers to follow him. He deployed them in an occupation of Köpenick town hall, arresting the mayor and confiscating 3,577 Marks from the council's coffers. His plan was very simple: it relied on the blind obedience of the soldiers he'd rounded up on the street—without his uniform he had no authority, and without that authority, he had no chance of getting to the money.

I think I probably felt much the same way as the Captain of Köpenick did when he began rounding up his troops. I was pretty nervous, but a uniform is like a coat of armour—I was shaking inside, even if nobody looking at me would be able to tell. The military cut of the green jacket and trousers, the shiny shoes, the peaked cap, all straightened my spine and lent me an arrogance I would not normally want. I strode confidently down the Mauerstrasse—a Captain of the *Volkspolizei*.

My ragtag troop of punks followed in silence. They'd been busy during the night: I had sworn them in to the service of the Republic, toasting them with beer. Each had a strip of red material tied around their left arm, white letters spelt out *HelferIn des RS*—RS auxiliary. Most of them had flowers, crude representations of peace doves or the national *Swords to Ploughshares* emblem daubed below the letters. Beside me I had Laura, Klaus and Erika, each of us caught up in the drama of the situation.

I walked up the steps and pushed in through the main doors of the Ministry of the Interior. Pulling myself up to my full height, adjusting my voice to fit the uniform, I commanded the porter to call the Central Round Table and the Round Table's Committee for Internal Affairs, requesting that they convene immediately here at the Ministry. Behind me, the squatters streamed into the building, ignoring the cops standing by the door. I waved an impatient hand at one of the policemen who tried to stem the flow of punks—a curt gesture, slicing the blade of my hand through the air. The guard came to attention, eyes front, ignoring my squad. Before me, the porter, who had been about to question my order, similarly stiffened and picked up the telephone. Karo was standing beside me, and I asked her to stay here with the porter, make sure he didn't make any other calls.

Turning to the cops, I ordered them to lock the main doors and to accompany me. Erika, Klaus and Laura were still with me, but once the front doors had been locked, they split up, each leading a small crew of punks to seal off the other exits to the building.

I took the two policemen up the stairs to the Minister's office—we barged in through the door, but the Minister wasn't at his desk. Out again, this time through the other door to the secretary.

"Where's the Minister?" I demanded.

The secretary looked up from her typing, nonplussed. "He's in his office–"

"Call the Central Command of the Border Police—see that he doesn't cross the border," I snapped at the policeman by my side, telling the other to guard the office, then headed down to the main hall at the bottom of the stairs.

"The Minister's done a runner—but we need to check whether he's still in the building. Can you form a search party?" I asked some of the punks who were still in the porter's office with Karo, they ran off shouting and sliding over the shiny parquet. I turned to see Laura at my side, looking embarrassed.

"Sorry, Martin, that's my fault. I went into the office this morning, and when Bärbel asked why nobody was in I just said where we were going, I didn't think–"

"Someone needs to phone the chair of the Central Round Table, tell her what's going on, that we need her here, now," I said, trying to hide my anger, and going back up the stairs to the Minister's office. I'd just reached the top when the policeman came out of the secretary's office, saluted and reported.

"Border Police have been informed, comrade captain!"

"Thank you, comrade *Wachtmeister*. Now go to the personnel archives and get whatever files they have on Hagenow, Evelyn and the Minister: Hartmann, Benno."

I didn't really think that the files would contain anything useful, but I wanted to get rid of the policeman, I needed to sit down for a moment, unobserved. And I was curious about Evelyn, why was she on the scene again, and how come she was at the Ministry? I went into the Minister's office, told the cop there to go and stand in the corridor, then sat down at the desk. What now? No Minister, no evidence; and the Central Round Table about to descend on us, wanting to know what the hell was going on. It couldn't get much worse. If the Minister had already crossed the border, or come to that, was hiding out somewhere in the Republic then we wouldn't find him in time, if ever.

A knock at the door, and the cop came in with the files. I ignored the Minister's file, and idly thumbed through Evelyn's: 1988 in-service training in Moscow, then attachment to the Ministry of the Interior. Before that she was an administrative worker at the State Opera. If she was just a cultural administrator, how did she end up getting a prestige posting to Moscow, followed by a position as case handler in a ministry? And if that wasn't enough, what was she doing serving drinks at a party thrown for the *Bonzen* all those years ago when I first saw her? And why did she come to my factory a few months later, wanting to see the works' Party secretary? To me, it sounded like a pretty thin legend. It certainly looked like she wasn't just some petty IM informant, but was somehow more involved. Reading between the lines it sounded like she'd been put in place in the Opera to spy on Party *Bonzen* when they attended performances, later on liaising with Party bigwigs in the factories, before being transferred into the Ministry at the same time the task force was formed around OibE GÄRTNER. But this was wasting time. I needed proof, and unless I found it I would be in deep shit. Alternatively, if there were no proof, if I was just plain wrong, well, same result.

I was mulling over this possibility when there was another knock at the door.

"Comrade *Hauptmann*! The Minister has been stopped at the Friedrichstrasse Border Crossing Point. The Minister and a woman, also in the vehicle, have been detained."

"Very good, have them brought to me immediately."

The Friedrichstrasse border crossing wasn't very far away, they'd be here in just a few minutes. In the meantime, we had to search the building for anything that might confirm my suspicions, and it made sense to start in this office. Going to the door, I asked the policeman standing outside to fetch Karo and Laura from downstairs. While I was waiting for them, I looked around the office. If I were the Minister, where would I hide potentially incriminating material? I started opening and closing cupboard doors at random, poking through files, just getting more and more frustrated with myself. I was desperately casting around the office when Karo came in.

"Karo, we need to search the building for any clues about what the Minister was up to. Do you think you could get your crew to go and safeguard the archives? We need all the staff out of there, and to make sure that nobody touches anything."

"Sure thing, Martin. But what about the computer?"

I looked around, and, sure enough, in the corner of the room, on its own little table was a big square box, beside that a television sitting on top of a smaller steel box. I pushed the big red button, and a red light came on, with a green light flickering alongside it. The green light went out, but nothing seemed to be happening on the television set. I shrugged and looked at Karo, who laughed at me.

"Try turning on the monitor, too—the button's on the left hand side, underneath. But wait a moment, I'll go and fetch Schimmel."

As Karo went out the door, Laura came in. I explained to her what we needed to find, and asked her to organise a quick search of the secretary's office next door, as well as the secretariat and archive downstairs.

"Worth a try, since we're here," she responded thoughtfully. "But it's a bit of a long shot."

I turned back to the computer, which didn't seem to be doing much. Just like me.

Karo came in with another punk, this must be Schimmel. Like all the punks here today he was young, with ragged hair and a ripped leather jacket. He took one look at the computer and gave a shriek.

"Cool, a P8000 compact! I wonder if it's the triple processor? Let's see what operating system they've got—aha! Wega."

I peered over Schimmel's shoulder at the screen: "WEGA login:" it said. Schimmel looked at me.

"What's your minister's name?"

"Benno Hartmann."

Schimmel typed in the name Hartmann, then: "What's his date of birth?"

I opened up the Minister's file, and read out his date of birth, Schimmel typed that in too.

"We're in! Most people use their date of birth as a password because that's what the manual says they should do, it's easy to remember. Ha! Right, what are we after? OK, so let's have a quick look at what files he has in here," he typed a few letters and looked at a long list of gobbledygook. "Any of these file-names look interesting?" he asked over his shoulder.

I peered at the screen, there must be hundreds of files, and with a few strokes of the keys, Schimmel made another screenful appear. He looked at me, and just as Karo had, laughed at my helplessness. A few more quick taps of the keys, and the printer on the floor started screeching, paper turning out of the top. Schimmel reached down, and tore off a couple of sheets from the long roll, handing them over to me.

"Here, that may be easier to read. Just look through the names there, see if anything sticks out."

He was right, it was easier to look at the print-out than the flickering green letters on the screen. I just scanned through, most of the names looked boring: LetterRT or LetterRT2, Rota17 and the like. I was about to give up again when I spotted ProjGart—that could be short for *Projekt*

Garten, and if Garten was the garden, maybe the OibE GÄRTNER was the gardener in charge of this project ...

"That one, let's look at that."

I watched him type "file: md(0,1600)ProjGart", then a load of random letters and shapes came up on the screen, and the computer beeped a few times.

"Fuck!" he groaned. "It's been hashed somehow ... like a code. It hides the contents of that file," Schimmel tapped away at the keyboard a bit more, then: "OK! I've got the programme that does it, but we still need a password. I've already tried his birth date, it's not that. If we can guess the password then we can read the file—easy as that!"

It didn't seem that easy to me—what would this password be? It had looked so promising for a moment, but maybe it was a waste of time after all. I slumped back down into the Minister's chair, putting my feet on his desk.

A knock at the door, and one of the cops came in, "Herr Hartmann has just arrived, comrade captain. Shall I bring him in?"

I didn't much like the idea of being confronted with the Minister. Even though he'd just been caught trying to leave the country, his word would still count for a lot more than mine; in his position I'd probably try to bluff it out, order our arrest, something like that.

But it was time to face him—I'd given up hope of finding any real evidence to back up my suspicions about the Minister.

"Who was the woman who was detained with the Minister?" I asked the policeman.

"Fräulein Hagenow, comrade captain."

There was just time for one last throw of the dice.

"Schimmel! That password we're looking for, try: *Evelyn*!"

EPILOGUE
Friday
8th October 1993

Görlitz: Following days of protests the West Silesian government has lost a vote of no confidence in the Region's parliament. The vote last night followed the exposure last week of an alleged plot by former Stasi officers to destabilise the GDR. The West Silesian Round Table has invited representatives of the Central Round Table in Berlin to negotiate terms for the full reintegration of the Region into the GDR.

Moscow: Soviet President Gorbachev continues to consolidate his position after surviving the failed coup attempt last week. Elections for both Soviet Parliaments have been announced, and several ministers in Gorbachev's government have been replaced. The Soviet Ministry of the Interior has announced an investigation into the role of the KGB during the crisis.

11:32

Erika, Klaus, Laura and I were sat in an ante-room in the old Party Central Committee building. We were all nervous, waiting to be called in to the Central Round Table to account for our actions. Dieter had come back from his annual leave, and was sitting there with us too—there was no need for him to be there, he hadn't been involved in the case at all, but he wanted to be with us, and we appreciated that. He wasn't just a reassuring presence: he had helped us sort through the aftermath too. The work hadn't stopped last week with the arrest of the Minister and Evelyn—we'd spent a lot of time analysing both the file that Schimmel had decrypted and the KGB file Dmitri had given us. Along with other papers from the Minister's office we had more than enough information on the Stasi task force. The encrypted file was a running report, written by the Minister for the leader of the task force, GÄRTNER—a comprehensive detailing of all his actions during the West Silesian crisis. It started last year with the Minister encouraging the West Silesian League to campaign for autonomy from Saxony, channelling money from a numbered Swiss bank account into the League's party coffers. The plan was to destabilise the GDR with the threat of West Silesian secession, making it possible to recentralise power structures, as Dmitri had predicted.

But once the West Germans had also started pouring money and technical support into the breakaway Region the threat of secession became an all too real possibility. That would have bankrupted the GDR, leading inevitably to a full takeover by the West Germans. Maier had spotted an opportunity to feather his own nest, and had become an overenthusiastic supporter of the plans for secession. He had started negotiating a power deal—both for political and electrical power—with the West Germans, hoping that with their protection he could outwit the task force he had been part of. It couldn't have been easy for Fremdiswalde to carry out the orders he had been given, to save the plan by silencing his lover. Maybe that's why he botched it so badly, leaving the body on the tracks rather than disposing of it properly.

Dmitri's file provided more general background detail to the beginnings of the operation. As we'd already worked out, the Minister was TRAKTOR. But BAUM wasn't Evelyn as I'd suspected: it was none other than our secretary Bärbel, who hadn't been seen since last Friday. Bärbel, always sitting quietly in the corner, making notes about absolutely everything, and never really noticed by any of us.

Last week I'd assumed the OibE was in position in West Silesia, but the Stasi officer in charge had actually been here at the Ministry all along, keeping tabs on the operation, and on me. Her time in Moscow had been spent preparing her to lead the task force—GÄRTNER was none other than Evelyn.

We hadn't yet worked out who ZIEGE and SPATEN were—whoever they were, they were still out there, but finding them was a job for the cops, not for us.

We'd spent a lot of time wrapping up this case, and we'd had lots of discussions about the state of our Republic. We'd had to confront some of the key issues our society faced: the way attitudes in the police force hadn't changed since the days when they took their orders from the Party, the way Chris could be beaten up and die at the hands of prison warders. His death was more than enough proof for me that there were still connections between the current security apparatus and their ex-colleagues who had been in the Stasi.

It was ironic to think that the same police force and prison service currently had custody of Benno Hartmann and Evelyn Hagenow. I was glad that it wouldn't be for us to decide what was to happen to them—that was a problem for the courts. Nevertheless we couldn't help but think about what kind of punishment they might deserve: prison or exile seemed the most obvious options, but neither seemed particularly palatable. Exile was the way the old regime dealt with those it considered too troublesome; an exclusion from friends, family and familiar landscapes. Prison represented another kind of exile, an exclusion from life without actually having to take that life. A sadistic punishment wrapped up in the language of protecting the population.

"How are things with Annette?" Erika asked me suddenly.

I looked over at her. I could have answered. I could have

said that I hadn't seen Annette since that Thursday in the Rigaer Strasse. That I'd spoken to her just once, on the phone, that she'd asked me not to contact her, that she would call me when the time was right. I could tell Erika that Katrin had suggested she talk to Annette on my behalf, but that I'd been too proud to accept the offer. But I didn't say anything.

Erika had already gone back to staring at the opposite wall, her legs and arms crossed, one foot tapping nervously, her question idle, empty, already forgotten.

I thought of Katrin. I'd seen a lot of her this last week. Somehow the events had brought us closer. I think Katrin had been glad to play some small part in what happened, it made her feel that she'd finally contributed in some way, made up for leaving the country in 1989. I think Karo and her friends had a similar sense of pride. They'd celebrated last Friday after the Minister and Evelyn had been arrested. I'd bought them a few crates of beer, and they'd partied far into the next morning, proud to be a part of this great social experiment of ours.

My thoughts returned to the present, and I restlessly flicked through my copy of the report we had prepared for the Round Table, recommending that all senior ministerial positions should be held by a committee rather than an individual. We argued that ministerial mandates concentrated too much power in too few hands, and were therefore unaccountable and open to abuse. We suggested that a small and accountable team should take responsibility for co-ordinating the work of each ministry. Other chapters of the report observed that there was an acute need to democratise the police force, recommending the presence of civilian observers in any potentially controversial operation, to be decided in each case by a standing sub-committee of the local Round Table. The problems of violence against prisoners was also addressed, and an independent investigation of Chris's death called for. We'd discussed the need for re-education efforts in the police and prison service, but the very phrase, with its Stalinist shadows, made us hesitate to include it in the report.

The document had been signed by every single member of the different branches of the *Republikschutz* and an outline of the suggestions had been published in the newspapers.

But now we had to personally account for what we'd done. Although the files we'd found at the Minister's office were more than enough to vindicate our actions, we were unsure how we would be received by the Round Table members—we had seriously exceeded our authority by detaining a democratically elected member of the government.

The door opened, and the five of us looked up, wondering whether we'd be called in. Instead of an usher, a Russian officer walked in—Dmitri. He smiled broadly, arms outstretched, including us all in his welcome.

"Comrades," he cried jovially. "The naughty comrades! What a brilliant plan, an instructive subversion of authority! But, my friends, don't look so worried, I think all is well!" He considered my anxious face for a moment, "I have given the Central Round Table of the GDR a full report on the activities of GÄRTNER and her team. I explained her links to the KGB faction which attempted to overthrow President Gorbachev last week. I impressed upon them that without your revolutionary vigilance GÄRTNER and her crew would have destabilised the GDR to the extent that West Germany would have simply taken over policing responsibilities in the interests of keeping order. Now the West Germans will have to find another excuse to interfere in your country."

"But what are you doing here? How did you get to address the Round Table?" I asked.

"Well, my friend, I thought you could use a little help. After all, you very kindly took the minor problem of the OibE at the Ministry off my hands—and that meant that I had

225

enough capacity to make my plans against the anti-Gorbachev forces here in Germany. As soon as the coup in Moscow failed I could round them up and make sure they didn't do any further harm." Dmitri looked very pleased with himself.

"There's something else, isn't there?"

"Yes, there is." A theatrical pause, then: "You are now looking at the senior liaison officer between the KGB and the government of the GDR. I have requested that you be my contact here in Berlin." A little bow, "I think, *tovarishch*, that you and I will be working together again. But right now I think the Round Table is waiting for you," and with a mock salute, Dmitri marched out of the room.

Read on for a preview of the next book
in the East Berlin Series: *Thoughts Are Free.*

HISTORICAL NOTE
The Point of Divergence

Historically minded readers will have noticed the point in time at which the narrative presented in *Stealing the Future* forks from reality. It is true that on the 4th of November 1989 there was the largest independent demonstration in the history of the GDR, but the *For Our Country* statement talked about by Martin and Margrit at the communal lunch on Sunday didn't actually make an appearance until the 28th of November 1989, when it was almost overshadowed (at least in Western accounts) by Helmut Kohl's '10 Point Plan' for German re-unification.

In *Stealing the Future*, however, both the Statement and the 10 Point Plan are launched on the same day as the mass demonstration—five days before the fall of the Wall.

This slight change to history resulted, in Martin's world, in increased awareness of West Germany's plans for a hasty annexation of the GDR, and in turn, of the issues that were considered in the *For Our Country* Statement.

The result: a continued existence for the GDR, and the grand social experiment that forms the backdrop to this book and its sequels.

More information about the point of divergence and the *For Our Country* Statement can be found on the author's website: www.maxhertzberg.co.uk

CHAPTER 1

OF

THOUGHTS ARE FREE
Book 2 of the East Berlin series

Monday
14th March 1994

The noise was neatly quarantined. A hundred people were marching—they were chanting, shouting, jeering.

But in the surrounding streets: silence.

Windows and doors were shut. Shops darkened, shutters rolled down. The only movement was the slow, snaking column of the demonstrators; the only sound was the chanting: *Foreigners go home! German jobs for Germans! Tear down the Wall!*

The skinheads marched at the head of the demonstration, a waddle of goose-steppers leading the pack. Shaven heads, faces contorted with hate, bomber jackets, paraboots with white laces. Behind them bullish men in ill-fitting suits. At the back, a few dozen people, normal people—the kind you could meet on the street, at work or in the queue at the tram stop—shepherded along by a fistful of skins carrying black-red-gold placards: *Germany: one Fatherland.*

How could anyone take them seriously—their self-importance, their stilted arguments? But they'd managed to tap into the fears of our time, they were gaining in strength and numbers. Many people in the GDR were unsettled by current immigration levels—higher than at any time since the end of the war: Russian Jews fleeing persecution, the Vietnamese and the Algerian contract workers stranded by the shipwreck of the Communist regime, the refugees from the Balkan wars, the idealists arriving from other countries, eager to support our cause. And we needed them all; without their support the labour shortage would bankrupt the country within days.

And a bankrupt GDR would suit the fascists just fine.

Behind the marchers came half a dozen cops, shields dangling from left hands, helmets clipped to their belts.

In the wake of them all came the police lorries. I stood next to the operational commander and his lieutenant on the back of a W50 truck, the tarp pulled back to give us a clear view of the demonstration. A police radio dragged at my shoulder, the earpiece keeping me abreast of the reports being made and the orders being issued.

Concentration anti-fascist repeat anti-fascist demonstrators Jessnerstrasse, crackled the radio. *Concentration Antifa repeat anti-fascist Pettenkoferstrasse.*

"Numbers?" demanded the police lieutenant next to me.

The static stirred, snapping and whistling. We were following the march down Frankfurter Allee and the wide railway bridges over the road ahead of us interfered with radio reception.

"Say again! Say again!" The lieutenant shouted into the microphone, but there was no need. We could see over the heads of the marchers—a black-clad knot of Antifa had run out of a side street on the right. About a dozen of them were wearing motorcycle helmets.

The march in front of us disintegrated. The skins from the

back were moving up through the ranks of the followers who cast about themselves, unsure what to do, where to go. A few looked back at the police lines behind, as if seeking advice.

"Squad C into position," sighed the captain behind us. Without hesitation the lieutenant repeated the order into the radio mike, looking over his shoulder to watch the riot cops jump down from their transports.

In front of us a second group of Antifa emerged from a street on the left, running across the central reservation, spearing into the demonstrators, isolating the skins from the other marchers scattered along the roadway. The cops headed towards the skins encircled by punks and squatters.

There was a moment of sudden stillness—the skins stood in the roadway, facing outwards in a ragged square, placards ripped off poles to make wooden staves. Around them the anti-fascists, just out of reach. A loose ring of police kettled both groups.

With a shout the action started. The Antifa clumped together and pushed against the skins, who hit back with fists and poles. The police used their truncheons, lashing out without discrimination.

"Disperse them," murmured the captain. He had turned away and was watching the group of fellow travellers being directed by the couple of cops left near the trucks. A few wanted to stay and watch but most seemed relieved, almost happy to be sent home.

"Disperse, disperse!" shouted the lieutenant into the radio microphone, but there was no-one to hear him. The cops in the mêlée didn't have radios. There weren't enough of them and they had no plan. They were pumped up on adrenaline and were reacting only to what was happening around them.

It was a mess.

★

I was in the canteen when the sergeant came to get me. Sitting at a table, all by myself, leaning against the wall and ignoring the cup of coffee and the slice of poppy-seed cake before me. The other tables had been pushed together and cops sat around them, slapping each other on the back and drinking beer.

"Shoulda left them to fight it out! All as bad as each other," laughed one. "But did you see the fascists' faces when the Antifa stormed across the road?"

This country was going through so many changes, yet I still found it hard to work alongside those who had once been against us. Before 1989 the police had played their part, shoulder to shoulder with the Party and the Stasi, repressing social and political dissent. But now the Party was no longer in power and an uneasy dance of reconciliation had started, a wooing between the police and the politicised population. Somehow I'd been caught up in the machinery, assisting the Central Round Table but assigned to the Ministry of the Interior, often working together with cops.

"Comrade Captain Grobe?" A sergeant stood in front of my table, saluting. "We thought you might be interested in something. A detainee we're interviewing. The duty officer suggested you come to see for yourself."

He led me up the stairs and down a long corridor of brown polished lino, institutional green walls with heavy, padded doors down one side. He stopped at one of these and pressed the bell set to one side.

While we waited I looked through a grimy window at the courtyard of the police station. A row of trucks were parked up, in front of them stood a dozen or so green and white liveried police patrol cars. There were no signs of life down there, just concrete, becalmed vehicles and the blank windows opposite. Last time I was here—just a few months ago—the yard had been boiling with movement and exhaust fumes as a squad assembled in preparation for a raid on a squat. It hadn't been a pleasant experience for me, even less so for those who were in the squat when the doors were kicked in.

Behind me I heard a door open, and I followed the sergeant into the interview room.

A police lieutenant in uniform was sitting behind a large desk—empty except for a phone and intercom device, and a buff file lying in front of him. The lieutenant held a pen, which he laid down on the thick file as he looked up to see who had entered. In front of his desk a table was set end-on, a couple of chairs to either side.

At a nod from the lieutenant we moved into the room. He didn't say anything, and I kept my silence too. It wasn't until I turned to shut the door behind us that I saw the detainee, sitting on a low stool behind the door; his hands pressed on his thighs, his knees drawn up tight to make room for the door that was pushed against his legs. I quickly looked away, but not before taking in the stone-washed jeans, the white t-shirt showing arms sheathed in dark tattoos and the heavily greased short-back-and-sides haircut.

The sergeant went to the lieutenant, leaning over his desk to whisper something. A curt nod from the officer, then he left, opening the door carelessly so that it rebounded off the prisoner's knees. I sat down at the table, and the lieutenant slid the file over to me. Flicking through it, I could see the first page was a custody record, presumably for whoever was sitting behind the door. After that were a handful of unused statement forms, followed by a few dozen blank pieces of paper. I looked at a virgin, ash-grey sheet, my eyes tracing the splinters of wood in the fibrous paper, then I thumbed back to the custody record, checking the personal data: Andreas Hermann, born Leipzig 1976, detained at the demonstration this evening. An initial charge of rowdy behaviour under paragraph 215 section 1 of the criminal code was being investigated and prepared. I tried to meet the police lieutenant's eye but he was staring at the man on the stool.

"Where were you yesterday at 1600 hours?" he snapped.

The detainee flinched slightly, I wouldn't have noticed if he didn't still have his knees pulled up so tight. The slight jerk of the man's head travelled down his torso and limbs, making his feet tremble. But he gave no answer, continuing to stare at a point somewhere above the lieutenant's shoulder.

"Fine. Tell me: when was the last time you went to Alexanderplatz?"

Again silence, the same stare over the lieutenant's shoulder.

It was a familiar set up. The sterile interview room, the implicit offer of the comfort that a simple chair with a back could provide: a seat at the table versus the reality of the hard stool. The discomfort, the prohibition against leaning against the wall, the indignity of sitting behind the door. Or alternatively the interviewee might be placed in the middle of the room, back to the door, unable to see who was coming in, whether they were bearing a message, choke cuffs or a cosh.

"Do you go to the Alex often? Meet your friends there? Or do you prefer to hang out in Lichtenberg?"

Silence.

How often had I sat in rooms like this? The endless questions, sometimes in relay, one interviewer replacing the next, only the detainee remaining the same, required to answer the same questions, again and again, hour after hour, day after day.

"But you don't live in Berlin-Lichtenberg."

The lack of sleep was worse than the arbitrary beatings. The lack of sleep played with your mind. You no longer knew what time of day it was, whether it was even day or night. You lost track of what you'd said or not said, what you'd meant to say or not say.

"Spend a lot of time there, do you?"

The lack of sleep made you paranoid, unable to trust yourself. It didn't take long, only a couple of days before exhaustion broke you.

"So you stay at a friend's?"

But they couldn't be using those tactics any more? These new times must have put an end to torture?

"Because it's true, isn't it, that you spend quite a bit of time in that part of town?"

I looked at the custody record again, as if it would show me what interrogation methods were planned for this Andreas Hermann.

"How much time do you spend at the premises Weitlingstrasse 122?"

This time there was a reaction. The detainee slowly moved his head, away from the spot above the interviewer's shoulder, slowly sweeping across desk and table, until he was facing me, his hard eyes challenging me.

"Think you're clever, don't you? But we have him," he said, in a slack Berlin drawl, his words whistling through the gap left by missing front teeth. "We know who he is, your *Zecke*, your little informant. And you know what? We know who you are too. You'll be next. No worries, you'll be next." His head slowly tracked back to its original position, facing the wall, above the lieutenant.

I continued watching the detainee, but out of the corner of my eye I could see that the lieutenant hadn't reacted at all.

"How long have you been registered as living at your mother's address?" the policeman asked.

Silence.